Murd
at a
Scottish
Social

Books by Traci Hall

MURDER IN A SCOTTISH SHIRE
MURDER IN A SCOTTISH GARDEN
MURDER AT A SCOTTISH SOCIAL

And writing as Traci Wilton

MRS. MORRIS AND THE GHOST
MRS. MORRIS AND THE WITCH
MRS. MORRIS AND THE GHOST OF CHRISTMAS PAST
MRS. MORRIS AND THE SORCERESS
MRS. MORRIS AND THE VAMPIRE

Published by Kensington Publishing Corp.

Murder
at a
Scottish
Social

TRACI HALL

Kensington Publishing Corp.
www.kensingtonbooks.com

I would like to dedicate this book to my family, which is growing all the time.

From my ninety-two-year-old grandmother, Sunny Brannigan, to my aunts, uncles, and cousins, to my mother, Judi, my son, Brighton, and my daughter-in-law, Cecilia; my daughter, Destini, my granddaughter, Kennedi, and my heart, Christopher.

Acknowledgments

To John Scognamiglio and all the staff on the publishing team. I appreciate all of the work that goes into a title and it's an honor to be part of Kensington's cozy lineup.

To Evan Marshall—you are a rock star agent!

To Sheryl McGavin for being my knitting guru, and dear friend.

To Allan Thornton for your assistance with Nairn and Scotland. Any mistakes are my own!

Thank you so much, readers, for taking this journey to Nairn with me.

Chapter 1

Nairn, Scotland

Saturday morning Paislee Shaw left Cashmere Crush, her sweater and yarn shop, in the wrinkled but capable hands of her grandfather, Angus.

"And dinnae forget tae bring back snacks—the larder is empty, lass." Grandpa patted his flat stomach as he watched her pack another shawl into the box for the Nairn Food Bank fund-raiser.

By larder, he meant her bin of crackers, crisps, and sweets in the shop that he tended to pilfer like a silver-bearded mouse.

"If you're hungry, tape the sign on the door and get something healthy tae eat besides junk food—a new Indian place just opened behind us." She'd noticed an increasing stream of empty biscuit packets in the trash at home as well. "A vegetable curry would do ye good."

She balanced her donation of a girl's cashmere sweater set in light blue on top of the other knitted items for the table at the Social Club and Art Centre.

Grandpa made no promises about fresh veg as he eyed the box. "Givin' away the merchandise is no way tae make a profit," he advised, sucking at his teeth. Though seventy-five he still had them all. He kept his silver-gray hair combed back from his forehead and his beard trimmed. Glasses slid down his long nose.

"This will raise money tae feed our neighbors. A local cause." Paislee braced herself for another round of Grandpa's opinions on getting something for nothing.

"Keepin' our own bellies full is verra local." He thumped his again to make his point.

"Have you never gone hungry?" He'd spent two weeks in the woods and she figured he'd have a wee bit more empathy toward the comforts of a stocked pantry.

"Naw." Grandpa lifted his hands. "Because I know how tae fish. Mibbe instead of soup, they should offer fishing poles."

"Och, I don't want tae argue. I'm donating the sweater, and doing my part for our community. It won't affect your paycheck." This wasn't the first time she'd noted the prickly combination of Scots pride mixed with age.

"Let me get the door for ye." He opened it wide and half-bowed.

She headed out the back to where her Juke was parked in the alley. "Ta."

Paislee took a deep breath of the warm morning air. Mid-May was pure magic in Nairn, with fine aqua-blue skies. The sun didn't set until after nine and was part of the reason tourists flocked to their seaside town for the summer.

"What time will ye return?" Grandpa stood in the threshold of the back door on the stoop, arms crossed loosely at his waist.

She shuffled down the four cement stairs, opened the hatch with one hand, and set her items inside before coming round to the driver's door. Paislee shrugged up at him. "Half past six at the latest." The highly advertised event was ten to five both days of the weekend, but being a vendor meant setting up and breaking down. "I'll bring ye back something chocolate."

He gave her a thumbs-up and ducked into the shop.

She pulled out to the street and drove toward Silverstein Real Estate Agency to pick up her best friend, Lydia Barron. They were going to share a vending table with Blaise O'Connor, who had recently moved to Nairn with her golf pro husband, Shep, and daughter, Suzannah.

Blaise fit right in at Paislee's Thursday night Knit and Sips where her crafters got together to knit and gossip. She was a step beyond beginner in her knitting, but did it to relax.

Her mobile rang and Paislee answered via Bluetooth. "Hello!"

"It's Blaise." Panic laced her voice. "Please tell me ye're on your way."

"I am. I thought you wanted us there at ten?" It was just nine thirty. Paislee wasn't even close to late for once.

"I do—you're fine. I'm a complete disaster." Blaise's exhale ruffled through the phone line. "What was I thinking, agreeing tae enter a baked sweets contest? I should've just handed over a couple thousand pounds tae the Buchanans and been done with it."

"What's wrong?"

"Kirsten is oot for bluid. My bluid." Blaise's tone lowered. "She tried tae hide our table in the corner by the loo, can ye believe it? I've talked tae the person running the show, Anders Campbell, and it'll be sorted any second, or I'll move it meself."

Blaise had kept them in stitches during the Knit and Sips as she joked about the competitive "ladies who lunch" from the golfing social circle. The Queen Bee of all the wives was Kirsten Buchanan. She ran everything from the Golf Charity to the Parent Council at Highland Academy where Blaise's daughter was enrolled.

The horror stories of ridiculous competitions, from whose child had the highest marks, which mum made the best biscuit, to whose husband earned the most money, made Paislee very glad that Fordythe Primary wasn't like that, or if it was, that she'd been too busy working to notice any cliques.

"Count tae three," Paislee advised. "Take a deep breath. We'll be there soon. Can we bring you anything? Scotch for your tea?"

"That wouldnae go over well, but it sure is tempting. I'm no Christina Baird."

"Who?"

"I'll explain later. Here comes Anders—hurry, before I lose me temper!" Blaise hung up without a proper goodbye.

Paislee parked before the Silverstein Real Estate Agency and

Lydia strode out, cherry-red head high. Her bestie changed her look every six weeks or so as the mood struck. The super-short style on one side was beginning to grow out in a wave with a swoop of bang over one gray eye. Lydia's impeccable makeup was something Paislee admired but would never dare attempt.

Paislee hopped out to help Lydia as she juggled paper cups, her large tote, and a shiny black box in one arm. She rescued the coffee, which smelled like mocha, and nodded at the box. "Morning— what's this?"

"Newest model gaming laptop. Dell Alienware Area-51m."

"What happened tae the trip for two tae Paris you were going tae donate?"

"Blaise is under a lot of pressure tae provide amazing items for the auction, so . . . I got Silverstein tae add tae his donation. He paid almost four thousand pounds for this beauty." Lydia strapped the box in the rear passenger seat as if it were a person.

For a laptop? Paislee could get all-new kitchen appliances for that. "Under pressure from whom?"

"Kirsten Buchanan. As ye know, Blaise's husband, Shep, is the newest golf pro in Nairn, so there are *expectations* from the other ladies in regard tae her participation. Kirsten requested only the best, or dinnae bother."

"That's ridiculous. Every little bit will help the food bank."

"It's the circle she's in, love. Blaise married a golf celebrity, who was endorsed by Gerard Buchanan, and she cannae let Shep down."

"How'd you get Silverstein tae up the ante?" Paislee climbed behind the wheel and plopped her coffee in the drink holder on the console. The scent of chocolatey goodness rose from the lid.

Lydia buckled up in the front seat. "I reminded him that Blaise is a potential client who hasnae closed on their new home yet. The bait is still on the hook, tae put it crudely."

Paislee laughed. "Yet, very nicely done."

"Natalya helped."

Natalya Silverstein was twenty years younger than her seventy-something husband, and had taken a liking to Lydia. Everyone in the business knew that Natalya would inherit the agency one day.

"She's a good ally tae have." Paislee left the agency and drove toward the club.

"Aye. So where's my prodigy today?" Lydia sipped her drink. "At work with Grandpa?"

Bennett Maclean, Brody's best mate's dad, owned a comic book store/arcade and had offered to keep Brody for the day. "Hanging out with Edwyn . . . I gave Bennett cash for at least four pizzas. Cheap at half the price."

"It's great that ye dinnae have tae worry aboot him. And Grandpa?"

"He doesn't understand why I'm givin' away the store. His idea is tae hand out fishing poles instead of food parcels."

Lydia chuckled. "What a character. Because ye know he'd share his catch with any who asked."

"You're so right. He's a grouchy old fraud." She glanced at Lydia. "Blaise called. Kirsten tried tae put our table in the back and she's not pleased."

"Blaise needs tae get away from that snobby school and those catty women. I've asked around and Highland's got commendable marks but a snooty reputation—as in, enroll with yer bank statements on display or forget aboot it." Lydia whistled. "Twenty thousand a year for day school, thirty for boarding students. Who can afford that?"

Paislee shuddered at the cost. "Not me. Drumduan will be a walk in the park for them in August." Drumduan was a private school with a less formal learning structure than Highland Academy.

"That's what I keep telling Blaise—she just needs tae hang on."

Lydia and Blaise had become friendly as Lydia helped the O'Connors find just the right house (mansion) in Nairn.

"I'm anxious about meeting the ladies in person—they can't be that bad, can they? Maybe you should have driven both days,"

Paislee said, thinking of Lydia's pretty red Mercedes. "I don't want tae embarrass Blaise with my Juke."

"There's nothing wrong with your SUV." Lydia set her coffee in the holder after another drink. "Just no, on principle."

The GPS directed them to go left and they headed away from the sea to the hills a few miles inland. Five minutes later they arrived at an old Victorian spa that had been refurbished into the twenty-first century to be used for public rooms that could be rented.

The car park was so new the orange-yellow lines separating spaces hadn't had a chance to fade. The clientele targeted for the fund-raiser was evident in the selection of parked SUVs: Range Rovers, Mercedes, Lamborghinis, and a Bentley.

"This is a sport utility vehicle mecca," Lydia observed. "Corbin would be ecstatic right aboot now."

Lydia's friend Corbin was in reality Laird Corbin Smythe. Paislee had met him once—he was handsome, no question, and he'd seemed genuine. He was only moderately rich, which for some reason mattered to Lydia. She didn't want to be "friends" with someone so wealthy they were out of touch.

Just friends, though, Lydia had claimed with a glimmer in her gray eyes.

"Will he drop by today?"

"Mibbe. There's Blaise's car," Lydia pointed, changing the subject.

Paislee parked between her friend's black-and-silver Range Rover and a bronze vehicle with huge shiny rims. She felt very out of place as she retrieved her boxes from the hatch. Her donation of the cashmere ensemble belonged, though, and this was for the Nairn Food Bank, for heaven's sake.

She lifted her chin as she and Lydia walked toward the front entrance. The old spa doors had been replaced with double glass and brass panels, with brass knobs. Planters full of bright red begonias brought vibrant color to both sides of the porch.

A friendly man in a chauffer's uniform and cap opened the door for them.

"Cheers, love," Lydia said.

Paislee nodded and wondered which designer SUV he belonged to—she'd put money, maybe as much as a pound note, on the Bentley.

"Wow." Lydia's eyes widened with appreciation as they entered the lobby. "I havenae been here since they gutted the place—brilliant choice in the new design. I wonder who the architect was?"

Paislee liked the large open foyer, white tiles, and natural light from all the windows, but it never would occur to her to wonder who designed it.

"Welcome tae the Social Club and Art Centre." They were greeted by an elegant woman in a dove-gray dress and white-blond hair. "You must be here for the Nairn Food Bank event. Doon the hall tae the left, and the conference room tae your right. You'll hear the commotion as things are set up, tae be sure. If ye have any questions regarding future room rental, I'm Sonya Marshal, director."

"This is fantastic!" Lydia exclaimed when they'd reached the room and peered inside. "I'll have tae bring Natalya for a possible new venue tae entertain."

Paislee followed Lydia through the open door. The tile in the gymnasium-sized conference room had been covered with thin beige carpet. Indoor palms in wicker pots brushed the high ceiling. Tall windows at the rear afforded a view of an emerald lawn and a thick beech tree provided shade over a patio reached by a back door, propped ajar as people brought in larger items for sale, like TVs and paintings. Tables teemed with opulence, luxury in each silk fabric swatch.

A dais had been raised to the left against the wall. Shelves showcased auction items. Along the right were the restrooms that Blaise had been worried about, but honestly, there wasn't a "bad" table to be had. Each was clearly visible, the aisles wide enough for browsers and shoppers once the sale started. Paislee checked the time on her phone. Fifteen minutes until it began.

"I've never been tae a sale quite like this before." She was surrounded by chic objects not in her budget.

"It's magnificent." Lydia surveyed the tables, effortlessly glamorous in a silk sleeveless charcoal blouse, fitted checked gray-and-black pants, a cherry-red belt and black boots. There was no doubt she fit in.

Paislee wasn't as confident in her cashmere lavender cowlneck short-sleeved sweater as she'd been when she'd first put it on, though it was perfect for spring weather. Her belt and shoes were both distressed brown leather, custom made for her by James Young, who had a leather shop next to Cashmere Crush. Her large leather bag was the same material and color. She'd twisted lavender cashmere into a bracelet with leather accents, and done the best with her too-thin auburn hair by braiding it loosely.

"You're here!" Blaise smiled but there was a frown between her reddish-brown brows when she reached them in a strawberry-jasmine mist of Marc Jacobs Daisy.

Paislee liked perfume in theory but didn't wear it—who had time?

"And hello tae you, too." Lydia calmly kissed each of Blaise's pink cheeks. "Where are we set up?"

"Hiya Lydia, hi Paislee—in the center now instead of the back, thanks tae Anders—Kirsten is so mean. Did she really think I wouldnae protest? Anytime someone went tae the toilet the door would hit our chairs."

Blaise's reddish-brown bob was so smooth it flowed to her shoulders like silk, her makeup appeared professionally done and her clothes were right on trend with the latest fashions according to the magazines Lydia left at Cashmere Crush.

They bypassed dozens of tables until they reached one in the middle of the back row. Other people were already seated on either side and Paislee smiled her hellos. Each new person might be a potential customer.

"This looks really pretty," Paislee told Blaise, who'd covered the table in silver sparkly fabric. Dishes of thin almond biscuits, a recipe that Blaise had been practicing since the last Highland Academy bake sale in February, were arrayed on tiered shelves, covered in clear wrap and tied with a raffia bow. "And the cookies, delicious."

"I've never won the stupid contest," Blaise muttered between clenched teeth, after a careful glance around. "Just once I'd like tae come oot ahead and show Kirsten that she is *not* the best baker. God, that makes me sound childish and shallow but I cannae help it." A vein pulsed at Blaise's temple.

"You're neither of those things," Lydia assured her. "Once you have Suzannah at Drumduan what they think willnae matter so much."

"I hope so, but their husbands all golf. I cannae get away from them completely just by switching schools." Blaise sighed. "Shep tells me tae ignore them but he doesnae realize that the wives hold a lot of sway in where a husband spends his money. And if I dinnae play along, then things will be bad for him, and for Suzannah, and we just moved and—"

"Ah." Paislee put her box of items down and gave Blaise a quick hug. "It'll be fine."

"You realize that Scotland has the most famous golf courses in the world? We cannae move away tae start over." Blaise rubbed her bare arms. "Can you see me livin' in Florida? Shep got an offer there once at Sawgrass where they have alligators on the green." Her eyes couldn't get more round. "No lie!"

"Calm doon, lass." Lydia put her arm around Blaise's shoulders. "Now, where should we put our things?"

A tall man with blondish-brown hair strode toward them, his untucked camp shirt billowing over slacks.

"Here's the person in charge now," Blaise said.

"Hello, ladies!" The man clasped first Lydia's hand, then Paislee's, letting his warm grip linger. "I'm Anders Campbell, fund-raising chair for the club."

"Nice tae meet you." Paislee pulled her hand free, noticing that his manicured skin was softer than hers, his nails shiny with clear polish. Grandpa would no doubt have something to say about *that,* she thought.

"Do ye have anything for the auction that I can display for you?" His friendly gaze settled on Lydia, and the shiny gaming laptop box.

"Aye!" Lydia held it up and grinned. "This sweet prize is from Silverstein Real Estate Agency."

"Oh, that should go for a lot." Anders eyed the picture on the side with approval.

"It's very powerful, with state-of-the-art graphics and a large screen," Lydia explained.

"Do you game?" Anders asked with interest.

"No." Lydia winked. "I shop."

"I'm glad you're here." Laughing, Anders turned to Paislee. "And what have you got for the auction?"

"A bespoke cashmere sweater set," she said. She unwrapped it from the tissue she'd packed it in to show him, proud of what she'd done—including her signature tassel at the end of the matching scarf.

"I brought a velvet hanger," Blaise interjected, "tae showcase the craftsmanship. Paislee Shaw is the designer."

Anders admired the soft sweater as he put it on the velvet hanger, and set it across the gaming box, then lifted the items. "Wonderful! These should bring in quite a bit for the Nairn Food Bank."

"What time will you do the auction?" Lydia asked.

"We'll have the bidding live through tomorrow, in order tae raise the most money." He smiled at them over the pile. "We'll even have the items available online for those that cannae make it in person. Gerard Buchanan does a similar fund-raiser at the school his son goes tae, so he's in charge of the whole operation—but if you have a question, I'm chuffed tae help. Thanks again, ladies."

Anders shuffled off toward the dais and the shelves.

"Well, he's a cutie," Lydia observed.

"Single, too—but you can do better than that," Blaise informed Lydia. "He's flirted with every woman in here so far."

Paislee elbowed her bestie. "Sounds just like Lydia."

"Two flirts in one relationship always equals trouble." Lydia crossed her arms and searched the room. "Where are your viperous ladies?"

"Shh!" Blaise joined Lydia to observe the front entrance. "Kirsten and Mari must've stepped oot."

While they stood watch, Paislee unpacked the other knitted goods from her box and displayed them, making sure they all had price tags.

"If only I had a smidge of your talent." Blaise turned around and smoothed a tassel on a shawl. "That's why I'm doing the cookies rather than attempting tae knit anything meself."

"You're learning!" Paislee hated for Blaise to doubt herself. She believed that the more you practiced the better your stitch. "You've got a fine eye for color."

"These jackals would tear apart anything less than perfection. Dinnae stare, but here come Kirsten and Gerard. The Highland Academy power couple."

Paislee oh so casually shifted toward the front entrance of the conference room and squinted to bring the man's black hair and trim mustache into focus. He grinned and laughed as he chatted with everyone.

"He seems nice," she said.

"He's the guid cop in the Buchanan marriage but no prince. Gerard married Kirsten when she was at the height of her modeling career tae take her off the market and boy does she resent it."

Kirsten had long, ebony hair, and a slender figure. "Kids?"

"One. Their son, Maxim, is in Suzannah's class." Blaise wriggled her shoulder. "When we first brought up moving and switching schools, Suz begged tae finish her year with her friends. I've had tae suck it up, but I am counting doon the days."

"For what, Blaise?"

Blaise whirled guiltily, her fingers to her mouth. "Och! Christina—sheesh, you startled me. Christina Baird, I'd like you tae meet my friends, Paislee Shaw and Lydia Barron."

"Pleased tae meet you." Christina offered a pretty smile, then turned to Blaise. "We really miss you at our after-meeting lunches. I ken ye've been busy with the move and all, but you cannae just disappear altogether. You're one of us."

The blond woman might have stepped out of a boating magazine, in white and navy blue. Paislee guessed somewhere in her mid-thirties, like Blaise. No popping out bairns at eighteen for finishing school lasses. "Hi."

"My son, Robby, is in class with Maxim and Suzannah. P3." Christina rested her fingers lightly on Blaise's wrist. "Where's Shep?"

"At the golf course, where else?" Blaise chuckled. "Will John be here today?"

"Naw—he's also at the golf course. Standard Saturday appointment with the green." Christina waved her hand airily. "At least your husband is making money—mine just likes tae spend it."

Blaise winced at the dig but rallied with a broader smile. "Where's your table?"

"Kirsten, Mari, and I are sharing one at the front there."

Paislee noted that it was the most favorably placed table, in the center, with an aisle on either side.

Christina studied Blaise's cookies. "I'm glad ye took my advice and tried a different recipe." She shrugged apologetically. "Going shortbread tae shortbread with Kirsten was a mistake—her private chef specializes in desserts, as you know." She sighed again. "I've given up on ever moving beyond third place." With that, she finger-waved and sauntered off.

"At least you make the top three!" Blaise mumbled to Christina's back.

"Why does Kirsten having a private chef matter?" Paislee watched the blonde go, the slightest weave to her stride. "Isn't she supposed tae be the one that bakes them?"

"She swears she does, but . . ." Blaise gave a slow blink. "I feel sorry for Christina withoot me at those lunches tae take the sting of Kirsten's and Mari's barbs. She's sweet, but boneless. Drinks vodka like water."

"That's so sad." Paislee patted Blaise's back. "Well, you have us now."

Kirsten ambled toward them, a too-thin lady at her side not even wide enough to be a shadow.

"You remember Kirsten," Blaise murmured. "Mari Gilmore is her very best friend. She could use a dozen steak-and-kidney pies."

Paislee half smiled and braced herself for the introductions.

"Cheers! You must be the friends who stole away our Blaise." Kirsten embraced Blaise, and offered a very limp finger shake to Lydia, then Paislee.

Mari squeezed Blaise in a hug. "We've missed you at school, but I'm so glad we can still count on you for the golf committee— you cannae get rid of us that easily." Her fake laugh suggested that Blaise wanting to would be unbelievable.

Kirsten caressed a long, manicured fingernail over a yellow scarf of merino wool. "Cute." Kirsten observed Paislee and Lydia just as carefully as the scarf. "Dinnae let Blaise's sweet face here fool you. She's got secrets."

What did that mean? Paislee schooled her features to remain neutral. She felt sorry for Blaise, whose pink cheeks turned red.

"Dinnae we all?" Lydia drawled. "They're the spice of life."

Paislee admired Lydia's ability to not trip over her own tongue when it came to confrontations in shark-infested waters.

Kirsten whispered loudly as she walked away, "My maid could knit a scarf better than that."

Mari's brow lifted and she tagged after Kirsten. "And those biscuits? Please. No competition, as usual."

Paislee started to go after them and forget all about Gran's teaching on being polite, but Lydia tugged her back and told Blaise, "I see what you mean aboot toxic."

Chapter 2

At ten sharp, Gerard took his seat on the dais and opened the computerized bidding while Anders welcomed the wealthy shoppers waiting in the hall. He strode through the aisles eager for someone to need him. Paislee was amazed at the turnout for the Nairn Food Bank fund-raiser and felt a spurt of pride in her hometown.

"Hi," a tall woman with brown hair said as she stopped at their table. "I'm Lara Fisk, Mrs. Buchanan's assistant. Blaise, can I collect your cookies for the competition?"

"Sure—what time will it take place?" Blaise handed over a dozen wrapped almond biscuits from a separate bag, having sold quite a few dishes of cookies already. "I'm a nervous wreck."

"The judges will sample all of the entries—there were over thirty—and then choose the final three." Lara spoke like a polished robot. "We'll have a taste-off beneath the tree oot back at six, with biscuits and a dram for all the kind folks donating their time here today."

Lydia perked up at the idea of a drink. "How nice."

"The Buchanans are verra thoughtful." Lara didn't crack a smile as she moved on.

"I wonder who the judges will be?" Blaise tapped her forefinger on the table. "At the school bake sale it was the teaching staff and the principal."

Paislee imagined Hamish McCall in such a position at Fordythe Primary and knew instinctively that he'd be fair. A wave of people arrived, interested in her knitted wares, and there was no more time for chatting.

By three, the sweaters on her table had all been sold and Lydia offered to drive back to Cashmere Crush for more.

"It's all right." Paislee thought to her inventory with surprised pleasure. "I'll need stock for tomorrow. Blaise, you'd better get baking tonight. You're almost out of cookies."

Blaise reached beneath the table for a bottle of water and took a quick sip. "I would say this event has been a success. The Buchanans should be happy."

"People are interested in seeing the refurbished Social Club and Art Centre—everyone's talking aboot how beautiful the building and grounds are," Lydia said.

Anders happened to be walking past and stopped with a grin, rubbing his hands together. "Sorry tae butt in, but that's wonderful tae hear. Renovations of a historical landmark are never easy."

"Or cheap," Kirsten said from his far side. The woman smiled at Paislee as if she hadn't just insulted her hours ago. Unbelievable. Gerard was racking up bids on the screen for the auction items, and Mari was in conversation with Christina at their table. Where was Lara? She could never relax her guard with these ladies around.

"Kirsten and Gerard are premier members of the club." Anders kept his fingers on Kirsten's elbow.

"We adore the arts." Kirsten put her palm to her heart.

"I didnae know you could *buy* memberships." Blaise leaned forward and placed her elbows on the table.

"Oh, aye," Anders said immediately. "Our center is made for community. The theater can hold a hundred people. We have a dozen private offices. The loch behind us makes an amazing wedding venue. But," he gave a shrug, "it is privately owned. We gladly accept sponsorships."

Paislee wondered if that had something to do with Anders's

flirty nature—he never knew when he might need to hit someone up for a donation.

Kirsten hooked her hand through his arm. "The events here are high-end and we want our services tae reflect that. Why, I spoke with the Earl of Cawdor just last week tae congratulate him on a job well done. Nairn is growing, and attracting the right kind of wealth."

"The right kind?" Paislee straightened in her chair, crossing her ankles. What did the woman mean by that?

"We want tae welcome those who are searching for a place tae unwind and get away from the stress of the world." Kirsten lifted her shoulder, her gaze dreamy. "Just like what the Victorians envisioned a hundred or more years ago. I'd like tae see the auld shacks torn doon and new housing built in a quaint style."

"There's been a lot of talk in Silverstein's office aboot this," Lydia said. "Paislee, your house would fall under that zoning."

"My house is not a shack!" It was old, true, but it was hers, thanks to Gran.

Kirsten's mouth pursed in distaste. "Well." She focused on Lydia. "You work for Natalya?"

"Aye." Lydia was coolly polite.

"Tell her I said hello." Kirsten tossed her long ebony hair. "Natalya used tae be friends with my mother. Anders, you might want tae contact her regarding a sponsorship of the club. She married verra well."

Lydia's cherry-red spikes quaked. "Natalya is a successful estate agent in her own right."

Paislee's gaze just happened to drop as Kirsten's and Anders's fingers grazed. Neither pulled away. The furtive act reminded Paislee of when she and Lydia used to pass notes in school. Was that a square paper?

"And when her much older husband dies, she'll be sitting pretty. Like I said," Kirsten purred, "Natalya married well."

Lydia shot sparks from her eyes but said nothing more. Kirsten brought her hand to her throat and simpered. Anders sighed. The fool had a crush, if Paislee had to guess. And what did Gerard Buchanan, Kirsten's husband, think of that? The pair strode off toward the back of the conference room.

Blaise blew out a breath. "That woman makes me mental. Her ego is so big that she doesnae even realize when she's making an arse oot of herself. Apologies tae both of you on her behalf."

Paislee scoffed. "You don't have tae apologize for an ex-friend, Blaise. Is Kirsten always so sharp?"

"Aye." Blaise organized her remaining dishes of cookies. "When she's on your side, it's great. And when she's not, well. I dinnae need her as an enemy. It could hurt Shep, or Suz."

"Karma," Lydia said. "What goes around, comes around."

For the rest of the afternoon, Lydia made sure they were fed with savory snacks and sweet homemade treats from the other folks with goods for sale. By quarter till six, Paislee and Blaise had sold out of sweaters, scarves, and cookies.

Christina cruised by, sipping on a water bottle, and Paislee recalled what Blaise had said about it being vodka. Mari and Lara were with her.

"Hiya," Christina said. "How's it going all the way back here? I thought we'd be table neighbors so that we could catch up, Blaise."

Mari rolled her eyes with impatience. Lara glanced from Christina to Blaise, shoulder to shoulder with Mari.

"We've sold oot of everything," Blaise answered with a pleased smile. "We'll have tae restock for tomorrow. How aboot you?"

"Och, my homemade macaroons are long gone. I've just been texting with my husband for dinner plans."

"I didnae know you were chatting this whole time with him. And how is *Doctor* Baird?" Mari asked.

Christina blushed. "Stop it." She sipped, then explained, "John is a psychiatrist, and Mari thinks it's funny tae call him doctor. I dinnae. John doesnae. He went tae university!"

"It is, just a wee bit," Mari jabbed. "Considering."

Lara covered a smile with her fingers. Paislee got the sense that

Lara had taken the fourth place in the clique that Blaise had vacated by her move. "Let's catch up later," Christina said. The three slowly walked on. Blaise didn't commit.

At ten to six, Gerard spoke into a wireless microphone. The shoppers had gone already with the promise to tell their friends and return the next day. There would be more items for sale to support the food bank. "Thank you, vendors, for coming today!"

Paislee turned toward his booming voice. Gerard owned the cushioned leather chair as if it were a throne, and he King Buchanan addressing his people.

"This is our first year supporting the Nairn Food Bank fundraiser, but I'd like tae kick off the opening of the new Social Club and Art Centre by suggesting we make this an annual event."

The crowd of about sixty all clapped and Paislee did, too. What a boon to her business this would be, in addition to the yearly parade.

Anders's mouth thinned as if Gerard Buchanan had overstepped. Anders looked to Kirsten, who also applauded her approval—he would get no support there. Christina, Mari, Lara, and Kirsten were grouped together before the dais.

"The biscuit competition was verra popular . . . we had thirty-seven entries." Gerard stood from his chair like a consummate showman, success and confidence in every gesture. "We've narrowed the field tae three, and will hold the final tasting outside with a wee dram from my own whisky reserves. For your generosity today, Kirsten and I have also supplied shortbread cookies for everyone."

More applause sounded.

Gerard cleared his throat dramatically. "Our three finalists are: Mari Gilmore, for her orange oatmeal lace, Kirsten Buchanan, for her shortbread, and . . . Blaise O'Connor, with the almond wafer."

Blaise squealed from her seat at the table. Paislee saw a very dark expression cross Christina's face, while Kirsten and Mari exchanged a conspiratorial look.

"I made the cutoff—I've never been top three. Oh, this could finally be the year. If I could leave Highland Academy on a win that would just make everything sweeter." Blaise, both hands to her chest, sank back in her chair.

Paislee wanted to say something about what she'd seen—it was a setup, but to what purpose? Kirsten's vanity? Were they trying to reel Blaise back into their clique?

"Everyone file ootside tae the tables where the judging will commence." Gerard applauded some more and hopped off the dais.

"I suppose her husband is the final judge?" Lydia commented dryly.

"Gerard? I wouldnae be surprised," Blaise said. "But no, that really would be too obvious. It's supposed tae be impartial."

Paislee didn't think so, from what she'd seen.

They followed the surge of folks out the back door to where eight tables for eight people were set up. There was a long table and three chairs behind it for the judges. Two big bottles of Scotch. Plastic glasses. Cookies wrapped and stacked in preparation.

As part of the final three contestants, Blaise was invited to sit up at the front table with Paislee and Lydia behind her. "I have tae text Shep!"

Blaise quickly sent a message off to her husband, who called. "'Scuse me a sec," she said, stepping away to speak with him, her voice giddy as she went inside the now empty conference room.

Gerard was not an actual judge, but Anders was, and so was Sonya, the director. Paislee didn't recognize the third judge.

Mari and Kirsten conversed at the table, Mari's voice rising. Kirsten stood up and searched the group, her hand on her hip. "Where's Blaise?" Kirsten asked irritably. "I thought this would be important."

"Here!" Blaise proudly joined the other two ladies.

Christina watched at a table across from the winners, her water bottle at her fingertips, her face pale.

Fergus Jones, a man in a chef's hat that didn't quite cover copper hair and wearing plaid black-and-white pants, was asked to bring up the cookies once the judges were blindfolded.

First was Blaise's almond wafer, then Mari's oatmeal lace. Last was Kirsten and she eyed the chef's offering with confusion. "Let me see those, Fergus."

He lifted the tray for her perusal.

Kirsten stared at the dish and lifted a biscuit, sniffing it. "These arenae mine, you imbecile."

"They are too," the chef said, his body rigid and embarrassed. "I helped ye plate them."

Kirsten licked the topping. "Brown sugar." Her mouth pursed as she nodded, as if to say the flavor was right. She bit into the shortbread and swallowed. "All right, then. Why did ye switch my plates? Ungrateful idiot. I wanted the one with three individual wafers. Presentation is everything! I dinnae care if the judges are blindfolded!"

"Now they'll know which is yours," Christina whined. "We have tae mix them up again."

"Ma'am." The chef trembled with indignity. "I did not—"

Kirsten's face turned red and she brought her hand to the hollow of her throat. Her eyes widened as she made a mewing sound.

Gerard shifted toward his wife, alarmed.

Paislee stood in concern. "What's wrong? Is she choking?"

Everyone just stared in bewilderment as Kirsten crashed into the table where her husband gaped. "Babe?" Gerard caught her shoulder and yelled to Fergus. "Get her EpiPen!"

Chapter 3

Paislee heard Gerard shout for what sounded like a pen before he smacked the chef in the arm so hard the man spilled the tray of cookies. "What are in those, Fergus?" Gerard gathered Kirsten to him and patted her back, stroking her long ebony hair. "God help ye, man, if there are peanuts."

Kirsten glared at Fergus and gargled something unintelligible.

"This was the tray labeled for Mrs. Buchanan." The chef transformed from angrily embarrassed to scared in an instant. "These shortbread are hers—no peanuts! I helped her plate them before we left the house."

"Kirsten, love?" Gerard reached for Kirsten when she dropped as if taken out at the knees, hitting the chair on her way to the grass, but his fingers missed her body. "Find her EpiPen, now!"

The judges all removed their blindfolds and rose at once.

"Hey!" Christina cried. "That voids the contest."

"Where's her purse?" shouted Mari. The thin woman left her position near Christina and the judges, her hands clasped as she checked the table by Gerard. "She always has one with her."

"EpiPen?" Paislee asked Lydia, who only shrugged.

Anders jumped around the table to where Kirsten choked and gagged, hunched over as she sprawled legs-out, her dress climbing from her knee to her thigh. A red-soled pump had loosened from her slender foot.

Gerard and Anders collided as they each tried to sit her up, Gerard caressing her shoulder, Anders tilting her head back as if to keep her passageway clear.

"She needs her medicine, Fergus!" Gerard yelled like an enraged monarch. The chef was frozen in place, the tray of cookies in a cluster around his black clogs. "Find Hendrie—I know there's an Epi in the car."

The chef ran for the lot where the SUVs were parked, smacking into tables and guests as he called, "Hendrie!"

The man who'd helped them with the door in the chauffer's cap appeared from where he'd been lounging in the shade. "I'm here, Fergus. What's up?"

"Mrs. Buchanan. Anaphylactic shock. Where's her injector?"

Paislee couldn't hear them anymore but then the door of the Bentley opened hard enough to slam into a neighboring SUV.

Shouts rose as the two men argued.

Hendrie and Fergus were back in less than minute. "Gone," Hendrie panted. "It's not in the glove box, sir."

Mari lifted the tablecloths and searched the chair backs. "Where's her purse?"

Christina seemed to realize that this was actually serious and moved away from the judges' table. "This is terrible—you're right—she always carries one in her handbag."

"Kirsten's purse must be at our table, then," Mari said, in shock. The thin woman ran inside the back door.

Blaise joined Paislee and Lydia, her mouth trembling.

"What's wrong?" Paislee asked.

"Peanut allergy—Kirsten is verra sensitive tae it." Blaise shuffled nervously. "We all know not tae bake with peanuts—she certainly wouldnae use them in her own recipe. The EpiPen is epinephrine and will stop the attack."

Paislee looked over at Kirsten as the woman made frightening sucking noises. "This is awful." She raised her voice toward Gerard. "How can we help?"

"We have an emergency EpiPen in the office." Sonya's manner was very controlled. "I'll get it." She immediately hurried into the building.

"Should I call 999, sir?" Hendrie held his mobile phone.

"Aye," Gerard cried, his hand on his wife's lower back, her head against his shoulder. "Hurry."

Mari returned with a red rectangular purse, the metal clasps open, teardrops sliding down her cheeks. "Gerard, it's not here."

"Impossible." He glanced up from his wife to Mari.

"It's true." She held up the purse as more tears welled. The long bag was slim and had just enough room to hold a few knitting needles.

"Check everywhere—bloody hell, she needs tae breathe!" Gerard's voice broke on a sob. "Back up, Anders, you're crowding her."

Mari dumped the purse upside down on the table. Mints, credit cards. No medicine.

Paislee scooted around the chairs and table to where Gerard hovered over Kirsten in a protective manner. "I know CPR. Let me help."

Kirsten scratched at her throat, her eyes bugging wide as she gasped, struggling to draw in air but it was as if something was caught. Paislee imagined a fishbone or chunk of scone. Big red blotches spread over her collarbone. Hives dotted her skin. Her lids fluttered and her face turned purple-red, her nostrils flared before her eyes rolled back in her head, her mouth slack.

Paislee quickly stretched her out on the grass, using two seconds to assess the situation, calm her own blasted nerves, and consider the treatment—this was much different from a rubber doll with no arms or legs that she'd learned on during class. It was better if she thought of the doll rather than poor Kirsten. "Elevate her legs."

Gerard knelt at his wife's extended legs and put her feet on his lap.

No exhale. No inhale. She'd learned to give two breaths per thirty compressions.

The air was not going through Kirsten's airway so she tilted the woman's head back and tried again. There wasn't anything caught, but the woman's body was swelling and causing the blockage.

Paislee imagined her breath finding a way into Kirsten's throat, her lungs.

One breath, two breaths. There.

Kirsten's mouth quivered . . . Paislee positioned her interlaced hands on her chest and compressed thirty times. After thirty, she gave two more rescue breaths.

She repeated this, concentrating on the motions, not able to think of anything other than the action of pressing down, or listening, or breathing—all the while praying to Gran for heavenly assistance as Kirsten remained unconscious.

Sonya arrived with the EpiPen from the office, her face flushed from her run back to the beech tree. "Where, Gerard?"

"Her thigh. Give it tae me." Gerard uncapped the stopper, raised his wife's dress a bit more, and stabbed down.

Paislee's arms trembled. "Should I stop?"

"Keep on doing it," he said shakily.

Paislee willed Kirsten to rouse and come back to life but it was the medicine that caused Kirsten to shake, and her eyes fluttered open as she gasped inward with a wheeze. She pushed out her left hand.

Paislee fell backward, surprised by the primal strength in the action, then stayed on her knees at Kirsten's side. Was that a breath? Yes! *Don't die, Kirsten, don't die. You have a son. A family.*

She was aware of the blaring sirens hurrying across the green field behind the beech tree because the SUVs had blocked a clear passage behind the club. The medics parked so close they knocked over a table. Within moments, Kirsten was strapped into the gurney and whisked away.

Gerard remained behind, handsome face flooded with worry for his wife. "Where's Hendrie? I need tae reach the hospital!"

Fergus shrugged.

"Consider what you and Kirsten discussed void." Gerard stalked toward the car park. "I better never see you again."

Fergus yanked off his hat and scrubbed his copper hair. "But sir . . ."

Lydia and Blaise gathered around Paislee, shaking like a tree in a storm, and brought her back to the table where she sank down into a folding chair. She touched her fingers to her lips. Kirsten had to be okay.

The ambulance left but a police officer stayed, joined by a second car. Paislee didn't recognize the officers.

"How are ye, love?" Lydia asked, handing Paislee a bottle of water.

"I . . ." Her body quivered. "What an awful thing tae have happen."

"I willnae pretend that I liked Kirsten but I dinnae wish her ill. She has tae rally, for Maxim and Gerard." Blaise's amber eyes filled with unshed tears.

"Modern medicine can do wonders," Lydia said matter-of-factly. "I'm sure she'll be fine. Well done, Paislee. Quick thinking."

Paislee briefly bowed her head and added more prayers to the ones she'd already sent. When she looked up, she couldn't miss how Anders Campbell and Gerard Buchanan glared at each other, and Mari cried on Lara's shoulder.

Where was Fergus Jones, the chef? And Hendrie? Paislee put a chair over the cookies on the grass so nobody accidentally stepped on them—they could be evidence, something she'd learned from Detective Inspector Zeffer was important when discovering what happened.

Christina, who had wandered inside the conference room, shouted from the back door to where they were all mingling, talking to the constables, consoling one another beneath the tree.

"Blaise O'Connor! How could you?" She leaned heavily against the doorframe.

Drunk? Distraught?

Paislee rushed toward Christina, questioning if she was all right after watching her good friend collapse. Blaise and Lydia were at her heels.

Christina brought them, and others who had heard her cry, inside the conference room. The blonde stood over Blaise's silver-clothed table, her face accusing as she waved a cylindrical yellow object with an orange cap that reminded Paislee of a permanent marker. "I found this on Blaise's chair. I know ye hated Kirsten, but tae hide her medicine?"

"I wouldnae do that!" Blaise flung her arms out to her sides.

"I think ye did. You wanted tae win the cookie competition that bad?" Christina's icy expression folded. "I thought better of you!"

Paislee and Lydia joined forces on either side of Blaise. "She was with us the whole time," Paislee said.

But she hadn't been. There'd been the few minutes when Blaise had ducked out of sight to talk with Shep. Could she have taken the medicine then? But why?

"Officer!" Christina called out in a singsong voice. "I found the EpiPen right here."

A constable in white shirtsleeves, black slacks, and a yellow vest said, "Dinnae touch anything!"

Christina immediately dropped the injector on Blaise's table like a hot potato.

"Where did ye find that?" the constable asked.

"On Blaise's chair—she took it," Christina announced.

Blaise turned crimson. "I did not."

"Ma'am," the constable scolded Christina, "you cannae just accuse folks like that."

"It might have fallen out of Kirsten's purse and someone just put it there," Paislee suggested.

"I highly doot that." Christina pointed to Blaise's seat, which was partially tucked beneath the table. "It was almost hidden but I saw the cap."

"What were you doing over here anyway?" Blaise asked with suspicion.

"Looking for the pen, obviously." Christina straightened and blinked red-rimmed blue eyes.

"And you just happened tae find it on Blaise's chair?" Lydia gave a delicate sniff. "I dinnae believe it. Did *you* put it there on purpose?"

Lara, standing to their right with Mari, gasped. The constable listened with interest.

"I did not." Christina raised her chin in a haughty manner and faced the constable, tapping the toe of her shoe impatiently. "Well?"

The constable's mobile rang and interrupted the tense scene. "Dinnae touch anything else," he warned them and stepped away to answer a call. "Dean here. Yeah?"

Paislee had a sinking feeling in her stomach when his back went rigid.

The officer turned around again, grim-faced. "I'll need ye both tae come tae the station for fingerprints." He pulled gloves from his pocket and a plastic bag that he put the injector pen in.

Paislee's body filled with trepidation as her mind raced to supply reasons for the change in the officer's demeanor. Kirsten had been alive . . . what if . . . ?

"What's the matter?" Lydia asked.

"Is she . . . ?" Mari trailed off.

"Mrs. Buchanan is dead." Constable Dean's jaw tightened. "If this was a prank gone wrong between you ladies—I heard yer bickering—there will be serious repercussions."

"I didnae touch that pen," Blaise said. "I'm happy tae give you my fingerprints."

Christina stared in horror at her hands and the bagged pen. "You know I touched it—you saw me. That's not fair!"

"Fair?" Blaise shouted. "You just accused me of stealing my

friend's medicine—were you jealous because I placed in the biscuit competition instead of you?"

Christina paled. "Kirsten was not your friend—you hated her, and she loathed you."

"Christina!" Lara said.

"Really?" The constable pulled his tablet from one of his many pockets. "I'll need all your names, phone numbers, and relationships tae the victim." He gestured to a female officer. "Butler, help me get statements. Start outside. We're gonna be here a while."

Gerard choked out a cry from the opposite table as the tall officer told him the terrible news. "Where is my chauffer? Hendrie!" His gaze landed on Mari and Lara. "Will someone drive me? I dinnae have keys." He stumbled backward. "God, I'm too late for her. My Kirsten."

Mari sobbed. "I rode with you, Ger."

Lara dragged in a breath and patted her purse. "I will."

Blaise leaned into Paislee and Paislee put her arm around her. "Dead," Blaise whispered in disbelief.

Paislee's stomach churned. *Dead.*

"What is it?" Anders asked, joining them with a worried expression.

"Back off, numpty," Gerard growled. "Kirsten told me aboot your unwanted advances. I'm going tae have your job on the line."

Sonya's calm manner slipped. "What? Anders, is this true?"

"No, it's not—I loved her." Anders's voice quavered and his hand snuck in the pocket of his slacks.

"Love? Haud yer wheesht, lad, or I'll break yer bloody teeth." Gerard held up his fist. Paislee flinched at the man's temper.

"She loved me, too," Anders said tearfully.

Mari, eyes wide, shook her head. "She did*nae.*"

"You knew?" Gerard demanded from Kirsten's best friend as if betrayed.

"I . . ." Mari said, then clamped her lips closed.

"Enough," Constable Dean declared with a swipe of his hand. "Rory, have an officer drive Mr. Buchanan tae his wife."

Christina stepped backward, her hip bumping the table. "I want tae go home."

"You have tae stay here and answer a few questions," Constable Dean informed her with strained patience.

"I want me husband!" she cried.

"Your husband?" Mari asked. "Over a few questions? Really, Christina, dinnae be so high and mighty, married tae a *doctor*."

"Stop saying that!" Christina brought her hand to her chin.

Hendrie arrived with the keys to the Bentley up high. "Mr. Buchanan? I have the car ready—it was blocked, sir, sorry for the delay."

"Aboot time, Hendrie." Gerard listed as if overcome.

The tall, young officer righted him with a steady hand to his shoulder. "You've a ride, then?"

Gerard gave a curt nod. "God, we have tae find Fergus and make him explain what happened. Where is he? Has anybody seen him since . . ." Broken-up, he turned to Lara, who half hugged him awkwardly.

The constable patted his tablet. "We'll find him. I'll have an officer there at the hospital."

"Thanks." Gerard's body hunched forward as he made his way to Hendrie. The chauffer offered no personal touch or condolences as he gestured his boss away from the social club.

"The wife had a peanut allergy?" the constable summarized. "And the private chef is gone? Odd, that. We must find him."

Christina nodded rapidly, obviously happy to have someone else in the hot seat. "His name is Fergus Jones," Christina said. "He brought the cookies tae the front table tae be judged in our baking competition. Kirsten always wins—it's her attention tae detail that makes her such a fine baker." Her voice was high and tinny. "She noticed that something wasnae right with them."

"So she took a bite?" The officer's voice rose in doubt.

"She could be . . . feisty," Anders said, knuckles to his lower lip.

"She knew what she wanted," Mari clarified defensively—then her body sagged. "Poor Maxim."

In contrast, Lara straightened her posture as if a rod was up her spine. "Say what you will aboot Kirsten Buchanan—we all know she was a right bitch—but she loved her son tae the moon and back, and wanted the best for him. I tutor him on the side."

Paislee's tummy did another twirl. She'd wanted to save Kirsten but hadn't. She'd offered her breath, her strength. It hadn't been enough.

Her head grew fuzzy.

"Hey, darling, I've got you." Lydia hooked her arm through Paislee's. "Can we go, sir? It's been a rough afternoon."

The constable peered up from his tablet. "How did ye know the deceased?"

"We just met today." Paislee gulped hard. "We didn't know Kirsten personally." Her throat burned and her vision blurred with spent adrenaline.

"Didnae I see ye by the body?" He jerked his thumb toward the beech tree.

"I . . . I tried to give her . . . CPR."

Paislee glimpsed compassion as he said, "You kept her alive for the ambulance." He studied her and Lydia. "Leave your names and contact details, then you may go."

His gaze shifted to Blaise.

"I'm Blaise O'Connor," she said quickly.

"You say you did *not* touch the injector?"

"No, sir."

"I'll need your fingerprints to verify that, which means a wee trip to the station." His tone let them all know that he doubted they'd find Blaise's prints but he had to check, as it was his duty.

Christina huffed, insulted.

Paislee reached for her purse and dug around for a business card, one of hers and one of Lydia's, to give to the constable. Lydia shouldered her tote bag. Mari and Christina stood on opposite sides of the room, with Lara in the center, near Sonya and Anders.

"I bet you willnae find the chef." Mari sniffed, but it was in anger this time rather than sorrow for Maxim.

"Why is that?" the constable asked.

"Kirsten told me last night at dinner that she planned tae fire him this morning." Mari dabbed at her lashes with a bony knuckle.

Paislee swallowed over the lump in her throat and scanned the conference room, as if she might find the red-haired man hiding somewhere. Having witnessed his shock, she'd like to make him explain himself. He hadn't expected Kirsten to collapse, or *die*.

The private chef's disappearance after being fired changed the viewpoint of those in the room from thinking it an accident, or a malicious joke, to something more sinister. Paislee watched as they each grew defensive in their own way.

Lydia ruffled the back of her hair. "Could he have added peanuts tae the shortbread, as revenge?"

"We dinnae know that there are peanuts," Constable Dean interjected . . . the cool voice of the law.

Blaise trembled so hard that she dropped her phone to the thin carpet. Paislee bent down to retrieve it and gave it to her, squeezing her fingers.

"But . . . she adored Fergus," Christina said, taking a half step back. "He was trained in desserts."

"She *fired* him." Mari raised her thin palm. "He lived at the house with them in his own suite. She paid him an above-average salary. What if this is how he repaid her for takin' it all away?"

Paislee reeled and pressed her hand to her stomach. Had she given CPR to a murdered woman?

Chapter 4

Paislee stumbled backward into Lydia, who straightened Paislee and faced the officer, Blaise, and Christina. Mari and Lara had come together to stare at Anders, who had lost all semblance of color.

"I cannae believe it." Anders shook his head. "I've had meals at their house. He's a talented chef."

"The chef knew she had an EpiPen. Who else?" Constable Dean asked.

"We all did," Mari remarked curtly. "It was no secret."

"I didn't." Paislee cleared her throat. "Nor did Lydia."

"People who *knew* her did," Christina said, righting the navy bow in her hair before it slipped out.

Paislee couldn't join the mob who blamed Fergus—she'd felt his surprise and fear, seen it up close. "Well, that means one of *you* who knew her might have added peanuts tae her biscuits. I don't believe it was Fergus."

Lydia raised her brow but didn't press Paislee for answers.

"Christina, please . . ." Blaise crossed her arms. "Must you always be so difficult? Now is not the time for yer dramatics."

"Och, that's rich, coming from you," Christina said. "Where did you learn your social graces again?"

Blaise turned on her heel to give Christina her back.

Constable Dean made a phone call, speaking low, then he returned to them and rocked backward, hands clasped before his yellow vest. "In light of this situation—the fired chef, and your commentary—I've asked an officer tae bring the portable fingerprint kits tae save time. Nobody may leave until after that's done."

Lydia gestured to the open door. "Except Paislee and I, right?"

"*Nobody*. This is now the scene of a suspicious death. We will need the prints of everybody who was inside the conference room tae help in our process of elimination."

"Against what you find on the pen?" Blaise whirled on the blonde. "I didnae put it there, Christina."

Christina blinked rapidly. "Mibbe Fergus did it."

Blaise brought her knuckles to her lower lip.

"We'll be dusting your table and the chairs, Mrs. O'Connor. Yours as well, Mrs. Baird," Constable Dean said.

"Kirsten had the highest regard for her chef. Why would she have fired him?" Anders's eyes were bloodshot. "Are ye sure, Mari?"

"That's what she said." Mari shrugged. "I dinnae ken why."

"Cooks are supposed tae be quite temperamental," Constable Rory offered.

"I, too, have eaten at the house often. Fergus thinks highly of himself," Lara said. "I've heard the two of them go at it over whose kitchen it was—his or hers. He'd have access tae the cookies."

"Have access?" Christina giggled. "That's one way tae look at it."

"*Och*, now, let's not jump tae conclusions." Constable Dean kept his thumb over his tablet as he took notes.

That order sounded familiar and Paislee glanced at Lydia, who tapped the toe of her boot to the thin carpet.

"Constable Dean," Paislee said to get his attention. "The spilled shortbread are still on the ground outside, from where Fergus dropped the tray. I put a chair over the area, so that they wouldn't be crushed, if you needed them for anything."

"Smart thinkin', lass! Rory, take care of the chair and shortbread, and get the tray for fingerprints."

The tall officer hurried out to the back and the constable nodded at her with approval.

Christina's phone rang and she answered in a rush, "Honey, the constable wants tae take my fingerprints. Can they do that?"

Paislee considered herself a compassionate person, but she was unmoved by the woman's sniffles—a prima donna, yet always third place to Kirsten's first. What was she thinking, to set Blaise up? Christina had been the one cut out of the final three in today's baking showdown. Had she wanted the attention on her?

"I didnae mean tae touch it—I found it on Blaise's chair." The woman, mom, wife—she heard Grandpa's voice in her head saying *wee clipe*, or tattletale—gave them a side view of her perfect profile, aware that they all watched her. Ending the call, Christina lifted her chin. "My husband said that I may give you my fingerprints."

"Well, that's just fine, then." Constable Dean smirked. "I'd hate tae have tae consider yer refusal an obstruction of justice."

Christina palmed her phone and slid it into her white pants pocket.

"We must speak tae everyone," Constable Rory announced from his position on the threshold, one black boot in the conference room, the other on the grass. "The sooner you cooperate with Constable Butler, the sooner you will be excused."

About forty folks waited at the tables outside, sipping water bottles that Sonya handed out, to give their statements. The individual plates of Kirsten's prized shortbread were stacked on the end of the judges' table, next to two large bottles of the Buchanans' fine Scotch and plastic tumblers. There were twenty people inside for the first wave.

A fourth police officer arrived, lugging in a black case on wheels. Paislee sucked in a breath when she spied the russet hair and blue suit of Detective Inspector Mack Zeffer as he entered from the back door behind the officer with the rolling case.

Trepidation, as well as a hint of relief, filled her. She and the detective didn't always see eye to eye, and the last month the DI had been scarce as Nairn had been mostly crime free.

Zeffer strode toward them, introducing himself to the officers on his way.

"Ms. Barron, Ms. Shaw," he said in greeting. "What's going on? I thought the neighborhood had been too quiet."

"Ha," Lydia replied.

"A woman, Kirsten Buchanan, choked . . . well, she has an allergy tae peanuts and she fell after a bite of shortbread, then . . . stopped breathing." The feel of the woman's lips beneath hers, the soft skin, the push of strength from Kirsten as she'd breathed in, made her queasy and Paislee gulped as her belly protested.

Zeffer watched her in question.

"She died after reaching the hospital," Constable Dean informed the detective. "They think that *someone* deliberately added peanut tae Mrs. Buchanan's cookies and then *someone* hid her pen with the dose of epinephrine. She'd supposedly fired her chef, and now he's missing. Fergus Jones. Looks guid for the perp, but . . ." Constable Dean shrugged self-importantly.

"Ah." DI Zeffer surveyed the posh conference room. Shelves were laden with donations for auction. Those who hadn't sold out of merchandise had tidied their stacks of goods on their tables as Sonya had hired a security guard to keep watch during the night. Jewelry, electronics, and artwork were valuable, and their profit would help the food bank. "Do you know for sure if there were peanuts in the shortbread?"

"My officers are collecting the biscuits now," Constable Dean said.

"Guid." The detective continued to appraise the situation in a noncommittal manner. He would want proof before condemning the chef, Paislee knew.

"Kirsten trusted Fergus—she raved over his culinary gifts. He had dishes featured in the newspaper. He won blue ribbons. I dinnae think he would . . ." Anders trailed off.

"In the paper?" Constable Rory asked.

"Kirsten Buchanan had tae have the best," Lara answered bitterly. "And everybody had tae know it was the best, or there was no point."

"Why did she fire Chef Jones—Fergus, was it?" The DI's tone was deceptive in its casualness. Paislee had always been impressed with his ability to remember details in an instant.

"She wouldnae say," Mari replied.

"Anders is right. Do we know if she actually let him go?" Christina asked. "She might've planned tae oot of a pique, mibbe he scalded the milk or something, but then she relented. He was her prize in the kitchen, even if they did argue."

Mari slowly shook her head. "I suppose it's possible. I only know that she intended tae do so in the morning, she didnae tell me why."

"I thought you were best friends." Anders went on the attack with his arms crossed. "According tae you, she told you *everything.*"

"Oh, she told me plenty." Mari and Lara glared at Anders.

Anders turned away from their accusatory looks. Sonya hovered uncertainly. What was her place in all of this? Paislee wondered if Anders and Kirsten had gone beyond a flirtation to an actual affair.

Paislee thought back to the scene outside beneath the tree . . . Anders had rushed to Kirsten's aid from the judges' table. Had Anders known about her allergy? Would he have wanted to hurt his lover? Even now he had his hand in his pocket. A lover's note?

"I hate tae be crass at a time like this, but should we cancel the fund-raiser for the food bank tomorrow?" Sonya asked with concern.

Constable Dean turned to the tall officer still standing in the threshold. "Did ye block off the area where Mrs. Buchanan fell, Rory?"

"Aye. I've taken pictures and bagged the biscuits."

The constable shrugged at Sonya. "We should be done in a few hours and you can continue with the auction as planned."

"It's just that we've put so much into the re-opening of the club . . ." Sonya said apologetically. "The Buchanans spent a lot on advertising."

"It's in *verra* bad taste," Anders declared. "Tae carry on as if nothing has happened here today. Tae Kirsten!"

"I dinnae think you should tell me aboot bad taste." Sonya arched her white-blond brow. The woman's body was tense as she glared at her co-worker.

"Consorting with Kirsten behind her husband's back is pretty low, Anders," Mari countered. "I'm with Sonya. We should continue for the sake of the food bank, in honor of Kirsten and the work she put into it."

"Nobody needs tae find out aboot the affair." Christina *tsk*ed at Anders as if he were a child.

"Who all knows?" DI Zeffer asked.

"We just found oot!" Lara said. "Can we keep it tae ourselves? It will only hurt Gerard and Maxim." Kirsten's assistant pleaded with the constable.

Detective Inspector Zeffer waited for the constable to answer and when he didn't, pressed ahead with his own questions. "Does *Mr.* Buchanan know?"

Anders shook his head. "Kirsten thought it best tae keep it hushed until we were ready tae move forward."

Flustered by where the conversation was going, as in away from Fergus Jones, the constable gestured to the fingerprint kits. "Will ye go first, Ms. Shaw? Then Ms. Barron, since neither of you really knew the victim."

"Aye, thanks." Paislee and Lydia waited while the fourth officer set up at a table cleared of items for auction. J. Gordon, according to the tag on his uniform.

The detective wandered toward Anders, who waited with Lara, no doubt to discover more about his relationship with Kirsten. If someone had deliberately killed Kirsten, Zeffer would get to the bottom of it.

Blaise joined Paislee and Lydia. "Thanks for your support today—I dinnae ken what I would have done without ye here."

"It's what friends do," Lydia said.

"I didnae put the pen on the chair," Blaise assured them.

"We know." Paislee wiped her hands on a disinfectant toilette the officer gave her, then allowed the man to press each finger and thumb down on a marked pad.

"Fill in yer information at the top of the form, there. Your turn, ma'am," he said to Lydia.

Paislee printed her name in block letters in the appropriate space. "Blaise, should we wait for you? Or call Shep?"

"No. I've sent him a text but he's with clients." They all glanced at Christina, who'd been snide about Shep working at the golf course, while her husband, the doctor, just golfed for pleasure.

Paislee stood between Christina and Blaise. "I don't feel right about leaving you." Among the jackals.

"I'm fine. Besides, you'll still be here tomorrow, aye?" Blaise clasped Paislee's wrist.

Paislee and Lydia exchanged a look of agreement. It wouldn't be pleasant but they'd promised. "I've already cleared my weekend tae be here."

"You both are *true* friends," she said loudly. Christina, Mari, and Lara glowered. The DI watched the drama with barely veiled amusement in his sea glass–green eyes.

Constable Rory brought in a box with all three ladies' biscuits—Mari's, Blaise's, and Kirsten's.

"What are you going tae do with those?" Christina asked.

"We'll be taking them tae the lab tae be checked," Constable Rory said.

"For peanuts?"

"Or any other kind of toxin," he explained.

Christina took on a greenish tinge.

Paislee's tummy rumbled with empathy. She'd been mouth-to-mouth with Kirsten if there had been actual poison.

"Hey, what aboot Paislee?" Lydia asked, obviously arriving at the same conclusion. "Could she have gotten something from Kirsten while doing CPR?"

DI Zeffer winged his groomed brow at her in that way he had of making her feel like she'd done something wrong.

"We'll let ye know what we find." Constable Rory used the marker to label the boxes with the ladies' names.

"How do ye feel?" Zeffer asked, at her side in a heartbeat. "Do your lips sting? Are they swollen?" He came toe-to-toe with her, his intense gaze on her mouth.

She swallowed nervously. "It's been almost an hour."

"Some poisons take time tae kick in," Constable Dean said.

That didn't help her anxiety level. "It happened very quickly with Kirsten . . . she licked the top, then took a bite of the short-bread, and then she dropped tae the grass." She glanced at the floor until Zeffer stepped back and she could breathe. "I'm fine."

Could his brows arch so high they might fly off his forehead? "I've heard that from ye before."

"I don't feel any different than normal." She crossed her arms in a defensive pose but then immediately lowered them.

"Ye willnae be alone for the rest of the evening?"

"Naw—I've got Grandpa and Brody, DI."

"Make sure your grandfather stays with you, just in case it's not the nuts," Zeffer said.

"Not the nuts?" Lara repeated in a detached tone. She brought her fingers to her throat.

The folks inside the conference room all stared at one another. What had started off as a day to raise money for the local food bank had taken a drastic turn. One of their special clique was dead, possibly murdered by her private chef. The man had said clearly that he'd helped her pack the biscuits. Christina had insinuated that Fergus might even be the baker, rather than Kirsten.

But what if it wasn't the obvious choice? What if someone else had done such a heinous deed? Who? Why? Anders . . . or Gerard? Christina?

Lydia rubbed a tissue to clean the residue of ink from her finger pads. "Let's go . . . we can stop at the Dolphin for a glass of wine. What time do ye need tae get Brody?"

"Bennett will drop him off after dinner." She'd called her grandfather to let him know she'd been held up, without going into specifics. It was almost seven, and Grandpa would be home by now. A large glass of wine sounded lovely.

She'd driven today, and Lydia would drive tomorrow so that Grandpa and Brody could have the Juke. "We both deserve a glass of wine."

"Just one for the driver now," the DI said, having eavesdropped into their conversation.

"I'm responsible, thanks," Paislee said, annoyed. The man flustered her beyond reason.

"I know that. I was teasin'."

"You don't tease." Which meant he was attempting to be friendly. What was he after?

"Fine." He patted his suit pocket. "That was quick thinking aboot using the chair tae cover the cookies. Constable Rory told me. Did you see anything that might be considered suspicious?"

Lydia elbowed Paislee and eyed the ceiling. The refurbished room had accentuated the Victorian crown molding, painted in an ivory shade. It was nice, but not Lydia's point. The detective and Paislee often butted heads about his cases when he wouldn't share information, but wanted it from her.

She flicked a glance toward Anders and lowered her voice. "If ye can find a way tae see what Anders got from Kirsten? I saw him put something in his pocket after they brushed hands. A note?"

Lydia gave Paislee a surprised look. "I didnae see a thing."

Paislee shrugged. "It seemed flirty, and I wondered at it, but let it go because Blaise said that he flirted with every woman in sight."

"She did say that aboot Anders," Lydia seconded. "And Kirsten's married, so you wouldnae immediately assume an affair . . . like we just found oot."

"Right." Paislee turned to the DI. "Since then, Anders keeps touching his pocket. As if tae make sure something is still there—perhaps a letter from his lover? But it could be nothing."

"Exactly." Zeffer raised his hands in exasperation. "Why do I bother?"

Lydia tucked the tissue into the side pocket of her tote bag, still slung over her shoulder. "Ready, Paislee?"

"You're really returning tomorrow?" the DI asked Paislee. "Despite the tragedy?"

"We told Blaise we would, and on a practical note, I sold all of my sweaters and scarves. Tomorrow is the actual auction—I've donated a gorgeous cashmere sweater set for a worthy cause."

"Ye hope tae get a lot for a sweater, eh?"

"At least a thousand pounds. It's quality cashmere." Paislee held his gaze, daring him to have a different opinion.

He rubbed his jaw. "And you, Ms. Barron?"

"I brought in the latest gaming laptop, a donation from Silverstein's Real Estate Agency. Do you game?"

"No. Too busy fighting real crime." His smirk was undeniable and unrepentant, and yet somehow charming.

From behind them, Sonya stifled a sob as if suddenly understanding the reality of what had happened today. "How can we expect Gerard tae run things tomorrow? He'll be devastated."

Paislee agreed that it would be too much for the man but she didn't offer to help. What did she know about running this kind of operation? If they were going to continue with the event, then she would do her part by bringing in more items.

"I'll do it." Anders drew himself up with effort. "Kirsten's life cannae be forgotten—this auction will be her legacy. We will make the event a triumph! If you can walk the floor, Sonya?"

"Aye." Sonya stepped closer to Anders.

Paislee wasn't the only one to sigh in relief at the solution—her sigh was followed by wondering if the legacy was to include Kirsten's husband, Gerard, or if Anders would focus on Kirsten alone.

Blaise was next for the fingerprints, and Christina lined up behind her. Constable Dean's radio went off and he clicked the volume high to answer it—they all heard the message that Fergus Jones had been spotted by the river.

The constable's expression brightened, then fell as he realized that he and his officers had to remain at the Social Club and Art Centre to do their part in apprehending the man.

"I'll be on my way," the DI said. "I'll be in touch, Constable."

"Aye, sir."

Paislee rolled her eyes and hoped the constable wouldn't hold his breath. How many times had she heard those words from Zeffer before?

Constable Dean rocked on his heels and gestured to Constable Rory. "Double the officers searching for Fergus Jones. He's wanted for questioning in the death of Kirsten Buchanan."

Chapter 5

That night, Paislee waited until Brody was in bed at nine to watch a movie in his room before sitting Grandpa down at the kitchen table with a cuppa, and Scotch besides.

Her fingers shook as she relived what had happened and her part in it. "I couldn't save her, Grandpa."

He patted her hand. "Have they caught the chef?"

"I'll be the last tae know," she said. "You know how close-mouthed Zeffer can be."

"Aye, but what aboot the other officers? They don't know ye, and might not be as tight-lipped." Grandpa slurped from his mug.

"Good idea. Constable Dean was actually very compassionate." Paislee recalled the officer's kind gaze. "And Constable Rory said they'd contact me if there was actual poison."

"It would be natural, I think, after doing CPR on Kirsten, tae want tae know what happened." His husky voice deepened. "You risked your own life."

Paislee shrugged uncomfortably. "But didn't save hers." She pinched the bridge of her nose. "Blaise feels terrible because Kirsten was so mean, and now there will be no repair tae their relationship. Lydia and I were treated tae Kirsten's acidic remarks ourselves."

Grandpa's head lifted at that. "Oh? I hope ye pushed back, lass. She sounds like a bully."

"We did not, thank you." Gran had taught the high road when possible. Paislee sipped her tea. "The other ladies are no better. Kirsten's best friend is an anorexic-looking woman named Mari, and then Christina, married tae a doctor, is third in their clique. She drinks vodka from a water bottle, no exaggeration. Lara, Kirsten's assistant who also tutors their son, Maxim, was going tae be the new addition tae the quartet—tae take Blaise's place."

"You tell Blaise she has no reason tae feel bad if those ladies are nasty tae her. This reminds me of the schoolyard when I was a lad." Grandpa's silver-gray eyebrows waggled as he peered over his black-framed glasses.

"I'm sure glad that Brody goes tae a nice public school." She'd have to tell Hamish—but she pulled that thought up by the scruff of the neck. She used to be friendly with the headmaster, but she'd realized that while Brody was still at Fordythe, she and the head-master couldn't even be friends. He would always choose the side of the school—rightly so—and she didn't always agree.

"Tell me why they think it was peanuts."

Paislee added a wee bit more Scotch to her cup of Brodies. "Kirsten was deathly allergic, and it was common knowledge."

"And she just bit into one?" Grandpa asked doubtfully.

"I think she thought the shortbread was hers, but the plating was off. She licked the brown topping, nodded, then took a bite. Then . . ." Paislee's pulse pitter-pattered at her wrists and throat. "She was angry about the lack of proper presentation."

Grandpa humphed. "And the husband, Gerard, he smacked the chef fella?"

"Well, it was more of him trying tae get Fergus tae drop the tray." She cupped her tea for comfort.

"How were he and the missus getting along?" Grandpa rested his elbow on the table, one knee crossed over the other. His long, skinny feet were bare, hair on his toes.

Paislee recognized his tone, and where his questions might lead. "Grandpa, we are not doing this." Their last foray into prob-lem solving had destroyed her "friendship" with Hamish.

"What?"

"Sticking our noses in this situation." She forced herself to sound like she meant it.

He tapped his nose and peered over his glasses. "Ye can't help it. There's no denying ye have a stake in the outcome. You were there at the woman's side, lass."

Paislee sat back and sipped from her cup—she'd given Kirsten her last breath; they were connected now. "We'll see. I don't know how well Gerard and Kirsten got on . . . but the fund-raising chair at the Social Club and Art Centre is Anders Campbell, and he told us all that he loved Kirsten. And that she loved him."

Grandpa's mug slammed down, golden liquid sloshing over the side. "How did that come up?"

Paislee blew back her bangs . . . past time for a trim. "Well, it was a bit of a scene, really, with Gerard upset and waiting for his chauffer, Hendrie, tae get the car ready—right after hearing that Kirsten had died on the way tae the hospital."

"So they're wealthy . . ."

"Very."

"Another man claims tae love his wife. Does he seem the type tae take that lying down, I ask ye?"

"Probably not." She tapped the table. "When Anders said that Kirsten loved him, too, Mari—"

"Who's that again?"

"Kirsten's best friend."

"Oh. More tea?"

"Aye, top me off, please." She held her mug out. "Anyway, Mari said that it wasn't true that Kirsten loved Anders back. Gerard got this weird look on his face, realizing that Anders and Kirsten might actually have something going on."

"Poor bloke just found oot. Shame."

"I saw Kirsten and Anders brush fingers before the auction started, and pass a piece of paper. Wasn't sure what it meant."

"How so?"

"Well, it could have been an accidental flirty thing." Paislee crossed her ankles. "I told the detective about it, in case Kirsten had given him a love note or something."

"Gotta trust your intuition."

"I know, I know." But she'd also learned that she had to take a minute before she reacted and made a fool of herself . . . again.

She got up for her bag of knitting to relax as they talked. "The officers took the cookies away tae test what was in them—the other finalists' cookies, too." She sank down on her chair.

"Tae see if they all had peanuts?" Grandpa asked, confused.

"I suppose." It was now ten . . . too late to phone the police station to satisfy her curiosity about the nuts. If it had been poison, surely someone would have called her with a warning. "I wonder if Blaise will bake any more of her almond wafers for tomorrow?"

"If I were her, I'd buy scones from the bakery and call it a day. When ye can't trust home cookin', what's the world coming tae?"

Paislee looped yarn over her finger to start the row. She could make a knit cap in just over an hour, and a matching scarf in two. She thought back to the inventory she had at Cashmere Crush, which was low thanks to the booming tourist season they'd had.

"Who did Kirsten piss off tae want her dead?" Grandpa guiltily eyed the ceiling. "Sairy, Agnes. Make mad?"

Paislee chuckled at Grandpa's apology to his deceased wife, who hadn't cared for cussing. "Kirsten, according tae Blaise, was Queen Bee of Highland Academy where their children all went tae school. Though she had a sharp wit, she was revered. Gerard Buchanan is an avid golfer and a client of Shep O'Connor's, who is the new resident golf pro at Nairn Golf Resort."

"Blaise's husband."

"Right. Christina Baird was quite rude about his career—as in, her husband golfs for leisure. Blaise felt she had tae befriend the wives tae help Shep."

"Cannae Blaise just tell them that she's busy for the rest of their lives?" Grandpa had met Blaise a few times at the shop and taken a liking to her.

"Lydia understands the situation—she could be part of that crowd if she wanted. I'm so glad she doesn't."

Unless of course she and Laird Corbin Smyth ever got past being friends.

Naw, even then her bestie would still be Lydia. She continued her cap, knitting and thinking. Had what happened to Kirsten been deliberate? Was it possible to develop other severe allergies without knowing it?

"Lydia's got a braw head on her shoulders, that one." Grandpa's admiration shone like the sun.

Paislee smiled at him. "You'll have the Juke tomorrow. She's going tae pick me up at nine so that we have time tae stop by the shop for more items tae sell—I sold everything today."

"Guid fer you! Even the cashmere sweater set?"

"No—that will be up for auction tomorrow."

"And you willnae see a pound note of it." He shook his finger at her.

"Don't get started on that old song again. Where were we? Oh, yeah. Who would want tae put peanuts in Kirsten's shortbread . . ."

"The husband."

"Why?" Paislee finished another circular row. "He didn't know about the affair before today. Doesn't make sense for him tae want tae be a single dad. From what Blaise said, Kirsten was a trophy for him."

"A trophy that was steppin' out."

"He didn't know until today." Paislee glanced at Grandpa. "Unless he was lying about that."

"And he's got a temper . . ."

"True." There was no denying that. She'd been shocked at how Gerard had smacked Fergus in the arm so that he'd drop the tray. Fergus had been, too. The chef's face had gone from indignant to scared in the blink of an eye. Had Gerard done that on purpose, hoping to destroy evidence of the peanuts?

Paislee stopped knitting and took a deep sip. The tea with

Scotch warmed her from the inside. "I saw Fergus's expression. I know it's not proof, but he didn't look guilty. I mean, let's say that Fergus was fired this morning. Why would Kirsten then have him show up with the cookies? That just seems like she'd be asking for trouble."

"How can you find oot?"

"There's nothing I can do tonight. Maybe we'll have news on whether or not the chef was caught in the morning. I imagine that the powers that govern Nairn won't be keen tae have another murder in our little shire."

"Ye're right there. The Earl of Cawdor was on the telly with a warm welcome tae the tourists. Inviting them all personally tae see his castle and the new lunch menu with artisan meals made from his own garden."

Paislee started to laugh.

"It's no joke, lass." Grandpa grinned. "That's the world we live in now. Gourmet lettuce in an old castle, twenty pounds a person."

Still smiling, she asked, "What are you and Brody going tae do tomorrow?"

"My mate Georgie does fly-fishin' on the river. I thought we'd go see him, and try it oot."

"It'll be a bonny day for it. I'm a wee bit jealous." She made progress on the hat, opting not to do a pom on the top but keep the slouchy knit-cap shape.

"Ye're fast," Grandpa observed. "Guid thing."

"Aye, I'll do another of these before I turn in. You don't have tae wait up if ye're ready for bed."

"I'll finish this first." He lifted his mug, in a conversational mood.

Paislee started on the second cap. "How did Brody seem today?" He and Edwyn had gotten into a few scrapes over girls in the last few weeks, but they'd gotten it sorted out, so far, without Mrs. Martin, their P6 teacher, having to call in the headmaster, Hamish.

"He got home just before you, but he seemed in high spirits. In fact, here's a word tae the wise, they're dreamin' up a camping trip."

"Just the two of them?" Her voice rose high as she imagined two adventurous boys alone in the woods and all the danger that might entail.

"Yep."

She didn't even look at her grandfather. "Nope."

He chuckled. "Ye cannae raise a lad afraid of his own shadow."

She lowered her knitting and speared him with her Mama Bear eyes. "That is not the case with Brody Shaw."

Grandpa noisily drank the dregs of tea. "Like I said, just giving you a heads-up."

"What does Bennett say?"

"How would I know?" Grandpa bobbed his leg beneath the table. "Bennett didnae talk tae me aboot it. Brody was just going on and on. And I'll not tell you more if ye let him know I said anythin'."

She clamped her lips closed but nodded. Better to know than not. "And I suppose you'd let him do it?"

"I never said that." Grandpa stood and brought his mug to the sink where he washed it out and put it in the dish drainer to dry. "But mibbe, a tent in the back garden wouldnae be so bad?"

With that compromise offered, the wily old man snuck off to bed.

Paislee had dozed off on the couch, staying up a good portion of the night to finish two caps and a scarf. She woke with the dawn's light smack in her eyeball and groaned as she rose, a crick in her neck.

"And me not even thirty," she said aloud to nobody. She stumbled zombie-like into the kitchen and turned on the electric kettle.

She heard Wallace whine and scratch at Brody's door and climbed the stairs, avoiding the third and fifth out of long-ingrained habit so they wouldn't creak, and let their Scottish terrier out.

The black pup raced down in a hurry this morning, but Paislee dragged to meet him at the back door where he pawed.

"Hush," she said to him, and she swore Wallace winked at her,

forgoing his usual bark as he scurried across the screened-in back
porch and down the wooden stairs to the grass.

Pink and lavender dawn shone on the flowerpots alive with
color and she took a moment to say thanks for all she had, and, of
course, a good morning to her granny in heaven.

"You'll never believe it, Gran. Another murder—here in
Nairn. We're practically Glasgow now." The city was infamous for
its crime rate, and the opposite of sleepy seaside Nairn.

Her grandmother had been an English teacher in Nairn for
thirty years and had encouraged Paislee to be independent when
Paislee had come to Gran pregnant at eighteen, with her mum in
America and her da dead. Paislee made mistakes aplenty, but she
did her best to set a good example for Brody in spite of them.

Right from wrong would seem basic, aye, but there were many
shades in between. Paislee, single and with a bun in the oven in
old-fashioned Nairn, had a lot to prove by the choices she'd made.
She hoped that Brody wouldn't have to pay for them.

Brody knew he belonged to her, and now they had Grandpa,
too. Craigh, the uncle she'd never met, hadn't returned from the
oil rig, the *Mona*, as scheduled. According to the authorities, the oil
rig didn't exist. There was a story to be told about that yet.

Grandpa had been homeless for two weeks when he'd landed
on the doorstep of Cashmere Crush, and now he lived in the very
house he used to live in with Gran, before her granny had given
him the boot.

A ray of sunshine bathed Paislee's face—warm and loving.
"We'll have a laugh about it in heaven one day." She held open
the back door as Wallace raced back in, tongue lolling, eyes flash-
ing . . . and, most important, bladder empty.

She filled the pup's dish with fresh water, then added dry kib-
ble to his bowl.

Bringing the assorted knitted goods to the table, Paislee poured
herself some hot water over Brodies Scottish Breakfast Tea and let
it steep to a dark, hearty color guaranteed to get her day off to a
decent start.

Paislee rubbed the aching muscle in her neck and piled the knit caps on top of the scarf. She'd started a second scarf but saw where she'd dropped a stitch. "Oops," she said with a laugh. "Guess we'll have tae go back and pick that up. No holes in a Paislee Shaw original."

Two hours and two cups of tea later, she'd rectified her mistake. Wallace curled over her toes, his furry body warmer than slippers.

The dog jumped up when Grandpa opened the door from Gran's room—his room, not that they called it that. For some reason he refused to share with her, he preferred to insist the arrangement was temporary until Craigh returned.

She wasn't going to argue or make a big deal of it, but had resigned herself to the fact that something had happened to her uncle and Grandpa wasn't willing to admit his fears about it. Paislee had no complaints with him as a roommate, either—he was a tidy cook and cleaned up after himself.

"What's this?" Grandpa studied the mound of knitted goods on the table. "Santa's elves visited during the night?"

"Not Santa, thank you, but me." She wiggled her fingers and cleared space for him to join her, folding the items into a bag to be priced later. "Even Brody's aware that Santa's not real."

"Hey now!" Grandpa opened the fridge and stared into it as if food would magically appear. "That's no way tae get your stocking filled at Christmas."

The interior light flickered, then died. She'd need to get bulbs at the hardware store. "Ye mind shutting the door before the cold escapes?"

"Not sure what I want tae eat." He closed the door without choosing anything, then went to the pantry. "Did ye stop fer snacks?"

"Naw—it slipped my mind, all things considered. Sorry." She'd put Kirsten's death as far from her thoughts as possible all night, losing herself in music on low and knitting. Every time she'd started to close her eyes, memories of Kirsten's last moments rattled her awake.

"Fair, fair. I'll get the paper." He looked at the clock above the cooker. "Seven. Should be here, if they arenae using that new guy. Worthless. Brody could do a better job. Could be time tae put the lad tae work."

"These days you need a car tae make deliveries, so no. We can wait."

Grandpa returned and dropped the newspaper in the center. Kirsten Buchanan's death was on the front page.

Paislee's stomach knotted. "What's it say?"

"Let's unroll it and see, now." Grandpa brushed his palms together and slid the rubber band off, adding it to the pile next to the house phone.

Paislee held her breath as she read. " 'Kirsten Buchanan, model, actress, superior mother, active in her community, dead due to anaphylactic shock.' Her own shortbread did her in. God, that's so sad."

The article went on, painting Kirsten in sainthood. "Yer sure she wasnae Mother Teresa? Mibbe Blaise got it wrong." Grandpa jabbed the printed words.

Paislee had seen for herself that wasn't the case and shook her head.

"Or," Grandpa said, "mibbe Gerard paid off the editor."

"That's more likely, with all the Buchanan money."

He poured himself tea and then brought some wheat crackers and a banana to the table. The man loved to snack but he especially adored sweets.

"Since you'll have the car today, why not get the cash from the jar tae buy snacks?"

"Aye, I suppose we can stop after fishin'."

She could only imagine the smell from that but kept her mouth shut—she wasn't doing it and didn't want to stop the shopping from happening.

Paislee finished the article but there was nothing about the chef or Kirsten's death being deliberate rather than an accident.

Had they all gotten it wrong yesterday? Had the constable's

first reaction, that perhaps Christina had played a prank on Kirsten, been correct?

"It makes no sense that she'd have peanuts in her shortbread, or even in her house if she was that allergic tae them." Paislee didn't understand it.

"Call that friendly constable later . . . but I bet there will be plenty of blethering today at the club."

"You're right. I'm curious tae see what the ladies will do, her friends. And Anders." Paislee snagged a broken piece of cracker and popped it in her mouth.

"What's the building like after the remodel?" He peeled the banana and bit into the soft fruit.

"It's beautiful, Grandpa." She thought of how well they'd refurbished the outside to retain its old-fashioned appearance, and made the inside modern. "A nice place for our community tae enjoy."

"I hope it doesnae get shut doon because of this. I've been asked tae a dinner there next month." He finished the banana in four bites.

"By whom?" Whom did he know that she didn't? Why hadn't he gone to them for assistance when he'd been in trouble?

"I had friends before I knew ya, lass, dinnae look so shocked." Grandpa brought the banana peel to the trash, then washed his hands.

"Sorry." Not friends that he'd let know he was in a spot of bother, prideful old goat.

He turned at the sink to face her. "Some fellas from the fishery I knew before they closed it, reached oot—I was that surprised tae get the invitation in the mail, at the storage place."

He'd moved Craigh's things into a very small unit in Dairlee, and set up a post office box for any mail forwarded from his old address.

"I'm glad, Grandpa."

"It'll be guid tae see them and catch up. Mibbe they've heard something, y'know? Aboot Craigh."

Her heart ached in an instant. There could be no good reason for her uncle to have disappeared, but she couldn't blame Grandpa for hoping. "That'd be wonderful."

"Aye." His expression sobered and he bypassed the kitchen table, shoving his chair in to go to his room.

Brody hurried down the stairs, swinging from the bottom post. "Sunday Funday!" His face fell as he remembered the change in plan. "Where's Grandpa?"

"His room. Hungry?"

"Starved."

"Want me tae make eggs?"

"Nope—I want toast and jam."

"And cereal, too." If it were up to Brody he'd eat nothing but orange marmalade on toast.

"Okay."

He busied himself and she bit her lip about the spill of milk or the dropped Weetabix. Faithful Wallace lapped it up better than a mop.

"Me and Grandpa are going tae go fly-fishin'."

"You know what that is?" Paislee kept knitting and checked the time. Thirty minutes until she had to shower and get ready to return to the scene of Kirsten's death.

"Naw—but he says we get tae make our own ties. For the bait." Brody scowled and swiped a drop of milk from his lower lip. "We willnae catch flies, will we?"

"I don't think so." She hid her smile behind a fall of her hair, which was a tangled mess since she'd slept on the couch.

"Anyway, it'll be fun." He took a bite, partially chewed, and swallowed. "Are you sure ye dinnae want tae come with us?"

"I'm tempted, believe me. It's going tae be a full day of sunshine." A rare thing in Scotland. "And I'm indoors. Oh well, it's for a good cause—the food bank. If you and Grandpa have fun, maybe you can teach me next weekend?"

"Sure." Brody pointed at the picture of Kirsten Buchanan in the newspaper. "Who's that?"

"Someone I met yesterday at the club."

"And now she's dead?" He stopped chewing his cereal to stare at her.

"Aye, so sad. She had a peanut allergy." Paislee completed another row and stretched. "Do you know if anybody at your school has something like that?"

He shook his head and resumed eating.

"I didn't realize that it was so prevalent." She nodded toward the paper. "The article said that people with this allergy are on the rise, probably because of peanut butter, which Scots didn't use tae eat as much of—it's an American import."

"I dinnae like peanut butter," Brody said. "The Americans can have it. I like—"

"I know, I know. Two slices of cheese and a pickle on white bread. Jam on toast."

They shared a smile.

Grandpa came out again, this time fully dressed for his day on the river in khakis, rolled-up sleeves on his flannel shirt, and a fisherman's hat on his head rather than his customary tam. He'd added a sleeveless vest loaded with pockets and she winced at the stains—but again, kept the peace rather than suggest tossing it in the laundry.

"That pretty lady died from peanuts," Brody informed Grandpa. "Did you know the Americans are trying tae poison us with peanut butter?"

Grandpa hooted. "What're ye sayin'?"

Paislee tossed her napkin at her smart-aleck son. "That's not what the article said at all. Would you like tae copy it word for word before you leave this morning?"

"No, no." Brody shook his head.

She rose from her chair and her spine cracked. "Hear that? All from sleeping on the couch!"

"Ye better eat more dairy for your bones, lass, or you'll be one of those old hens walkin' around with your nose to the ground and a hunch in your back."

Brody giggled at the image.

"Fine, if ye say so. Ice cream for me." Just to be ornery, she took the carton of vanilla from the freezer, knocked off the freezer burn (Grandpa preferred chocolate) and dug in with her spoon for breakfast.

The shocked grin on her son's face at her not mum–like action was priceless and worth the awful taste in her mouth from the crystalized ice cream. His happiness was all she wanted in the world.

Chapter 6

Lydia arrived in her sporty red Mercedes, two coffees in paper cups, two muffins, and the paper open to the article on Kirsten Buchanan.

"Thanks, Lyd." Paislee waved goodbye to Grandpa and Brody on the front step, Wallace squirming to be free in Brody's arms. "Don't forget tae stop at the shop."

"Why—you have an entire bag full of goodies."

"No sweaters, though, just things I could do fast. I was so tired I dropped a stitch in my second scarf."

"Not Paislee Shaw perfection," Lydia joked.

Lydia parked before the shop and Paislee hopped out, leaving Lydia to read the paper in the front seat while she waited.

Her neighbor, James Young, saw her and hurried out. "Can ye believe the news, Paislee? You were at the social club yesterday, weren't ye?"

Paislee's first instinct so that she could get through the day without being an emotional mess was to focus on business and not what happened to Kirsten. "Aye. Next year, if they do this again, you should get a table. I sold everything, James. Your leather merchandise would fly out the door—way better than the parade because rich people are coming with their wallets open."

"I'll keep that in mind." James rubbed his wrinkled chin. "Did ye know the model that died?"

Paislee gulped as Kirsten's image filled her mind, and prayed the memory would someday fade. "Just met her yesterday."

"Peanut allergy. Who knew that could be so deadly? They should have medicine, in this day and age. I wonder if Margot at the lab knows of something?"

"They have an EpiPen, tae stop the shock, but by the time they found one, it was too late for her." Paislee couldn't bring herself to talk about her part in it and still function, so she went into her shop.

James followed. "Too bad, that. I never cared for peanuts anyway."

"Brody, either." She was not a big fan anymore.

"Smart lad. See ya!" James left, leaving the door cracked open.

Paislee piled together five pullover sweaters and two cardigans, keeping one of each at the shop.

She left Cashmere Crush, double-checking the lock to make sure it was closed, then stowed her goods in Lydia's narrow backseat.

"The sweaters fill it up! You could never have kids in this car, Lydia."

"I should hope not," Lydia laughed, closing the paper and folding it so Kirsten wasn't watching them.

"You know what I mean."

"I do, and I'm ignoring you. No kids. Can you believe that article?" Lydia tossed the paper in the back. "Kirsten was no angel like this implies."

"Not even close, but still . . . what good can come from speaking ill of the dead?"

"I suppose. I want tae know aboot the chef . . . but there wasnae a mention of it."

"Grandpa thinks Gerard paid the paper tae edit the piece."

"What is that saying . . . you know, that the first liar wins?" Lydia tapped the wheel and pulled into the empty lane toward the social club. "That way no matter what else is printed later, people will remember this tribute."

"Interesting plan tae protect Kirsten's reputation." Paislee eagerly bit into her muffin. "Carrot? But way better than carrot . . ."

"Isn't it flavorful? I was stress-baking last night. How'd *you* sleep?"

She rubbed her sore neck. "Not well."

"Understandable." Lydia patted Paislee's knee. "I hope they find oot what actually happened tae Kirsten. Paper confirmed anaphylactic shock. Peanuts. It had tae have been the chef. I mean, he lived with them, and had access tae her food. And if Christina's little digs are right, he might have been the one tae make them while she took all the credit."

Paislee shrugged. This was no longer her first foray into crime and death and trying to discover a killer. She'd learned to ask questions beyond the obvious answers.

"You didnae think Fergus was guilty yesterday, either," Lydia said. "So, who?"

Paislee finished the delicious muffin. Her friend couldn't knit a stitch or sew on a button, but she could bake and make appetizers that were restaurant worthy. "I've been asking meself the same thing." *Gerard* was on the tip of her tongue but she held the name back.

"Have you heard from Blaise?" Lydia checked the rearview mirror, then the side mirrors, before switching lanes. She led the traffic pack on this bonny Sunday morning.

"No." Paislee sipped her coffee. Lydia had added enough cream and sugar to it to make it drinkable. "This is perfect. Thanks."

"Welcome. Blaise wasnae exaggerating aboot how awful those ladies were tae her . . . I almost called her last night, but decided tae wait until today, just in case she'd managed tae put the incident from her mind for a few hours."

"Kirsten and Mari especially were *so* snarky. I'm not sure about Lara." She glanced at Lydia. "No wonder Christina drinks."

"I read an article in a magazine just last week that was aboot how those mean girls in secondary school and university grow up tae be the mums we have tae deal with in business situations, or school settings. It applies tae Blaise fer sure. You see any of that at Fordythe?"

"Naw. But I'm too busy tae join those social circles. I have tae take care of Brody and I don't have time for more."

"I know! Like dating, or . . ."

"I let you buy me wine yesterday at the Dolphin."

"Not the same. You need tae be kissed under the moonlight, on the beach with the surf at your ankles."

Paislee heard the catch in Lydia's voice and knew her best friend so well that she got the subtext right away.

"You've seen Laird Corbin! When?" Paislee studied Lydia hard. He hadn't come by yesterday as Paislee had hoped.

Lydia's blush just added to her beauty whereas when Paislee blushed she looked like she had a rash.

"He popped over last night after I'd shared the reasons for my baking and we walked along the sand. It was verra romantic, I dinnae mind saying." She flipped her cherry-red hair. "He left this morning."

"Brilliant!" Paislee couldn't be happier for her.

"I dinnae want tae talk aboot it anymore, now." Lydia raised her finger in warning. "I want tae enjoy the magic."

"You should!"

"Before it fades. The magic *always* fades."

Paislee clamped her mouth closed. She recognized the obstinate tightness of Lydia's jaw and knew it wasn't worth an argument. For now.

"We're here!" Lydia turned into the car park of the social club at precisely nine thirty and had to circle twice to find a spot. Word of the success—or was it the death of a socialite?—had prompted more people to show up. Shoppers weren't allowed until ten, and there was a security guard at the front glass doors checking their badges before he let them in.

Sonya wasn't at her reception desk, but Paislee remembered that the director would be in the conference room to help Anders operate the fund-raiser.

They entered the room. Unlike yesterday's organized high-energy activity, this was sheer chaos. Mari and Christina were nose-to-nose arguing over something at their table—front and center. Lara intervened with her arms outstretched between them.

"Stop!" Lara said, her face ruddy. "Do ye think Kirsten would approve of you behaving like this?"

"Probably so," Blaise mumbled—she'd been waiting by the door for Paislee and Lydia in a panic. "They've been yelling at each other for ten minutes straight, accusing each other of the most horrible things."

"Like?" Lydia enjoyed a genuine drama so long as she wasn't involved.

"Well, it started when Mari showed up and Christina was already at the table, crying, and Mari pounced on her for being a drunk, and a fake friend tae Kirsten. Then Christina accused Mari of being a bulimic bitch who couldnae think withoot Kirsten telling her what tae do."

Lydia's gray eyes glittered with amusement. "You're right. Horrible. Especially if it's true."

Paislee brought her hand to her mouth. Drunk? Bulimic? Awful.

"Then they went after each other's kids, and husbands"—Blaise gestured to Lara—"and here we are, with Lara trying tae calm them doon."

"We should have come earlier." Lydia slid the handle of her tote bag into her palm.

"Maybe they should go home?" Paislee suggested. "Let themselves grieve for their friend."

"Neither one will leave—it would be a point of weakness if one couldnae manage tae stick it oot today. Just watch." Blaise shook her head. "Poor Lara."

Lara was trying to get each lady to sit down at the long table with three chairs, leaving the center one empty. She attempted to sit in it, and both Mari and Christina rounded on her like rabid dogs.

"That is not your chair," Christina said.

"You are no Kirsten." Mari lifted her nose. "You're her assistant, which means you are now oot of a job."

Lara gasped. "I'm here for Maxim. For Gerard."

"Shouldnae that be 'Mr. Buchanan'?" Mari asked sweetly. "Or did you want *more* of what Kirsten had? I'll be watching you."

Christina's eyes widened as she studied Lara. "No . . ."

Lara bolted toward the shelves of items.

The women exchanged satisfied looks before remembering they were no longer allies.

"Unreal," Lydia said.

Paislee passed by the table toward theirs at the back, not bothering with a good morning to Mari or Christina since it obviously wasn't one. The silver cloth over the table was gone, revealing a bare wood surface. "What happened tae it?"

"I gave it tae the police in case they can find anything on the fabric." Blaise hugged her waist. "I still cannae believe any of this."

Paislee unpacked her bags of sweaters, hats, scarves, and shawls. "It's surreal. When did you get home?"

"Not until seven. Shep was waiting for me with a giant glass of gin." Blaise tilted her head back as if taking a shot. "I havenae done that since college."

"You earned it," Lydia commiserated.

"I just wanted tae forget—but that's impossible. Kirsten Buchanan was my first 'friend' at Highland Academy. She invited me into their circle and I felt so honored until I realized how things really went—backstabbing, gossiping, bullying."

Blaise dabbed at her eyes.

"I'm so sorry," Paislee said, hugging her.

"Isnae this sweet?" Christina said from behind them. "Why arenae you in jail, Blaise?"

Blaise gestured Christina back. "I didnae take the EpiPen, for the last time." She fired off, "Did your husband post bail for you?"

"I'm not guilty," Christina insisted.

"Your fingerprints are all over the injector." Blaise crossed her arms and stood her ground.

Christina paled and murmured, "I havenae heard anything from the police. Have you?"

Paislee realized that was why Christina had deigned to join them. She wanted information—she might have started out sweeter rather than attack-mode.

"No." Blaise relaxed her body. "Other than what was in the paper."

"Where are your cookies?" Christina asked. The table only had Paislee's merchandise on it. "I stayed up all night making more macaroons."

Blaise touched her throat. "I couldnae . . . I'm selling mints in decorative tins. I'll set up in a minute."

Christina rolled her eyes. "Hardly the rules."

"The baking competition is *over*," Paislee said.

Blaise shrugged. "I'm donating the proceeds tae the food bank. I already spoke with Anders aboot it and he said it was fine."

"He'd agree with anything at the moment, he's that frazzled." Christina lowered her voice. "Can you believe that he and Kirsten were . . . you know."

Blaise clamped her lips closed. "I dinnae know anything aboot it."

"You're leaving our group—your choice."

"I have no regrets." Blaise maintained eye contact.

Christina lifted her chin and then walked away.

"She seems worried," Paislee said. "Do you think she knows something more about Kirsten?"

"She has problems with anxiety." Blaise sighed and went around the table to sit down and unpack her box of prettily pre-packaged mints. "It's why she drinks."

"Is it possible that she hid the pen on your chair?" Lydia asked.

"I just dinnae ken why she would, unless she was trying tae frame me. But does that mean that she killed"—Blaise swallowed hard—"Kirsten?"

"Christina instead of the chef?" Paislee considered this and nodded. "Fergus Jones just seems too obvious."

"Doesnae mean he didnae do it, though." Lydia drank her coffee.

"True." Paislee stacked her items for sale in tidy rows so the colors tempted folks to touch the soft wool, and then buy.

Could Christina have acted out of jealousy when she didn't make the top three bakers in the competition? And hadn't she seen Mari and Kirsten collaborating about it? Maybe Christina had seen them, too, and overreacted by somehow putting peanuts in the shortbread, and setting up Blaise, who was no longer part of the group—Blaise had escaped the clutches of the clique.

It made sense in a sick way.

"Have you offered tae bribe Suzannah into leaving her friends?" Paislee only half joked.

Blaise straightened a bow on a mint box. "Not yet. I'll talk tae Shep . . . mibbe a new bike could take away the pain of an early goodbye?"

Anders was up on the dais today, working with the computer and monitors. The auction would end at five and the lines for bidding would be open until then. There were two large flat-screen televisions, a painting, three vacations, and, of course, Paislee's cashmere sweater set and Lydia's gaming laptop. Blaise and Shep had donated a vacation to Italy and a round of golf with Shep.

Sonya walked the aisles, ready to assist shoppers or vendors as needed. She eventually arrived at their table. "Hello! Thank you so much for coming back today. We had three people pull oot because of what happened. We at the club, in support of the food bank, very much appreciate your patronage."

Paislee could tell that this was not the first time she'd said this, and though it was sincere, it was also flat.

"We're happy tae do our part for the community," Lydia said. "How are you holding up, Sonya?"

"I'm all right." Sonya wore black slacks and a black blouse—she had not forgotten yesterday's tragic ending. "You're ready tae begin at ten?"

"Aye." Paislee nodded.

Sonya walked to the next table. "Hello!" she said, and began her spiel.

Paislee, on the right, looked at Lydia, in the middle, and Blaise on the other end. "The bags under Sonya's eyes suggest a sleepless night—something I can relate tae."

"I could show you how tae hide those shadows in an instant," Lydia offered. "A little cream, a little powder, and voilà."

"Lydia's a magician with makeup," Paislee told Blaise. "I'm like the toddler with a crayon coloring out of the lines."

"Stop." Lydia gave Paislee's arm a nudge. "I'm going tae bid on that Eva Ullrich painting. She's an artist tae watch, mark my words."

"It's pretty." Paislee tilted her head to study the piece on the wall. She had no interest or time to devote to art—she either liked it or not.

"It's a landscape." Her friend went on about the shadings and colors.

"Landscape of what?" The blue rectangle resembled nothing that was out her window every day.

"Abstract—it's art, Paislee."

Blaise chuckled. "I dinnae see it, either, Lydia, but Shep has a true eye—he buys our artwork."

"May you get the winning bid, Lydia," Paislee said with a laugh. To her the painting was made up of light blue swirls. That was all.

"I was thinking of bidding on what doesnae sell, in order tae up the profit," Blaise said.

"That's decent of you." Lydia shrugged. "But ye might end up with that sewing machine. It's only got a few bids."

"The important thing is tae make money for the food bank." Blaise scrunched her nose. "Not that I can sew. I send our tailoring oot."

"I can manage a hem and buttons." Paislee folded a last cap to provide an appealing appearance on the table. "No machine needed."

Lydia stood up and eyed the front entrance. "Sonya just opened the doors. Hang on, ladies. There's a horde of people ready tae race in."

"So long as they have cash, they're welcome!" Paislee patted her stack of knitted items.

A day had never passed so fast. Lydia kept them refreshed with water, tea, and snacks. It was like a plague of locusts had descended on the conference room and cleaned the place out.

"There went my last sweater," Paislee said, pleased. Blaise had run out of mints hours ago and had been helping Sonya keep the crowded aisles clear. About a quarter of the people who'd shown up wanted to talk about Kirsten's death—where had it happened, who'd found the body—while the rest wanted to support the food bank.

Paislee didn't engage in conversation but Lydia and Blaise both kept up their parts for the table while Paislee took money. Lydia wrapped and bagged for Paislee while she talked.

At five, Paislee wiped her hand across her forehead. "This is ten times better than the parade—I would do this again, tae be sure. Minus the dead person."

Her bank account would have a nice cushion in the event her pipes burst, or the roof leaked. With an old house there was always something.

"I cannae imagine that Gerard will back it with Kirsten gone," Blaise said. "She was the driving force behind it. Though Anders might find another premier member tae take it on."

"Like you?" Lydia suggested to Blaise. "As you say, it's a great cause."

"Not me." The flow of people had slowed and those in the conference room now were mostly waiting for the auction to begin. "Christina might, or Mari. I'm sure they'll make up soon. They're two of a kind."

"I wouldn't want tae manage it—there are too many big personalities." Paislee uncapped a water bottle and took a drink.

"Shep is quite brilliant at dealing with rich, entitled people— he was born with money, and talent, and chooses tae be a golf pro. Christina's husband, John, doesnae have the special gift for the game that takes a golfer to the next level, no matter how much money he has in the bank."

"Is that why she's so snarky about it?" Paislee asked.

"I think so." Blaise shrugged. "I'm looking forward tae this event being over and going home tae soak in a nice hot tub with a bath bomb. Suzannah's nanny makes herbal ones that smell amazing."

A nanny. Paislee lowered her head. She was grateful for Grandpa but didn't see any homemade herbal baths in her future.

"Ten minutes till showtime!" Anders announced from his seat on the dais.

Each big-ticket item had a box showing the bid beneath it.

"Watch oot," Lydia teased Blaise. "Someone just bid on the sewing machine."

They all laughed.

Lydia got up to scrawl another figure on the Eva Ullrich painting.

Blaise patted Paislee's hand. "How are you doing? It was a traumatic thing that happened yesterday, for you especially. There hasnae been a minute tae relax but I've been meaning tae ask all day."

"Fine." Paislee smiled to prove it.

"You're strong." Blaise touched the diamond on her ring finger absently. "I envy that."

"What are ye talking about?" Paislee turned toward Blaise so they were face-to-face, the dais at Paislee's back.

"You would never be in my ridiculous situation because you wouldnae be friends with mean people just tae be popular."

"It's not that I wouldn't," Paislee said, feeling like Blaise gave her too much credit. "I'm just so focused on raising Brody that I don't notice much else."

"The Buchanans' support of Shep is how he got offered the job here in Nairn." Blaise studied her manicured nails. "I mean, his talent and skill are there, but Gerard knows the right people. Spoke into the right ears."

The door to the conference room slammed open and Sonya, who'd been speaking to a vendor, jumped back. "Gerard! What are ye doing here?" She put her hand on his forearm and whispered, "Shouldnae you be home, with your son?"

"Dinnae tell me what tae do!" Gerard's face was ravaged with grief and rage. "Where's Anders?"

Anders stood and seemed prepared to bolt. Gerard's gaze lasered in on Anders, who remained frozen on the dais.

"You scum-sucking arse!" Gerard pushed Christina and Mari, who'd both run to him, aside to reach Anders.

Anders balanced on the edge of the dais, his hands out in a placating manner. "Calm doon, Gerard."

"Dinnae call me 'Gerard'—you snake in the grass. I invited you intae my home! You took advantage of my generosity."

"I didnae mean—"

Gerard yanked Anders's ankle and pulled him down with a clatter as Anders's head smacked wood on the descent.

"I'm going tae kill you!"

Paislee shook free of the spell she was caught in, and called her friend Amelia Henry, who answered the phones at Nairn Police Station, to see if there was an officer in the neighborhood before another person died at the club.

Chapter 7

The ten other men in the group of vendors inside the conference room were all over sixty and in no condition to pull Gerard off Anders as he repeatedly pummeled the face of the man who'd slept with his wife.

Anders had curled his arms around his head. "Stop, Ger—Mr. Buchanan!"

"Get off of him!" Sonya shouted. When Gerard didn't listen, she grabbed a coffee-table book by a local photographer and whacked it over Gerard's head.

Gerard fell back, stunned.

The security guard, the same man who'd checked their identification at the door earlier, raced into the room. "What's going on?"

Gerard stumbled to his feet and pointed at Anders. "That man slept with my wife!"

The security guard stood speechless—obviously torn on the right response. Buchanan's wife sleeping around? There might *need* to be some payback . . .

Paislee felt sorry for Gerard in the worst way, but violence wasn't the answer.

Lara arrived at Gerard's side, her manner calm. Paislee noticed that she, too, had dressed in black. "Come now, Gerard. Sit with me over here."

He broke down crying as he collapsed, head on his arms, at a table selling handcrafted ceramics. Thankfully, there was room as most had sold and none crashed to the floor.

Sonya studied Anders, the man she'd just saved from a beating. "Is this true?"

"I told you yesterday that it was love."

She slowly lowered the book. "And you and I?"

Anders snapped out of his daze as he realized what might be at stake. "I . . . I'm sorry."

"Och, what a tube," Blaise whispered.

"We arenae at all alike," Lydia declared. "For the record. There's flirtation, and then there's being sleazy. He's crossed the line."

Mari offered Sonya a bottle of water that the woman accepted with shaking fingers. She put the book back on the shelf of things for auction.

"I cannae believe this," Christina said, then focused on the crying man and tapped his shoulder. "Gerard, why did you come here just now? Maxim needs you tae be with him at the house."

Gerard raised his head and pulled a printout of emails from his pocket. "I was home, and found these! Sickening notes from Anders tae *my* Kirsten."

The police arrived—well, a single officer: the tall one, Constable Rory, from yesterday.

"This man threatened tae kill me." Anders pointed to Gerard and crossed his arms.

"That bloke was sleeping with his wife," the security guard explained to the officer.

"Wife's dead, and we're still investigating." Rory patted his vest—Paislee had no idea what the officer was searching for. Did that mean Fergus Jones remained free? Or had he been caught and released?

The security guard nodded and glanced around the room with renewed interest.

Lara took the printout from Gerard and read the emails, her mouth trembling. "Oh . . . how awful for you." She put a compassionate hand on his shoulder.

Mari sidled closer to Lara and Gerard. "Watching you, Lara."

"Stop it!" Lara snatched her hand back, her expression stricken. "I never wished Kirsten harm."

"You called her a bitch yesterday," Mari said, her gaze on Gerard. "We all heard her."

Gerard roared and straightened. "You did, Lara?"

Lara eyed the ceiling, then shook the paper at Mari. "You're a troublemaker. You and Christina will never be as beautiful as Kirsten, no matter how many meals you miss, or how hard you try."

Mari gasped at this show of spunk.

"Kirsten was a bitch, we all know it, but she'd earned her place at the top as a model, a wife, and a mother." Lara stayed near Gerard. "I stand by what I say."

"My beautiful Kirsten!" Gerard dug his hands into his hair and yanked.

"It's all right, now." Lara patted his back. "Let's get you home."

"He's *pished*," Sonya said, waving her fingers beneath her nose. "I can smell the whisky from here."

Paislee could, too. It was a miracle he'd made it here, and hopefully without hurting anybody.

"Where is Hendrie, Gerard?" Mari asked in a soft tone.

"Dunno. Didnae wait for him once I found the emails. I used the Fiat."

"I'll drive him home," Lara told the officer.

"Where is Maxim?" Christina asked, eyes round.

"Home with his nanny."

Paislee exhaled with relief. Thank heaven he hadn't piled his son in the car.

"You can take him to his residence," Constable Rory agreed.

"Arenae you going tae arrest him for assaultin' me?" Anders dared ask.

Sonya doused Anders with the water left in her bottle. "You've got tae be kidding—you need tae finish this auction. This is for the Nairn Food Bank and that is what matters right now."

Lydia clapped and a few of the other vendors joined her.

Mari whispered goodbye to Gerard when he and Lara passed. "Let me know how I can help." Gerard nodded and he and Lara left the conference room.

Even if Lara did have a crush on Gerard, she would see the heartbroken man safely home.

Gerard had suspected his wife of an affair . . . could he have been the one to add the nuts to the shortbread cookies, and then hidden the EpiPen?

Did the same person who added the nuts, hide her medicine?

Or were they two different instances?

This was a tragedy, to be sure. Paislee walked up to Constable Rory, who waited by the front door. He smiled, possibly recognizing her from yesterday—she would be a friendly face in this particular crowd.

"Hiya. Have you found the chef yet?" she asked casually.

"Naw. Thought we had him yesterday by the river but he slipped through our fingers." He held out an open palm, fingers spread wide.

"I read in the paper that Kirsten died from peanuts." She gave him a half smile. "Good thing it wasn't poison, since nobody called tae let me know. I was up all night."

"Och!" He smacked his hand to his forehead. "I'm sairy. We got confirmation late last evening. It slipped me mind completely that you should know, since you gave her CPR. We're not supposed tae discuss investigations."

Paislee, sensing the officer's sincere regret, asked, "Do you think Fergus did it?"

"I *cannae* say." Constable Rory refused to look at her. "He's wanted for questioning, that's all."

She gestured toward Anders and Sonya, who were rooted by the crooked dais where the fight had taken place. "If you need suspects, Gerard just found out that his wife was having an affair."

"We dinnae 'need' suspects." The officer tapped his walkie-talkie. "Tough way for a bloke tae find oot."

"Aye. He might be really angry." She cleared her throat. "You never asked me about Fergus yesterday."

"I didnae get your statement?" His brow furrowed and she could see that he was worried he might have missed something. Worried that he might have to *report* that he had missed something.

"Listen, I don't want you tae get into trouble, but you should know that I was standing right there and I saw Fergus's expression when Kirsten fell tae the grass after eating the cookie. He was shocked, Constable Rory."

She hoped that he might open up to her, but Christina joined them and interrupted their conversation.

"I want you tae know that I didnae put that injector on Blaise O'Connor's chair—why hasnae your boss called me yet?" Christina's blond hair was smoothed back in a bun, her attire in dark navy, from blouse to flats.

Constable Rory shuffled, uncomfortable. "You'll be contacted once we know more."

Paislee arched her brow at that blatant tale.

"Were all the cookies tainted with peanut? Were they poisoned?" Christina persisted.

"I cannae say, ma'am."

"Well, will you go find oot when you can, if ye please?" Christina crossed her arms. "We'll be right here for the next hour or so. This silent treatment is unacceptable."

The young officer actually left—probably glad to flee their barrage of questions. The security guard walked out of the conference room with him.

"I hope he comes back," Christina told Paislee.

"That would be too easy." She glanced at Christina . . . the woman was insistent that she was innocent. "Have you called Constable Dean yourself?"

"Aye—so many times that I think he's turned his ringer off. Left three messages. Next I'll have my husband call."

From what Paislee could tell, Christina seemed very dependent on her husband. Was it the alcohol? Or the anxiety? Both?

Paislee patted Christina's shoulder. "Christina, do you mind telling me exactly how you found the pen?"

Christina pulled back, defensive.

"I'm not accusing you of anything, believe me. You seem so adamant about it and yet . . . I know Blaise didn't do it. She had no reason tae want Kirsten out of the way, not since she was moving, right? I'm just trying tae understand."

The blonde studied Paislee's face. "Well . . ."

"We were all out beneath the tree . . . you had mentioned that you didn't think it was fair when the judges took off their blindfolds tae see what was happening with Kirsten."

"God, I'm so embarrassed aboot that. But I didnae know! And these competitions are cutthroat. They always have been." She patted her chest, her wedding ring sparkling. "Kirsten had tae win. And now, Kirsten is dead. I simply cannae believe it."

"Maybe you could help me pinpoint where people were. Blaise was right by me and Lydia. Then I did CPR, the ambulance came and rushed her off, and then . . . when did you go back inside the room? Fergus was outside the whole time."

Christina's eyes narrowed. "No, Fergus was in the kitchen of the club here—he'd brought the dishes oot after the judges finalized the three winners." She dabbed her forehead with the inside of her wrist. "Well, there is only ever one winner, as Kirsten used tae say."

"So, Fergus would have walked through the conference room from the kitchen, with the plates, right by our table?" She pointed to where Lydia and Blaise sat in conversation.

"Yes, he would have." Christina nodded slowly.

Had Fergus been so angry about being fired that he'd stolen the medicine from Kirsten's purse and plopped it randomly somewhere? Or was Blaise chosen on purpose?

"What are you two whispering aboot?" Mari arrived before them, painted red lips pursed.

Christina pouted, deigning not to answer.

"We haven't heard about the cookies," Paislee said. "Have you?"

"No." Mari blinked with worry. "I've left messages with the constable, but . . ."

"Me too!" Christina deflated and put her arm around Mari. "Oh, I'm sairy for fighting. We shouldnae, not now. We are the best friends that Kirsten ever had and we should put our heads together tae find who did this tae her."

Mari tearfully hugged Christina back. "I'm sairy, too. What will we do withoot her?"

The two ladies, fences mended, wandered off without another word to Paislee. Paislee returned to Lydia and Blaise as Anders continued the auction part of the fund-raiser.

"What was that?" Lydia demanded from her seat—which had a perfect view of the front entrance.

"Fraternizing with the enemy," Blaise said. "It had tae be for a sound reason."

"It was, it was. I don't think Christina put the pen on the chair."

"What?" Lydia and Blaise said in unison.

"I'm serious. Maybe the obvious answer is the right one. Christina mentioned that Fergus Jones had tae walk through the empty conference room tae the beech tree with the tray of cookies. He had ample time tae put the medicine injector on the chair."

Lydia and Blaise exchanged a look.

"Why would he?" Lydia asked. "Was it tae set Blaise up?"

Blaise shrugged but her face turned scarlet.

"What aren't you saying?" Paislee asked in a whisper.

"If I tell you, you'll think the worst." Blaise studied her nails. Not a single cuticle.

"We willnae," Lydia promised.

"I swear!" Paislee raised her palm.

"Well . . ." Blaise glanced at Paislee and Lydia and tucked her hair behind her ear. "Fergus used tae work for me and Shep, in Inverness. The Buchanans . . . hired him away from us."

"What?" Paislee rocked back. "Did the chef leave your house on respectable terms?"

"He snuck off like a thief in the night . . ." Blaise sounded angry and hurt. "We had no idea that he was unhappy. That didnae make Shep, or me, look guid at the private school, I can tell you. Kirsten lorded it over me."

"Kirsten stole your chef?" Lydia put her elbow on the table.

Paislee tried to wrap her head around having both a nanny and a chef, then shook the images away. Blaise was her friend even if she was loaded. "Was Fergus angry with you? Would he have a reason tae set you up?"

"No. He moved up in the world—more money, better station." Blaise blew out a breath. "See? You're staring at me funny, just like I knew you would."

"Did you tell the police this connection?" It would be something Zeffer might deem important, but who knew about the constable—Constable Dean ran a looser ship.

"No. Until this moment I hadnae put it together like you just did. It was two years ago."

Two years. That was a long time. But, if he'd just been fired? What kind of opportunities were there for a chef of his caliber?

Lara had said that she'd overheard arguments between Kirsten and Fergus in the kitchen, over whose kitchen it was. Could be the chef was all about the money or status. To be fired would be a terrible blow.

"Blaise, do you know where Fergus might be hiding? I'd love tae talk tae him and find oot what happened. Was he fired? Did he kill Kirsten by adding peanuts tae the shortbread? Or was he set up somehow?"

"The cook's looking more and more guilty. I know." Blaise shrugged. "Listen. Fergus worked for us for six months—I didnae really have much tae do with him. Shep handles the service people in our house."

"Why is that?" Lydia asked.

"Well . . . he grew up with servants. Staff. I'm not that comfortable with it, really."

Blaise didn't handle the art, either. Or have as skilled of a rapport with people, as her husband—according to her.

"You come from a different background?" Lydia leaned toward Blaise, across Paislee.

Blaise darted a nervous glance around the room. "I was not of the same, well, class as Shep." She touched her diamond ring again.

"That's not important in this day and age." Paislee came to her immediate defense.

Blaise's amber eyes filled with tears that she blinked away. "Somehow Kirsten found oot that I was raised in an orphanage and she made my life hell. I was never suitable enough after she discovered that."

"That's the secret Kirsten held over you?" Paislee squeezed Blaise's shoulder. "It doesn't matter!"

"That doesnae mean anything at all except tae prove that you're a smart woman tae move out of low circumstances." Lydia's tone was fierce. "You cannae help where you're born."

Blaise gave a limp smile.

Paislee clasped Blaise's hand. "Since we're coming clean . . . I know that you're proud of your cookie final in the bake-off, but you should know that I saw Mari and Kirsten whispering together after the announcement. I think they fixed the contest."

"Why?" Blaise jerked back from Paislee.

"Tae keep you in their clique." Paislee sat back to make room for Lydia to see Blaise. "They didn't want you tae go."

"Paislee, that's terrible—how can you be sure?" Lydia kept her voice low as she looked at Blaise, then Paislee.

"I can't be one hundred percent, unless we get Mari tae confess, but I know what I saw . . . in the commotion of Kirsten dying, I didn't think it mattered, but I hate for you tae feel bad about Kirsten in any way, Blaise. Kirsten wanted power over you and you were slipping from her grasp."

Blaise's knee shook so hard it moved the table. "I didnae win?"

Paislee sighed. "My guess is that the entire competitions were rigged so that Kirsten could be the best. You should talk tae the principal of Highland Academy and put the pegs in due tae Kirsten's death. I bet he admits that there was something extra in it for him."

Chapter 8

Blaise excused herself to the restroom after Paislee's suggestion that the competitions had always been rigged. Lydia tilted her head at Paislee.

"Way tae bring the lass doon—when did you get so cynical? That's something I might have thought of, if I'd seen it. But not you."

Paislee had grown a lot in the last few months since almost losing Cashmere Crush and having Grandpa in her life. Life and death had brushed closer to her and forced her to lift her nose from the grindstone.

"I didn't mean tae hurt her feelings . . . but while I'm at it, and since it's just you and me, Christina has hinted more than once that Fergus baked the winning shortbread." Paislee watched Anders, not an ounce of flirt left in him, add the final tally for the auction items.

"What are you getting at?" Lydia asked.

"It seems odd tae me that Kirsten would fire the chef the morning of the competition, *unless* she was sure that Fergus would keep quiet."

"You're right, that's a big risk—why wouldnae she wait until after the event?"

"We need tae find Fergus for answers." Paislee watched Anders. "If Blaise can't help us locate him, maybe Shep can?"

"Guid idea." Lydia checked behind them. "What do you think aboot Blaise being in an orphanage?"

"Me? I think it's great, how far she's come—but I'm a normal person, not a member of society, or a social climber."

"I'm a normal person, too, just like you," Lydia said. "Born and raised in Nairn."

"She needs us tae realize that she can be herself. Obviously Shep loves her and that's the most important thing for their family—not what Kirsten thought of her humble beginnings." Paislee scanned the conference room.

Anders jumped off the dais to speak in a murmur to Sonya.

The security guard returned and took up a position right inside the door, elbows out, legs braced, stern expression. Had Constable Rory asked him to keep an eye on things until the fund-raiser ended?

She turned toward Anders and Sonya as Anders scowled. "Anders looks mad," Paislee said.

"He's a complete *nyaff.* What was Kirsten thinking? I mean, yes, she's dead now and we cannae know that, but why risk your marriage over someone so contemptable?"

"I have no idea. Maybe she was bored with her perfect life?" Paislee couldn't even begin to imagine. "You know who else might know where Fergus is hiding?"

"Who?"

"The chauffer—I think his name is Hendrie."

"He probably knows a lot aboot the family." Lydia tapped her fingers on their table. "Want me tae chat him up?"

Lydia was a beautiful secret weapon that Paislee had no problem unleashing on the unwary. "Maybe. Let's think about it."

Sonya pushed past Anders, her nose curled with distaste, and stalked to the shelves.

"I feel sorry for Sonya, too," Paislee said.

"Sounded like they had different ideas of what their relationship was—and she got hurt. Never lower your guard. It's a timely reminder for me," Lydia said.

Paislee patted Lydia's arm in total, but silent, disagreement.

Sonya eyed the list of items for sale on a clipboard and searched the shelves again.

"Something's wrong." Paislee rose and Lydia stood, too, then they walked down their aisle closer to Sonya and Anders to listen in.

"Could it have fallen somewhere?" Anders asked, his tone concerned.

"Really?" Sonya remarked incredulously.

"The gaming laptop was there earlier." Anders crossed his arms but it didn't fend off Sonya's disbelief.

"When could this have happened?" Sonya demanded. "We've all been here, all day."

"I saw the system this morning," Lydia said, stepping forward. "On the shelf, next tae the television."

"When was the last time you saw it?" Sonya asked.

Lydia touched her finger to her chin. "For sure? I checked tae see how much it was getting, two thousand pounds, after lunch, but then I didnae look again. I've been monitoring the painting."

"So, noon?"

"Naw, more one." Lydia thought back. "Aye, that's right."

Paislee asked, "Who would steal items meant tae bring in money for the food bank?"

"The room is closed off!" Anders said.

"It's not, either—the back door was open for fresh air half the day," Mari said as she and Christina joined them. The pair was no doubt drawn in like magnets to drama.

"What a disaster," Christina declared. "This never would have happened if Kirsten and Gerard were in charge."

That statement lay flat between them and nobody said anything else. Sonya glared at Anders.

"What?" he sniped. "Just say it, then."

"We need tae fix this," Sonya said. "This kind of sensationalism will not help the club's reputation in this community, and that matters or it will fail. I have everything in this venture."

The security guard sauntered over. "What's going on?"

"A gaming laptop has managed to wander off," Sonya said in a curt tone. "Dinnae suppose you saw anything? I'm paying you, so I suggest you think long and hard aboot anything unusual or you willnae be hired back."

Well, that was plain-speaking, Paislee thought. Sonya had a backbone under her elegant exterior.

"Shiny black box, aboot this big?" Lydia demonstrated with her arms.

The guard lost some of his cockiness. "Well . . ." He brightened. "I didnae think a thing of it, since you're selling stuff, and I only remember because I'd never seen a Bentley SUV before, and this chap in a hat—big guy—loaded a black box intae the back."

Sonya gritted her teeth. "Anything else?"

He shrugged. "This is a sale; folks came oot with packages and bags. Didnae think it was a crime."

"It's not," Anders said. "Calm doon, Sonya. Help me go through everything tae see if something else is missing. Mibbe it will turn up."

Hendrie had been here, without Gerard. It was possible he'd bought something for himself, and the security guard was mistaken about the shiny box. Paislee checked the time—a half hour more until this long day was over. "Blaise is back at our table," she murmured to Lydia.

"I'll keep looking," Sonya said, her mouth drawn. "You finish with the computer bids—unless you're done?"

"Almost. Just need the final tallies." Anders returned to the elaborate computer system on the dais.

"We can help," Lydia told Sonya. Paislee matched items to the paper list. There was the cashmere sweater set, with a bid of a thousand pounds, but no gaming laptop in a shining black box.

"This is verra disappointing," Lydia said. "I know what the Silversteins paid for that."

"We'll do our best tae find it," Sonya promised. "I second Paislee's sentiment—who would steal from the food bank? No matter how you pretty things up, the truth is there are children who go hungry in our little town, bairns that need food."

"Children?" Paislee asked. For some reason she just thought of older folks, with tempers and bushy beards, needing sustenance.

"Aye," Sonya said. "When Anders and I were brainstorming for a worthy cause tae launch the reopening of the building, I discovered some alarming facts. Not only Nairn, but the outskirts, where poor families used tae fish for a living, or worked on the rigs. They need help—giving food is the simplest, fastest way until we can find a better solution."

"Like the Trussell Trust?" Lydia asked.

Sonya nodded. "You're familiar with them? They're the most notable source for collecting nonperishable food."

"'Five weeks too long.'" Paislee knew the slogan and had donated cans and nonperishables at Fordythe every time they had a drive.

"Over that long school holiday, kids that are entitled tae free meals go hungry and it isnae right. Since the new benefits system in 2017, there's been a thirty percent increase in families needing food parcels." Sonya lowered her arms but it was obviously something near to her heart.

"How did the Buchanans get involved?" Paislee asked.

Sonya flushed red. "Anders knew them from when we needed wealthy sponsors for the club . . . he thought they'd be a dynamic fit tae bring light tae the cause."

Paislee quickly changed the direction of the conversation away from Anders and Kirsten. "I think you've done wonderful work here."

"Thank you. Anders thought I'd gone mental when I told him what I wanted tae do with this property. I saved it from being torn down when I inherited a bit of money from my granddad."

"Why this place?" Paislee asked.

"I have black-and-white photos of my great-grandmother here when it first opened as a luxury spa."

"A personal connection tae it." Lydia nodded. "And now it's

beautiful again. It was in bad shape two years ago but it's come tae life."

"My brothers are in construction, which helped with the cost," Sonya said. "Anders and I did our fair share of painting."

"Is he your . . ." Lydia trailed off.

"We have an open relationship. I thought eventually we'd get hitched but that's all changed in the last forty-eight hours." Her eyes turned glassy. "You know why."

If you give away the milk, Gran used to say, why buy the cow? If it was marriage Sonya wanted, then maybe she should have been clearer.

"Oh! The constable is back." Sonya shook her head. "We should file a police report on the missing gaming laptop. Lydia, I'm so sairy aboot that." She led the way to the open conference door.

"Why's he back?" Lydia asked Paislee under her breath as they fell in step behind Sonya.

Blaise joined them as they walked to the front.

"Christina poked him hard about the biscuits, and urged him tae find answers—maybe he's been on the phone in the car park this whole time?" Paislee raised her brow. Far-fetched but possible. "He told me that they received notification last night of peanuts in the cookies—but no details, and only in response tae me saying I'd worried all night that I'd been poisoned."

"I cannae believe they didnae tell you, once they knew," Blaise said.

"I can." Lydia sniffed. "Police officers can be verra protective of what they share with the public, right, Paislee?"

Hadn't they learned that over and over? "I just hope the constable has answers." Paislee stayed next to Lydia and Blaise. Why else would he have come back inside looking so pleased with himself?

"Constable Rory!" Christina said, getting up from the table where she sat with Mari, the two forgetting their tiff . . . for now. She cut off Sonya.

"What did you find out?" Paislee asked when they all converged on him.

The constable winked at Paislee. "It took some doing, but the constable has allowed me tae share the results of the test on the cookies." Constable Rory patted his vest pockets, removed his tablet, and read: "The almond wafer—"

"That's mine," Blaise said, without the pleasure she'd had earlier.

"—had no peanuts or toxins."

Blaise briefly closed her eyes as if saying a little prayer. Mari took Christina's hand, scooting between her and Sonya. The constable read, "The orange oatmeal lace cookie. No peanuts." Mari exhaled.

"The macaroon," Constable Rory paused to eye Christina, "had no toxins, or peanuts." He took a deep breath and announced, "The shortbread had been topped with brown sugar . . . and peanut dust. There was no peanut in the cookie itself."

Christina and Mari gasped. Blaise, too. But Paislee's dismay went inward as she recalled how Kirsten had touched her tongue to the topping.

"It's really true. Somebody *murdered* our friend," Christina said. The ladies collapsed into tears.

Constable Rory sucked his lips inward as if to keep himself from saying one way or the other.

"Have you found Fergus Jones yet?" Paislee asked. The chef had to be questioned, and it wasn't looking good for him. A dusting of peanut crumble? Couldn't get more cheffy.

"No." Constable Rory placed his tablet in his pocket.

"I'm sairy, and now might not be the time," Sonya said, "but we've had a theft of one of our big-ticket items for the food bank."

Constable Rory shuffled his boots. "You'll have tae report this at the station."

"Oh." She stepped back.

The officer cleared his throat. "Christina Baird, I'll need you tae come with me. Constable Dean has a few more questions for you."

Christina turned the color of unbleached wool. "I didnae do anything!"

"You can drive your own car, and I'll follow you tae the station."

"Now?"

"Aye."

Silence ticked by in painful increments.

Mari patted her friend on the shoulder. "Go, love. I'll call John and have him meet you there."

Christina nodded and retrieved her purse, her lower lip quivering as if she were a little girl about to get in trouble.

Chapter 9

Paislee, Lydia, and Blaise remained near the door after Christina and Constable Rory exited. Mari tapped her lower lip as if in thought. Was she wondering if one friend had killed the other?

"Do you want me tae call John?" Blaise asked.

Mari blinked. "Naw, I will. Christina cannae go tae jail—she's just not verra strong. Mibbe he can bring her something tae calm her anxiety."

"That's smart," Blaise said.

Mari raised her brow, letting them all know that Blaise's approval wasn't needed.

"Is there anything I can do tae help?" Blaise plowed forward with her offer despite the chill.

The dark gray of Mari's blouse gave her skin a sallow hue as if her grief was taking a terrible toll. Her heel caught on the beige carpet as she had started to turn. "With what?"

"I dinnae ken . . . Maxim, or Robby? Mia?" Blaise spread her arms to the sides. "Our kids are all in the same class."

"You're leaving Highland Academy, Blaise, so the answer is no. Lara can step in. God knows she's been waitin' on the sidelines long enough. I wonder where she was during the cookie fiasco?"

Paislee admitted that it was a good question . . . maybe Lara thought that by getting rid of Kirsten, she could step in with Gerard.

"I want tae help, and now with Christina being questioned . . ."

"Stop right there, Blaise." Mari held up a hand weighted with rings. "Christina did not put peanuts on Kirsten's shortbread, I can guarantee that. She doesnae have the balls." Mari dialed and put the mobile to her ear. "John? It's Mari, aboot Christina . . ." She turned away, the bones of her shoulders visible through her silk shirt.

"Grr," Blaise said, shaking her head. "Even when she's nice she's mean."

"She'd probably feel better if she had a large shepherd's pie with extra gravy." Lydia patted her own flat stomach.

"She says she has stomach issues," Blaise shared in a whisper. "Worse than the gluten thing. Kirsten told me when they were teenagers Mari had been fat."

"I don't believe it," Paislee said.

"I think it's true because Kirsten would tease her aboot getting her a fat suit."

"Talk aboot mean!" Lydia said.

"I know, I know . . . but they were two peas in a pod, with Christina the third smaller pea just waiting for her chance to get bigger. Mibbe now, well." Blaise dropped her gaze.

"And where did you fit in?" Paislee asked.

Blaise made a humming noise in her throat. "I was the smashed pea. Smashed under their collective heels." She exhaled. "It makes me bloody well mad when I think of how Kirsten treated me. What's worse? I let her!"

"Dinnae say that too loudly or you might be next down at the station," Lydia warned.

Mari returned to their group and palmed her mobile. "John is on his way tae the station. I relayed your offer tae help—he said thanks, and he'll let you know if Robby needs something."

"Thank you," Blaise said.

Paislee nodded at her, glad that she'd passed on the message to John on Blaise's behalf.

"We have tae look oot for each other. This whole thing hasnae sunk in yet." Mari crossed her arms, the elbows sharp points. "I cannae think aboot it or I'll fall apart. We have tae ensure this Nairn Food Bank fund-raiser is a success for the Buchanans' sake. Gerard and Maxim will need something tae hang onto when the dust settles."

Sonya joined them. "Mari, that makes me very happy tae hear. Your support means everything. How can I help?"

"Well, for a start, you can be my intermediary with Anders." Mari lowered her arms. "I didnae know that they'd gone beyond a flirtation."

Sonya's jaw clenched. "It doesnae matter now."

"Just so you understand, Kirsten was struggling with her modeling career—her agent had told her that she was no longer relevant, at thirty-five." Mari swirled her finger in the air. "It sent her into a tailspin."

"When was this? How brutal!" Lydia said. "She was flawless—her agent is detestable."

"Agreed. A month ago, give or take." Mari dabbed the corner of her eye. "She wasnae used tae being turned down and thought she could pick up her career whenever she wanted tae—Gerard preferred that she didnae work at all, but she was restless."

Paislee imagined how useless that might make someone feel, after being at the top of the heap to be set on a shelf and admired, but not needed.

"Mari," Blaise asked hesitantly, "did you and Kirsten fix the cookie competition yesterday? Or at school?"

Mari's softness disappeared in an instant. "You care aboot the competition right now? It is *so* not important. Really, Blaise. Your upbringing is showing."

Blaise gasped.

"Hey!" Paislee said.

A buzzer sounded from the dais and the ladies whirled toward the blare. "And we have our final totals for the two-day event! Not including the ten percent from each vendor—oh, this is great—we have earned fifty-five thousand pounds for the Nairn Food Bank, and surrounding Highland towns!"

Paislee clapped, knowing that her percentage would add another two hundred pounds, at least, and if each table did as well, that might bring them past the sixty thousand mark.

"Kirsten would be thrilled. Her goal was fifty thousand," Sonya said. She left them to join Anders on the dais.

The open-relationship couple clasped hands and lifted them in victory. "Thank you for helping us fight hunger!" Sonya said. "Now, please see me on your way through the front and I will officially check you oot from the event."

Sonya stepped down and sat at a table near the door with a receipt book and a welcoming smile.

"She's on her game," Blaise remarked. "Rallying after an emotional blow. I dinnae know that I could do so well."

Lydia shrugged. "Has tae be, tae make the club a success. I like her. Ask her if she knits, Paislee."

"All right." Paislee elbowed her friend that didn't knit but never missed a Thursday night Knit and Sip. They had about six regulars but there was room for more.

Anders helped people stack up chairs and tables, his demeanor quieter and more subdued. Being punched in the face by your dead lover's husband might do that to a man.

Paislee collected her few unsold caps, and counted her money for the two days. "Two thousand five hundred. Not bad for a weekend." She couldn't wait to share the news with James, who also lived for tourist season to see him through the winter months.

The trio walked toward Sonya's table, the security guard by her side in case anybody got a bad idea to skip out without giving their due.

"I've got seven hundred from the cookies and tins," Blaise said to Sonya. "I'm going tae donate it all."

Lydia shouldered her bag. "I feel terrible aboot the laptop being stolen. Let us know how it works oot?"

"I'm going tae file a police report," Sonya assured her. "It's a valuable item and unique. Not everybody can get one, it's that new."

"Call me if you need any specific information," Lydia said.

"I will, I will." Sonya opened to a fresh page for the receipts. "I'm so sairy that you were outbid on that painting you wanted. I love Eva Ullrich, too, and have one in my house." She filled out the slip for the mints and gave it to Blaise with thanks, then turned to Paislee. "How'd you make oot?"

Paislee handed over the cash. "I had no expectations, so I'm very pleased."

"Two fifty is your share," Sonya said.

"I'll donate five hundred." Paislee was glad to be able to do a bit more. "And let me know if you do something for the food bank again? I didn't realize the state of things in our own neighborhood."

"Wonderful!" Sonya handed her the receipt.

Lydia cleared her throat. Oh! "Do you knit, Sonya?" Paislee asked.

"Not a thing—I've no patience for it, either. I appreciate your talent all the more for not being able tae do it." Sonya tucked a strand of white-blond hair behind her ear.

Paislee bumped Lydia's arm—she'd tried.

"How do you unwind?" Lydia asked.

Sonya grinned and pointed toward the water at the back of the property. "Fishing in the loch. I learned with my brothers."

Lydia shuddered. She was not a fan of the great outdoors, like Paislee and Brody and now Grandpa were.

"My son and his grandfather are out fly-fishing today, somewhere." Paislee shrugged. Grandpa hadn't told her where, actually. And they didn't have a mobile. A niggle of worry of what might happen settled in her tummy.

"It's a braw day for it," Sonya said. "Well, thanks again."

That was their cue to move on as others waited to check out. Paislee looked behind them, and it was hard to believe the place had been such a hive of activity even thirty minutes ago.

Most folks had dispersed, the tables cleared. No sign of Anders, who'd probably gone to lick his wounds in private.

"It was so crowded, anybody could have walked oot with it," Lydia said, still focused on the stolen gaming system. "Cheeky bastards. That would have added tae the pot quite nicely."

The three walked down the hall toward the front door. Paislee had a bag of caps along with her purse, but the others only carried their handbags and phones.

"Should we get a drink?" Blaise asked. "I could use one or more. Preferably more."

Lydia half smiled and blushed adorably. "I cannae today. I'm meeting Corbin for dinner."

"Corbin?" Blaise asked.

"Corbin Smythe."

"*Laird* Corbin Smythe," Paislee said, stressing the Laird part as she teased her friend.

"Ooooh." Blaise tugged on Lydia's arm. "Is it serious?"

"We're friends—never serious."

"Friends with benefits," Paislee said, laughing.

"Those are the best kind." Blaise chuckled.

"So, another time for a drink? And I'll call this week with an update on your house closing." Lydia pulled her keys from her purse.

"We should double-date," Blaise said. "Do dinner."

Paislee momentarily felt like the odd girl out but shook it off. She didn't date because she was busy being a mum to Brody and she had no time for anything else.

"Too soon!" Lydia cried, raising her hands. "We are taking things verra, verra slow."

Paislee was happy for Lydia, who deserved someone wonderful after her ex, who'd been rotten. It had taken a long time for Lydia to trust again. Maybe she needed more time, or maybe Corbin was the man to show her that she could lower the fence around her heart.

"Fine!" Blaise grinned. "Didnae mean tae pressure you. Is she always like this, Paislee?"

"Lydia knows what she wants and there is nothing wrong with that."

"Fair." Blaise shook her head. "I wish I'd met you lasses earlier in my life."

Lydia strode forward to open the door for them, letting in light from the sunny day. "You know us now."

A news van had parked in front of the steps of the Social Club and Art Centre, and a female reporter in slacks and a blouse held a microphone toward Anders.

"And how did the fund-raiser for the Nairn Food Bank go?" she asked.

"We raised almost sixty thousand pounds for our community— we thank everyone who participated here at the club or online."

"Did the death of Kirsten Buchanan, the sponsor for the event, hinder sales—or did it bring in more awareness?"

Anders choked up.

The reporter's eyes narrowed as she zeroed in on Anders's emotional state. "Were you close friends of the Buchanans? We read it was an accidental ingestion of peanuts, when she had an allergy."

Anders puffed out his chest and touched his black eye.

Paislee had a very bad feeling as he moistened his lips.

She could practically see him thinking over the consequences of his rash action, and yet in the end, he went for it anyway.

"I was *verra* good friends with Kirsten Buchanan."

The reporter's eyes took on a manic glint as she sensed blood. "Just Kirsten Buchanan? Not Gerard?"

"Gerard is an entitled goon who kept his beautiful wife on a pedestal. She gave him her best years as he emotionally strangled her."

"No," Paislee whispered from the open door but Anders didn't stop and it was like watching an oncoming train and not being able to get out of the way.

"We loved each other."

Blaise drew in a loud breath. "Oh, no."

"Gerard found some of our romantic emails and stopped by earlier tae deliver this shiner, right here." Anders tapped the bruise.

The camera crew surged closer. The vendors who hadn't left yet now took pictures with their mobiles from the car park.

"Gerard Buchanan hit you at his Nairn Food Bank fundraiser?" The reporter couldn't keep the excitement from her voice at the unexpected story.

"He's got a mean temper." Anders leaned in as if to impart a secret to the reporter, "I think he killed Kirsten."

Camera flashes blinded them and Sonya hurtled past the front door to grab Anders by his shoulder.

Sonya dragged him back. "What on God's green earth is wrong with you?"

Chapter 10

Paislee stepped out of Sonya's way and Lydia slammed the door closed before the reporter got inside.

"You cannae accuse someone of murder, Anders!" Sonya pleaded with her lover.

"He's the perfect suspect! He's a bully—he clocked me upside the head." Anders showed her his eye as if they weren't all staring at it already. "He threatened me."

"You slept with his wife." Sonya reeled back.

"Exactly!" Anders said. "So he killed her so that we couldnae be together."

"Is that so?" Sonya tapped her foot to the marble tile in the lobby.

"I'm sairy, Sonya, but we were going tae run off together." Anders bowed his head and wiped tears from his lashes.

"How dare you use me like that?" Sonya demanded, then she realized that she'd grown an audience—not only Paislee, Blaise, and Lydia but about ten vendors, including Mari, and the security guard. Christina was at the police station, and Lara hadn't returned after taking Gerard home.

"It was love." Anders held out his arms.

"It was not love!" Mari seconded what she'd said yesterday. "She was bored and you were entertaining. She wouldnae leave

Maxim for you, and Gerard wouldnae let his son go withoot a fight."

Anders said nothing to that, which meant Mari knew Kirsten well.

"Get oot of here, Anders," Sonya ordered. "You're fired."

"You cannae fire me—I helped you build this place."

"My brothers helped me—you rinsed the paint brushes. Now I know why you were so busy with the Buchanans. It was probably just Kirsten on those late meetings, wasnae it?"

"Not always. Gerard was needed tae reach the premier-level sponsorship." Anders gulped. "Give me another chance."

"Get. Oot." Sonya pointed to the door.

Mari opened it to the waiting reporter. The ladies crowded behind him until he was on the step, then Sonya shut it hard in his face.

"This is such a disaster for the club." Sonya sobbed.

Paislee gave the woman a hug. It had been a terrible two days and yet she'd handled it like a champ until now—everybody had a breaking point.

"Focus on the guid you've done," Lydia suggested. "You dinnae need that idiot. Seems like you were doing all the work anyway."

Sonya straightened. "You're right. I hope all I've poured into making this place part of the community again isnae destroyed. How could he be so thoughtless?"

"He was only thinking of himself," Mari said supportively.

"How can we help?" Blaise asked.

Sonya held her hand to her temple. "I'm going tae have tae address that reporter. Try and stop the bleeding of what he's just done. Accusing Gerard Buchanan of murdering his wife. Och." She swayed then straightened.

Mari peeked out the front door. "She's following Anders tae his car."

"Then why dinnae you all go, and I'll lock up," Sonya said with no small sigh of relief. "I've got a little studio in the back where I sometimes sleep over."

"If you're sure?" Paislee asked.

"Aye." Sonya cracked it wider and ushered for them all to go except the security guard, who was no doubt necessary because of all the money raised for the food bank. "Thank you so much."

"Stay safe." Paislee, then Lydia, darted out first, followed by Blaise and Mari. Most of the attention from the vendors, shoppers, and the reporting team was on Anders as he tried to get into his car.

"I'm dropping by the station tae make sure Christina's all right," Mari said, unlocking a brand-new Mercedes SUV. "See you at school tomorrow, Blaise. If you can, show up a few minutes early?"

They all waved. Blaise went to her Range Rover. "Tomorrow—what a nightmare that will be for Maxim and the other children. I should call the principal when I get home tae see how he wants tae handle this situation. Kirsten usually managed these things."

They all watched Mari drive away.

"Maybe you can ask Mari?" Paislee suggested.

"She's taking care of Christina. I need tae do my share." Blaise shrugged. "Let's talk tomorrow, ladies. Tonight, I'm having Shep pour me a double."

"You've earned it!" Paislee said, getting into Lydia's red Mercedes. Anders still held court outside his car.

Blaise left first, and Lydia stayed on the Range Rover's taillights.

"This was insane," Lydia declared. "I've never experienced anything like this . . ."

"Death?"

"No offense, but Kirsten's death is the tip of the iceberg when it comes tae all the weird drama."

"What do ye mean?" Paislee sank back against the leather. It was nice to have someone else drive every once in a while.

"Anders for one, accusing Gerard of killing Kirsten. Gerard, finding oot that his wife was shagging the fund-raiser coordinator, and telling him he was going tae kill him, then the fund-raiser still going on—it had tae, for the food bank, I get it—but there wasnae a break, or a chance to digest that someone put peanuts on Kirsten's shortbread tae murder her. *Murder,* Paislee."

Paislee's skin broke out in goose bumps. "When you put it like that . . ."

"And somebody stole the donation from Silverstein's, literally taking food from children's mouths—what kind of animals are we dealing with?"

"I wish they'd find Fergus." Paislee looked out the window and sighed. "But he's not the only suspect."

Lydia drove like a professional race car driver as she smoothly changed lanes and sped toward Paislee's house. "What do ye think of Kirsten's agent? Not relevant. That bombshell might explain why she hooked up with Anders, tae assure herself that she was still beautiful. I hope she fired him, too. Old at thirty-five. We're only seven years away from that magic number."

Paislee didn't mind her age. "I saw Fergus's reaction when Kirsten fell. I want him tae be questioned and cleared so we can move on tae whoever actually did it. It wasn't him."

"So why was he hiding oot behind the Buchanans' house?"

"Until yesterday, he lived there."

"True. What a mess." Lydia's fingers drummed the wheel and her voice hitched. "I wonder if I could whip up a batch of lemon bars before dinner tonight?"

Stress-baking, poor thing. "You'll be fine. Deep breath. Corbin will take your mind off of this tragedy."

Lydia patted Paislee's leg. "What are you going tae do?"

"Knit! I'm out of inventory."

Ten minutes later, Lydia dropped Paislee at home. The Juke was in the drive under the carport, which meant Brody and Grandpa were home. She'd missed her family, and her sanctuary.

"Sure you don't want tae come in?"

"Naw—but say hi from me. I plan on showering, lathering up

in expensive lotion, and allowing myself tae be wined and dined tae forget all aboot the last two days. I have no idea what Natalya will say aboot the laptop being stolen."

"It wasn't your fault. You deserve tae relax. Love ya!"

She grabbed her things from the small backseat and ran up the stairs and into the house.

The scent of rosemary potatoes greeted her. Wallace jumped on her legs to say hello, Grandpa popped his head up from the cooker, and Brody raced toward her with a giant red mark on his cheek that made her stop short.

"Look, Mum! I caught a fish so big we had tae wrestle it, and it got me in the face with his tail. I practically needed stitches but Grandpa put mud on it tae stop the bleeding!"

Paislee turned to Grandpa in alarm, thinking of all the germs in the mud. "Is that healthy?"

"Sure," he said with a shrug. "Georgie said it would work, and it did. No stitches or a plaster needed."

She eyed the wound closely. "Well, have ye showered?"

"Aye." Brody dropped back down to his heels.

"Let's get some antibiotic ointment on that. We can't have your skin fall off. You need it. You don't want a scar, either." Her boy was handsome with his auburn hair and smattering of freckles, if she said so herself.

"Wanna see the fish? Grandpa didnae catch one, only me, and we're cooking it for dinner."

Paislee grabbed the tube from the downstairs bathroom and slid ointment across the red mark before she admired the fish in rosemary potatoes and a cream sauce.

"This is wonderful . . . I didn't realize how hungry I was until I smelled that. Let me wash up."

When she returned, Brody had set the table for them.

"How was your day, lass?" Grandpa asked.

Better, now that she was home. "We made almost sixty thousand pounds for the food bank, which is pretty phenomenal."

"I'd say so!" Grandpa grabbed a mitt and opened the door, taking the pan from inside and placing it in the center of the table on a cork trivet. "Here we are."

"I cannae wait tae tell Edwyn," Brody said. "If I had a mobile, Mum, I could've taken pictures. Sent 'em to you, and Edwyn."

Paislee lowered her eyes. She didn't care about photos, but what if he'd needed medical care? They'd had nothing. The truth was, she'd been looking into a family plan, once Grandpa would decide what to do about Craigh. Would her family plan be two phones, or three?

She bit into the fish—thick, white, flaky. "This really is terrific—well done, both of you."

"Can I have a knife, Mum?"

"Don't start in on that either, Brody." Paislee cut another portion of fish with the side of her fork, it was that tender. "No phone. No knife. Let's enjoy our meal."

He rattled on for a full thirty minutes on how cool Georgie was, how fun fly-fishing was, how cold the river was, and how he couldn't wait to do it again.

"You said if I liked it you'd try, Mum. This weekend? Sunday Funday at the river?"

"We'll see." She hated to commit to anything just yet, as she was still unsettled about the murder.

After dinner, she did the dishes. Brody, picking up Wallace, went in to watch telly, while Grandpa kept her company.

"He had a good day," she laughed over her shoulder.

"A verra guid day." Grandpa picked at the remains of a chocolate biscuit he'd nibbled on for an after-dinner treat.

"I hope you can make this dish again." She rinsed the pan and set it in the strainer, then dried her hands, leaning back against the counter. "How are you?"

"It was a braw day. Couldnae have asked for more perfect weather."

"I was inside for a profitable cause, but it was crazy . . ." Paislee glanced toward Brody on the couch engrossed in his program.

"Nobody else died?" Grandpa's brow lifted.

She walked closer to the table to murmur, "Almost—Gerard Buchanan found emails from Anders Campbell tae his wife and he burst into the club swinging."

Grandpa straightened. "Is the man okay?"

"Aye. I called the police and Constable Rory arrived—he was the sweet one from yesterday. I asked him what he'd heard about the cookies, since I was up all night worried if I'd been poisoned. I may have laid it on a wee bit thick."

Grandpa grinned up at her.

"He's young and immediately apologized, admitting that there was no poison—but that was all before Christina laid into him about not answering phone calls, or letting her know the results of the cookie test."

"More theater than I thought." Grandpa tsked.

"I'm not finished yet." Paislee chuckled. "The constable left but returned within the hour, acting as if he'd done us all a favor tae get permission tae share the results. Blaise's, Christina's, and Mari's biscuits were fine but Kirsten's had brown sugar mixed with peanut on top."

Grandpa gasped.

Topping that Kirsten had licked, as if suspecting something was wrong, but then she'd been satisfied by the taste enough to bite it. "Constable Rory had Christina leave the fund-raiser immediately tae answer more questions for Constable Dean at the station."

"Christina's the one who drinks vodka from a water bottle? She accused Blaise of hiding the pen?"

"Aye, with the doctor husband. High drama." Paislee sat down across from Grandpa. "Do you know what an open relationship is?"

Grandpa turned red. "What do you want tae know that for? Who approached you? Let me know, and I'll bash heads."

"Not for me." Paislee settled back, wishing for a cuddle with Wallace, or her bag of knitting, but she was too tired to get up. "Anders and Sonya, the woman whose great-grandparents were at the house when it was a Victorian spa, had one and she assumed

Anders would come around tae want marriage one day. Instead, he fell in love with Kirsten Buchanan during their visits regarding the event for the food bank. There was a reporter there, and Anders told the reporter that he thought Gerard had killed Kirsten."

Grandpa closed his gaping jaw with a snap. "Och, no!"

"Aye—so after that, Sonya kicked Anders out." Paislee shrugged. "He was still gabbing tae the reporter in the car park when we drove off."

"Gerard Buchanan has the money tae slap him with slander. What an eejit." Grandpa leaned closer to Paislee. "Unless you think Gerard did it?"

"The truth is, he had motive. He kept Kirsten on a very tight leash according tae Blaise. He was devastated when he found emails between Kirsten and Anders, but Mari and Christina both say that Kirsten would never actually leave her marriage. She is—was—devoted tae Maxim, her son. If not Gerard."

"Gerard arrived at the club tae punch Anders." Grandpa scratched his full beard. "From what you've shared he's an emotional man with a short fuse. Probably not going tae have the patience tae make a topping for a cookie. Too premeditated for Gerard."

"You're right." Paislee forced herself to get up and pulled clothes from the drying rack to a basket where she could fold while they talked.

"Have you heard from the DI aboot the case?"

"Zeffer?" She folded a uniform shirt for Brody to wear to school tomorrow. "That would be a no."

Grandpa broke off another piece of cookie. "Did ye buy anything nice for yourself?"

"No time tae shop. I was too busy selling! I told Sonya I'd be happy tae help if she did it again."

"Your gran liked tae help, too. If there was anything at the church, she'd cook, or knit, or clean up. Didnae matter tae her. Lord's work, either way, she said."

Paislee held up a pair of pants. The cuffs were fraying. She would have enough to get Brody a new wardrobe without touching her groaning credit card. "She walked the walk."

"That she did, that she did."

"You mentioned a dinner at the club next month . . . was there any word from Craigh at the storage unit?"

"I woulda told you if there was."

Paislee wasn't sure she believed her grandfather about that. He was protective of his missing son and wouldn't give Paislee so much as a clue.

He'd gone to the storage unit in Dairlee twice on his own—always returning the Juke with the tank full of gas, but it was pulling teeth to find out if the unit had been disturbed, as he'd thought before.

Whatever. It was Grandpa's game and she didn't want to push—what if he decided to pack up his old suitcase and go?

"Are you ready for school tomorrow?" Paislee walked to the couch where Wallace lay flush to her son's leg. Brody was absorbed in television.

"Yeah."

"Did you read today?"

"Yeah!" He didn't so much as glance her way.

"Anything I need tae sign? Kites tae make?"

Brody said, "Ha ha." Then he straightened, his face losing color as he leapt from the couch and raced up the stairs to his room.

She and Grandpa exchanged a worried look when she returned to the kitchen.

The thump of Brody's backpack hitting the floor from his bed upstairs echoed, then the *clump, clump, clump* as he dragged it down the steps, then the hall, followed by the faithful Wallace.

Grandpa had finished his chocolate biscuits and washed the plate, clearing space for Brody to work.

"What is it, lad?" she asked, her chest tight. So much for relaxing.

Brody brought out a tube. When he unrolled it, she saw that it was a map. It covered the round table. "I have a project for extra credit."

"Why would Mrs. Martin give extra credit?"

Brody's ears turned dark red—only the tips, which meant he knew he was in trouble. "Well . . ."

"Out with it!" She'd let him play all day Saturday with Edwyn, and not a mention of the "extra" credit.

"I only have tae do this if I want tae—she didnae assign it," Brody said, lower lip protruding.

"And why would she do that?"

Brody dug his markers from his bag. For a moment Paislee was reminded of Kirsten's EpiPen, but she buried the memory. She couldn't deal with that right now. "It might be tae make up for a test grade." He offered a math test with a D on it. Only two of ten answers had been written in.

"Two? Explain." She tapped her toe.

"I know ye cannae take one more thing . . ."

Grandpa chuckled and Paislee gave him the eye.

". . . but me and Lucas were making this highway across the desks with sugar tae watch the ants march and . . ."

Grandpa left for his room before he got into trouble, too.

Chapter 11

Paislee arrived at Fordythe Primary at five minutes till nine. She and Brody had rolled his project back into a tube-shape that Wallace thought made an excellent chew toy. Paislee rescued the project from complete destruction, but there were actual tooth marks in the paper.

"You can tell Mrs. Martin that the dog *almost* ate your homework."

Brody didn't find that the least bit amusing. "Mum!"

"What? Is it my fault that ye left it on the couch where the pup could get it? You're lucky he didn't gobble the whole thing!"

She lowered the volume on the radio and when she looked up next, Hamish McCall was at the passenger side of the Juke. Brody mad-dashed for the blue doors of the school.

"Not late," she said defensively. Other cars were still in queue behind hers. Some were going around with an impatient beep of the horn.

"Guid day, Paislee. I thought I might have a word with you?"

She glanced at the clock at the dash. "Can it wait? Jerry's delivering yarn this morning at quarter after."

His brow tightened and his knuckles whitened where he gripped the open door. "All right. Actually, I'd heard a rumor."

"Not like you tae spread gossip," she said lightly.

"I figured I would do some digging around."

"And?"

"Here I am."

"What's the rumor, Hamish?"

"Brody and Edwyn have been fighting. We have a zero toler-ance policy here for violence, as you know." He maintained eye contact with her. "Since you've signed the parent handbook."

The man was deliberating poking at her, reminding her of that blasted rule book of his. What did he hope to gain?

"Mrs. Martin told me the boys had a disagreement," Paislee said, "but had worked it out. They spend time together on the weekends sometimes, so they're friends. Not bad kids."

"I didnae say that they were bad kids." Hamish raised his palm.

"What do you want from me?" There'd been a foolish few weeks where she'd imagined them as friends. Where if he'd asked her to dinner she might have gone. But that had all changed when she'd realized that he would always put the school ahead of per-sonal feelings.

She didn't blame him, but she wasn't a glutton for punishment, either.

He winced. "If you could talk tae Brody, I would appreciate it. Remind him that we have a code of conduct here."

She bristled. "And will you be letting Bennett Maclean also know that Edwyn is supposed tae behave according tae the rules? Or is it just Brody?"

Hamish lifted his chin. "I will make a call tae Mr. Maclean as well."

"I'll touch base with him later tae make sure that we parents are on the same page." There—that would let him know that she and Bennett would compare notes. Hamish had better call, or she would make an official appointment to ream him out on being fair to all parties.

Hamish opened his mouth as if to say something else, but then opted to nod and quietly close the car door.

Paislee denied the sting of regret and checked to see that nobody else was coming before pulling into traffic and driving toward Cashmere Crush.

Her job in this life was to be the best mum possible to Brody, and that meant focusing on what mattered—keeping a roof over their heads, and making a living to provide for them.

So far she'd managed, but Brody was only ten. There were still a lot of years to get through, and lots of pitfalls. Secondary school was said to be the hardest. He'd definitely want his own mobile, and then there'd be a job, and a car, and insurance—and by the time she parked behind Cashmere Crush in the alley, she was on the verge of a full-blown panic attack.

Jerry pulled in next to her with his delivery truck that was twice the size of her Juke.

"Hiya!" Jerry said. "It's a braw mornin', Paislee lass."

She blinked and eyed the blue sky. "I hadn't noticed."

"Shame on ye," he joked. "These days are the best of the year. What's going on? Grandpa trouble?"

Jerry had been there for the morning when Grandpa had been delivered to her door and knew all about the missing Craigh. She'd held onto her business by a stroke of luck, since her landlord was actually quite ill.

Still. Some said it served him right, but Paislee couldn't go that far. She missed her raspberry scones from the bakery on the corner that was now closed.

"Wallace tried tae eat Brody's homework."

Jerry chuckled. "And here I thought that was just an excuse."

"We saved it, but I'm sure he'll get marked down. It was extra credit because he was building an ant bridge during the test he was supposed tae be taking and didn't do so well."

"Sounds like a regular boy. Dinnae fash."

Paislee climbed the four cement steps to the back of her shop, and Jerry went around to his truck for the yarn.

She hurried inside and had just put her purse on the bottom shelf below her register when he brought in four cases of yarn.

"How did the sale go at the new club?" he asked. "I read that Kirsten Buchanan died from a peanut allergy."

Braw morning her behind, she thought. Maybe she was destined for a dark cloud kind of day. "Aye. I was there. Tragic, actually."

"Did ye know her?"

"Naw." That was the easiest answer to give without having to delve into more questions that he would surely have. They lived in a small town, and folks cared, which meant they could be a wee bit nosy.

Jerry handed her a sales slip and she wrote him a check for delivery. "Ta—and try tae get down tae the beach today, if ye can. Fresh air will put the roses back in your cheeks."

Paislee nodded. Sea air revived her spirits. "Grandpa is in at noon. I might walk over tae the bandstand."

"It's crowded, even on a Monday. Maybe head tae the other side if you want privacy."

That was the down side of being a tourist town—more folks disrupted the normal routine. "Thanks, Jerry."

Jerry left out the back. Nine thirty. Paislee didn't officially open until ten. She spent the next twenty minutes setting up the till, sweeping the polished cement floor, and pricing the skeins of wool.

Beige, or natural, was the most popular shade, then an emerald green. She'd also ordered chocolate brown that she'd once imagined the color of Hamish's eyes, and lavender for a custom cardigan from an online order.

She unlocked the front door at ten, turned the radio on low, and stocked the shelves. Grandpa said he could do it, but she hated for him to climb the ladder—though he was nimble as a Highland goat.

Humming a Belle and Sebastian tune, she set her knitting schedule for the week—in addition to the lavender cardigan she had to replace her inventory in store. Tourists loved the heavy fisherman sweaters, in beige, so she would make those a priority. Scarves, caps, gloves, pull-on jumpers, thick button-up sweaters. Shawls, neck warmers, infinity scarves, socks, handbags, backpacks—the list went on.

Being busy did much to lift her gray mood. The Shaw family would not go hungry. They had a roof over their head for business and home. Just maybe, she would research mobile phone plans for later this week. Get one for Grandpa and Brody to share—that way Brody wouldn't technically have his own, but could take pictures, and Grandpa wouldn't feel like he was obligated in any way. She would tell him he was doing her a favor. Bonus for her, if there was a true emergency they'd be able to call for assistance.

As she knit, thoughts whirled like a balled sock in the washer, making her dizzy. This morning over toast and Weetabix, Grandpa had informed them that Fergus Jones was still on the lamb. Kirsten's death had been second page, with Anders Campbell's accusation against Gerard Buchanan there in print.

Front page was from the earl and promoted the wonders of seaside Nairn.

Grandpa liked to walk the mile from the house to the shop—claimed it kept him limber and healthy. She was thinking of doing it herself, once she didn't need to drop Brody off at school for the five weeks of summer holiday.

She'd just finished her third lavender row of merino wool when her front door opened and Blaise entered in a rush of frenetic energy that disrupted Paislee's hard-earned lower-key vibe and immediately put her on alert.

"Are you all right, Blaise?" Paislee looked behind her friend—no Suzannah, which meant the lass was at school as she should be on a Monday morn.

Blaise reached the counter with the register on it and dropped her designer bag to the floor, then buried her hands in her smooth bob and leaned her head back, whirling once before freezing in place. Her amber eyes were rimmed in red—her mouth agape though no words escaped.

Paislee released her knitting, rushed around the counter to get a stool, and urged Blaise down on it. "What is it?"

"I . . . I . . ."

"Hang on." She went to the back sink and poured a glass of water for her friend, then brought it to her. "Here."

Blaise used both hands to hold the cup and sipped.

"Better?"

She nodded. "I hate her."

Paislee motioned for Blaise to have another drink. "Who?" Mari, or Christina? Lara?

"Kirsten. It's guid she's dead." Blaise set the glass on the counter.

"What did she do?" Paislee watched Blaise carefully.

Blaise drew herself up and steadied herself with a deep breath. "Kirsten fixed the baking competitions. All of them."

So it was just as Paislee had suspected. "Oh no. How did you find out?"

"Well, after my feelings were stupidly hurt yesterday when ye told me what you saw, with Kirsten whispering tae Mari, and me not winning, like, honestly taking third would have been a win in my mind." Blaise put her hand on the counter. "You understand that I know how mental that makes me sound?"

Paislee offered her a piece of toffee from the jar.

Blaise shook her head. "I decided tae find oot for meself if it was true. Mari would lie tae cover up for Kirsten, so would Christina. I looked for Lara today, but Maxim wasnae at school."

"Understandable, poor lamb."

"Aye." Blaise sucked in her quivering lip. "So. I marched into the principal's office tae confront Master Horace Johnson. Placating and condescending—how did I never notice before?"

"Might be something in the leadership role that gets tae them." Paislee shrugged and tried to be fair about how she saw Hamish.

"It's the first time I've ever challenged him. He threatened tae call my husband! How archaic is that?" Blaise folded her arms. "I wasnae accepting no for an answer. It took me threatening tae call Shep and the other parents in for a meeting before he cracked."

"Nice turnaround."

"Thanks. I thought so." Blaise drank the rest of the water. "Horace had the nerve tae say that aye, Kirsten had gifted him and his wife two weeks at her summer cottage each year. Nothing was written, of course, and what was the real harm? Her shortbread was amazing and he would have chosen it anyway."

"That's awful."

"Kirsten gave him a list of the moms she wanted tae win. Of course, this was only the third year. Now she's dead. He willnae do it again. So he swears."

"He's a pig."

"But I'm the idiot. Why didnae I see?" Blaise held up her hand. "No. I saw but looked away, for my own selfish reasons."

"Stop being so hard on yourself. It's done now. I can see that you're not like that at all. You've changed."

"Have I?"

Paislee nodded. "I hope so . . . otherwise what does that say about your new friends, me and Lydia, specifically?"

Blaise relaxed and allowed herself to laugh. "All right. Give me some knitting therapy. What are ye making?"

"A bespoke lavender cardigan for an online order. I got a new pattern in for the most adorable coin purse for little girls you might like." Paislee dug through her files and pulled out the pattern that had rabbit ears, eyes, and whiskers.

"It's so cute! Suzannah would love it." Her nose wrinkled. "Is it hard?"

"Nope. It's for beginners. I'm right here if you want tae start it. I was losing myself in knitting tae forget everything, too." For her own sanity, Paislee had banished Kirsten's last moments.

They chatted companionably. Paislee helped a customer find yarn and needles, and a pattern for a shawl. After the woman left, she sat down with Blaise again.

"So, did you ever talk tae Shep about Fergus? I guess he's still in hiding somewhere."

"I brought it up but then Shep received a call from one of his golf clients and we never got back tae it. He'll be home at noon for lunch. Want tae join us?"

Paislee thought about it and accepted as Grandpa walked in, not a bit out of breath. His silver-gray hair was free-flowing as he removed his tam. "That would be fun."

"Guid day tae ye, Blaise," he said courteously. "Whatchya making?"

"A coin purse for Suzannah."

Grandpa pulled a coin from his pocket and slid it on the counter. "Canae have an empty purse. For when you get it finished."

Paislee hid her smile. That was sweet but she'd never say so.

"Why, thank you, Angus. I'll let Suz know where the coin came from."

"How was your walk?" Paislee asked.

"Fine, fine. Sun is shining, birds are singing. We should take a picnic dinner tae the beach tonight. I've got it all planned with chicken sandwiches and pea salad."

"That's a terrific idea. Let's see what Brody has for homework." She and Grandpa exchanged grins. "Mrs. Martin might have sent home extra-*extra* credit if the boy wants tae leave P6 tae reach P7 next year."

Grandpa told Blaise the story of Wallace and the half-eaten map like a bloody comedian and even Paislee was laughing so hard it hurt.

Blaise checked the time on her phone. "I'm going tae steal your granddaughter away for lunch, if you dinnae mind? I'd like for her tae meet my husband, Shep."

"Not at all, not at all."

As if he had a say, the old codger. What he had was a wee crush on Blaise. Paislee got her friend's address of the rental they were in until their home closed, saying she'd follow right along.

"Your picnic sounds perfect," she told Grandpa as she gathered her purse and keys to leave.

"It's too bonny tae be inside." He rubbed his hands together.

"Fergus Jones hasnae been found yet. Are you going tae grill ol' Shep O'Connor for information on his previous chef?"

Paislee gripped her keys in offense, but settled down as she admitted he had the right of it. "Aye. I'll stop at the florist across the way tae pick up some flowers. Can't go snoop empty-handed."

Chapter 12

Paislee parked before a gorgeous single-story home on the golf course that Blaise and Shep were renting until their new house was ready.

Golf in Nairn was a very big deal but it wasn't a sport she'd ever taken up. Brody was more into football, though if he expressed interest, she'd gladly sign him up for lessons.

Cleats and a ball were less expensive than golf clubs and a membership, which didn't hurt in her current situation, knowing that she wasn't a millionaire.

Chuckling to herself, she exited the Juke and walked up the stone stairs to a broad porch with wicker furniture, colorful planters, and a wall fountain. Long chimes tinkled musically in the breeze.

Blaise opened the etched glass door with a smile. "You made it! Oh, you didnae have tae," she said, accepting the bouquet of fresh-cut lilies that Ritchie had quickly put together in an artistic way light-years beyond anything Paislee might try.

"They're lovely. Liza?" Blaise called.

A smiling maid in gray slacks and a white blouse with capped sleeves emerged from a door down the hall. "Ma'am?"

Blaise handed the maid the flowers. "Will you please put these in the crystal vase that Mr. O'Connor bought for my birthday? I think the bouquet will fit perfectly."

"Aye. It's just the right height. Would you like them in the dining room?"

"Is that where we're lunching? The kitchen would be no bother."

"Mr. O'Connor requested the dining room."

"Then yes, let's see the flowers there. Thank you, Liza." Blaise turned to Paislee. "Lunch in the dining room it is. I cannae wait for you tae meet Shep. We're having a simple chilled shrimp salad."

"I'm not the least picky."

Blaise grinned. "I'm not going tae waste time giving you a tour of the house since we're moving next month—at last! Lydia is bringing the paperwork over later, when Shep is home for dinner. The man works such long days."

"It isnae work if you love what you do," a masculine voice echoed on the open tile and preceded the man down a short flight of open stairs. The interior was very modern. White and sleek.

Paislee had seen pictures of Shep O'Connor, but the reality of the man was overwhelming to the senses. Trim goatee and mustache in golden brown, his hair longish in the front, highlighted blond—a tribute no doubt to the amount of time he spent outdoors. He was lean, his brown eyes inquisitive and confident. He wore cologne, and smiled with bright white teeth against his tan skin.

He was a man's man, Paislee could tell right away—kind to women, yes, but more comfortable on the green with his mates. Cigars and Scotch. He ran the show.

Blaise crossed the floor to him once he reached the bottom step. He took her hand and tucked it in the curve of his elbow.

"I happen tae agree with you," Paislee said.

He and Blaise waited for Paislee to come to them and he extended his hand, clasping her fingers warmly. "I've heard nothing but great things aboot you, Paislee Shaw. It's a pleasure tae finally meet you."

She could see why Shep was a sought-after celebrity golfer. He was the whole package. Beautiful Blaise on his arm, and their daughter, Suzannah, completed the image for him as a man who had it all.

Paislee understood this was calculated—and yet it didn't detract from Shep's charm. She would bet that if he gave you his word on something, it would be done.

He wasn't flirty at all, but proud of his wife as they walked into the dining room overlooking an oval pond as well as the golf green. This was next to a screened-in porch the size of her living room and kitchen combined, which led out to a pool. There was a parked golf cart on a cement slab and a wooden shed that she imagined held golf equipment.

Plates had already been set with their meal and frosty crystal glasses of water with lemon.

"I have an hour," Shep said, "before I have tae get back. You ladies are welcome tae take your time. I can have wine brought out for you?"

"Not for me, thank you." Paislee noticed the lilies already in the vase. "Grandpa is minding the store so I don't want tae be too late."

"Cashmere Crush. Blaise said you were an immense help for the Nairn Food Bank."

"I was happy tae be there. It was a success." Paislee's polite smile faltered. "Except for what happened, I mean."

"Tae Kirsten Buchanan." Shep sat at the head of the table. Blaise took the chair not facing the view, and Paislee was on the opposite side, with the view.

Blaise shook out a cloth napkin and placed it over her lap. Paislee did the same. The "simple" chilled shrimp salad was actually five large prawns on a bed of ribboned romaine, slivered radish, and scallions.

"Dig in," Shep said. "Would you care for bread?"

Paislee didn't see any on the table, so shook her head. "No thank you." There were two slender sesame bread sticks on the side of the dish.

He probably had to be healthy as part of his job, and Blaise got to benefit with amazing meals. Made by a private chef.

What a life.

"So, Blaise mentioned that you wanted tae ask me aboot Fergus Jones."

So much for being stealthy. Paislee laughed at herself. "Aye . . . he's wanted for questioning in regards tae the peanut topping on Kirsten's shortbread cookies. Blaise said that he used tae work for you as your chef? Might he have had a reason tae put the EpiPen on Blaise's chair?"

"The Buchanans stole him away." Blaise trailed the tip of her breadstick through the cilantro lime dressing. "It was very rude. Fergus had no reason tae hold a grudge. Shep found us another chef, end of story." She glanced with admiration at her husband. "He's so nice he didnae want tae make a big deal of it."

Shep swallowed his bite of prawn. "Well. There is a little bit more tae it than that. I didnae want tae bother you with it at the time."

Blaise frowned slightly. "Why not?"

"You were doing so much already with Suzannah at school that I didnae want tae add tae your concern."

In other words, he'd handled it without her input.

"Shep, I . . ." Blaise glanced at Paislee and sipped her water. "So," she said in a light tone, "tell us now, then."

Paislee could see that he didn't really want to but he was in a corner with his wife. This was how polite educated people fought. Privately. Her mum and da had gone at it at times loud enough to rattle the walls.

They'd also hugged and laughed. She'd forgotten that.

"How long did Fergus work for you?" Paislee asked.

Shep folded his napkin on his lap. "You remember, Blaise, when we lived on the course in Inverness? You were overseeing the remodeling of the downstairs parlor, thinking we'd use it for Suzannah's playroom, for her fifth birthday?"

"Yes."

"So, that's when I hired Fergus Jones. Margaret had retired. Fergus was out of school three years, mibbe, but he was quite skilled in fine dining. I guess I thought by hiring someone young that he'd be on staff for decades." He shrugged.

"How old was he?" Paislee asked.

"Not even thirty then."

"So what happened, Shep?" Blaise frowned. "Why didn't he stay?"

"I paid a fair wage, with the plan of his being with us. He had his own rooms. Set hours. But not even a month had gone by when I caught him with the pool girl, getting high."

"Oh." Blaise turned to Paislee. "Shep doesnae condone drugs. It's not guid for his public image."

"Did Fergus know that?" Paislee asked.

"He'd signed a contract," Shep said, "which was then void when he broke the rules."

Like Hamish, with his rules. "Did you let him go right away?" Paislee speared a sliver of scallion.

Shep rubbed his forehead. "He begged for another chance . . . which he failed, another month later. I knew the Buchanans werenae as . . . rigid in their views and so I talked Fergus up and allowed him tae be 'stolen' from us. He got a higher wage, his own room, and access tae a car—they also have a chauffeur."

Paislee laughed softly. "Well played!"

"Shep!" Blaise's eyes twinkled with amusement. "And all this time I thought we'd been tricked. You tricked them!" Then her laughter faded. "What if Fergus really did kill Kirsten? I had no idea he did drugs."

"I dinnae think he did it." Shep sliced another piece of prawn. "He wasnae a bad guy—he just wasn't up tae the standard that I try so hard tae hold for myself. It isnae easy." He chewed the bite and swallowed, holding Paislee's gaze. "You must think I sound like a hardhead."

"I don't," Paislee quickly said. Controlling maybe, but as he said, he had an image to uphold to bring in high rollers for his business. Where did that leave Blaise and Suzannah? Was there room for mistakes?

Blaise said, "Paislee doesnae think Fergus did it, either, which is why she wants tae find him. The police are after him."

Shep studied Paislee more closely. "You dinnae? Why not? It's in the paper so it must be true." His lips twitched.

Paislee chuckled. "My granny taught me tae think for myself. It's been a blessing, but it can also create obstacles."

"Well said." Shep lifted his water glass to her.

"I was there when Kirsten collapsed tae the ground. Fergus wore a look of complete shock, and fear. It wasn't the expression of a man taking revenge over being fired that morning."

Shep nodded and placed his hand over Blaise's with a gentle squeeze. "Blaise said she told you and Lydia aboot her childhood?"

"Aye."

"If she trusts you enough with that after what happened, then I will trust you with this:" He raised his index finger. "Fergus Jones's mother had a small house in Elgin where he used tae send money from his paycheck."

"He did?" Paislee asked in surprise.

"Aye. Like I said, I wanted tae give him a chance. He's not a bad man. I'd say Gerard Buchanan is more cutthroat. Blaise told me that Anders accused him of killing Kirsten. I could believe that far more than Fergus doing it. Kirsten was a trophy for Gerard . . . one that had acquired a tarnish."

The maid knocked on the open door of the dining room, holding a phone in her hand. "The call you were waiting for, Mr. O'Connor."

He got up and put his napkin beside his half-eaten lunch plate. "You ladies continue. I'll have that address for you, Paislee, before you go."

He left, taking energy with him from the room.

Paislee smiled across at Blaise. "I like your husband, Blaise."

Her mouth trembled. "I don't know what he ever saw in me, but I am grateful every day tae be his wife."

"How about because you're amazing?" Paislee crunched down on a breadstick.

"We met at university. Shep was there on golf scholarships due tae his talent. I was there on a math scholarship—otherwise I wouldnae have been able tae afford tae go."

"You're so smart—math? Brilliant."

Blaise shook her head. "I studied my brains oot tae make it. I didnae want tae be one of those kids that never left the squalor behind. I helped Shep with calculus and the rest is history."

"Good for you. How on earth could Kirsten take your success and turn it around tae be anything less than stellar?"

"I wasnae born with the silver spoon. Shep was, of course. And Kirsten, Mari, and Christina. Gerard. Mari's husband, Charlie. Ugh. I've had tae listen tae the stories of them all being friends since childhood. I felt so left oot. I want that solidarity for Suzannah, too. I guess it's why I've kept her at the academy."

"What does Shep think?"

"Och, he's left that up tae me. He knows I struggle with confidence against those women. He's incredibly supportive."

Paislee finished the last scrumptious bite of prawn, dressing, and romaine. "There is nothing simple about this salad."

"Our chef was trained in Edinburgh. Nice mid-forties man. I cannae believe Shep never told me the truth aboot Fergus." Blaise cupped her chin in her hand, elbow on the table.

Paislee kept her opinion about that to herself and wiped her mouth with her napkin.

"I'll think aboot it later . . . right now, let's go tae that address in Elgin and see for ourselves if Fergus is there? If not, mibbe his mother will know where he is."

"Are you serious?"

"Why not? You think he's innocent, and so does Shep, which means we wouldnae be in any danger."

"I . . ." Paislee really wanted to find Fergus and prove his innocence, but she had responsibilities. The shop.

"Your grandfather can wait another hour, eh?"

Paislee allowed herself to be persuaded. "I'll call him—but it'll be a wee bit longer. Elgin is an hour round trip."

"Fifty minutes, less if traffic is light."

Shep, still on the phone, walked into the dining room and placed a neatly printed address to Paislee's right, waved, and walked out again.

"Is he speaking Spanish?" Paislee asked.

"Aye. He's got a few high-profile Latin customers he's working one-on-one with. He really loves his job," she said in an adoring tone. "He says he willnae always be at the top of his game, so he wants tae bank as much as he can and retire at fifty. He promises tae take me and Suz all over the world."

"That sounds terrific."

"I'm verra fortunate."

"So is he, math star."

At that, Blaise laughed.

Paislee called Grandpa to let him know she'd be a while longer.

"I can handle the shop, lass. Have some fun. I'm just watching telly."

"Grandpa!"

"Just jokin' around. You're so easy. Cheers!"

She shook her head and stood up. "I'm ready. Should we take one car, or two?"

"Leave yours here. I'll drive the Beast."

Petite Blaise hopped behind the wheel of her Range Rover and drove onto the main road leading out of Nairn toward Elgin.

Twenty-three minutes later, they arrived at a decrepit stone building with an abandoned air. Yet, Paislee saw a yellowed lace curtain in the kitchen window move.

"Is Mum still alive?" Paislee asked.

"I hope so." Blaise snickered. "Otherwise, this place is haunted."

They got out of the Range Rover and walked up the cracked path to the front door. There was no porch, and the lawn was dead grass.

"Someone's here." Paislee pointed to the muddy mat before the door.

Blaise nodded and knocked. The door was thin, like plywood, and she feared one solid gust off the Firth could blow it down.

No answer.

Paislee rapped her knuckles with a wee bit more force. She got the strangest feeling up her spine. "Let's check the back."

The two ladies went around the side yard. There was a wooden fence, as tall as Hamish McCall, but the panel door was open a crack.

Paislee pushed at it. She saw a man in jeans and a hoodie hoofing toward the back fence as if to leap into the neighbor's yard.

"Wait!" she called.

"Fergus Jones!" Blaise shouted.

The chef stopped and turned around, his hoodie falling back to his shoulders to reveal a defiant expression beneath coal-black hair rather than copper.

"Mrs. O'Connor."

Chapter 13

"Stop right there!" Blaise instructed, very much lady of the manor in the forlorn back garden.

"I heard ye." Fergus shoved his hands into his front pockets. His jeans were loose and he didn't have any extra fat on him to show his love of food.

If Paislee were a chef, she'd constantly be sampling the wares—it was a better option for her to knit or her extra weight would *really* be extra.

Fergus had dyed his hair black as well as changed out of his professional chef's garb. He wore a baseball cap that he removed, beseeching them with his earnest gaze. "I didnae add the nuts tae the shortbread."

"I believe you," Paislee said. "I was there and saw Gerard hit your arm so hard you dropped the tray of cookies."

His face screwed up. "You gave her CPR. I remember. Tell them tae stop huntin' me doon like a bloody criminal!"

"I already told them that I don't think you're guilty."

"Fat lot of guid then, eh?" Fergus glanced to the side of the yard. An old dog bowl lay on its side, years forgotten.

"Is your mum here?" Blaise asked.

"Dead. Thank the lord. Her son on the lamb accused of murder woulda killed her." He shrugged. "I inherited the place a few months ago. Thought I'd have plenty of time and money tae do it up for a rental toward me retirement."

Life could change at the drop of a hat.

"Come with us tae the police station," Paislee said. "Tell them you're innocent. Where were you that morning?"

"Did you bake the shortbread?" Blaise interjected. "Tae win the contests, even at school?"

Paislee realized that Blaise was still hurting from the deception.

"Naw," Fergus answered. "Mrs. Buchanan had her own recipe. And her kitchen had no nuts in it. I dinnae ken how they got into the recipe."

"A crumble on top," Blaise said.

He studied the brown grass, mouth pursed. "She had a dusting of brown sugar that she'd caramelized for her topping. I suppose nuts could've been chopped verra fine in a processor, then added. The shortbread appeared identical. I saw them with me own eyes."

"She said the presentation was wrong." Paislee sighed. "You didn't notice when you brought the dishes from the kitchen?"

"No. They were covered in the same cling film that I'd helped her with earlier that morning."

Blaise stepped toward the chef. "Were you fired?"

Fergus gulped and pulled one hand from his pocket to wipe his eyes. "Aye."

"What for? Drugs?"

"Naw, Mrs. O'Connor." He scuffed at the lawn creating a poof of dirt. "I'd rather not say."

Paislee cleared her throat. "Is it about the affair between her and Anders?"

Fergus dropped his shoulders. "If ye know so much, then who killed Mrs. Buchanan?"

Paislee and Blaise exchanged a look. "We're trying tae find that out. And save you in the process."

"Who are you?" Fergus shifted his attention to Paislee. "Not one of them fancy ladies at the academy."

"No. Just a regular lady. I'm Paislee Shaw."

He bobbed his head. He'd been around good manners long enough to be polite, but where did this situation fit on the decorum scale? "I need tae get into my rooms at the Buchanan house."

"You were spotted around their property," Paislee said. "The police just want tae talk tae you."

His voice took on a desperate tone. "My money is there. I was given two weeks' notice, with pay. I had every expectation tae go back tae the house after the biscuit competition and work oot my time. I had a deal with Mrs. Buchanan."

Paislee remembered how angry Gerard had been, telling Fergus to forget about any agreement he'd had with Kirsten. "And you can't call Mr. Buchanan?"

"I tried that already but he just screams at me. He knows I wouldnae do it, but he seems to have lost his mind—understandably." Fergus looked longingly at the fence and Paislee got the feeling he'd love to bolt.

"Let's go inside and sit down, maybe have a cuppa," she suggested.

"Not a guid idea." He shoved his hands in his hoodie pockets. "Have ye talked tae Hendrie? Ask him what happened that afternoon. He was probably sleeping on the job when the EpiPen was stolen. I walked right by him and he didnae see me."

"You don't like Hendrie?"

"He's all right, but we're not best mates or anythin'. Mr. Buchanan hired him for his size, not his brains."

"I hardly recognized you with your hair dyed," Blaise said.

"Guid. I need tae get oot of Scotland."

"If you didnae kill Kirsten," Blaise said, "there's no need for you tae be on the run."

Sweat broke out on his forehead. "I just . . . it's personal." He lowered his shoulders. "Mibbe we better talk aboot this inside. You willnae let it go, huh?"

Paislee held his gaze. "I believe you're innocent."

He nodded and stepped forward, urging them to go on ahead. "Door's open."

Paislee and Blaise walked to the back of the house.

After a few paces, Paislee glanced behind to suggest going to the nearest bakery for a tea and sweet just in time to see Fergus launch himself silently over the fence and out of sight.

"Fergus—no!"

Blaise had the back door open when she looked around. "What?"

Paislee was mentally kicking herself. She should have had him walk in first. "He's gone."

Blaise clicked her tongue to her teeth in frustration. "Guilty behavior . . ."

"Aye." Paislee stared at the back fence. "If not of killing Kirsten, then what? Why wouldn't he tell you why he was fired?"

"We can talk tae Hendrie—he'll know." Blaise waved her hand beneath her nose. "Should we go in and have a poke around? It's musty. Fast, and then let's come up with a plan tae help that eejit Fergus."

Paislee had her mobile out to dial the station. "We should let the police know we've seen him."

"We will . . . after. It's not like the constable called you right away, is it?"

Blaise had a valid point. "All right." Paislee pocketed her phone and followed her inside.

The interior of the small house was poorly lit but there was a sleeping bag on the sofa, a kitchen with outdated appliances. Nothing was on, and she assumed there was no power.

"He was hiding here," Paislee said.

"Laying low." Blaise walked down the hall and opened a door. "Bedroom—still full of his mother's things, poor soul." The next door she pushed wide and said, "Bathroom—with black dye all over the tub; the container is in the trash." She circled back to the living area. "That's the whole place."

Paislee rubbed her arms. She'd been taught to do the right

thing and this felt like breaking and entering, even if Fergus had suggested they go in. "We should go."

"Wait now . . . what do we have here?" Blaise lifted a duffel bag, opened, that had the name of the private school Blaise's daughter went to. The initials HA were on the side.

"We need tae let the police know about Fergus's new appearance," Paislee said. "They're searching for a redhead."

"Why does Fergus have a bag from Highland Academy?" Blaise peered inside. "Clothes. With tags on."

Paislee voiced the obvious. "He had tae buy new because he couldn't get back tae his room at the Buchanans."

Blaise did another circuit around the small home. "Dinnae look so pained, Paislee—we were invited inside, weren't we?"

"Well, technically." Paislee scrunched her nose. "As a distraction so Fergus could run away from us." She glanced out the open back door, hoping that Fergus would return. "Do you think he'll come back?"

"Not while we're here." Blaise placed her hands on her hips. "Where did he get the money for new things?"

"Fergus probably had his wallet with him that day. He made a good wage working for the Buchanans and likely has credit cards."

"You're right," Blaise said. "He's crashing here because he's hiding from the police. He owns the place, he said. No crime in that. Why does he want tae leave Scotland?"

"A fresh start? Maybe his passport and severance check are in his rooms at the Buchanan house." Paislee sighed, hating not having answers. "We should go."

Blaise scooped her loose hair behind her ear. "Should we find Hendrie?"

"Hendrie won't talk tae us," Paislee said, feeling dejected. "He doesn't know us."

"I have cash for a bribe." Blaise patted her purse. "And if that doesnae work, Shep can ask Gerard why they fired Fergus."

"That's a great idea. Let's just do that, and avoid bothering Hendrie. Would he?"

"Aye. Shep is all aboot fair play." Blaise shut the back door when they left, making sure that it was locked. "You phone the station while I drive."

"All right." Paislee left a message with receptionist Amelia Henry for Constable Dean, who was out on patrol. Constable Rory was also unavailable. She thought of leaving one for the DI, but she was pretty sure Constable Dean was in charge of the investigation.

"You tried," Blaise said. "I just keep wondering aboot that duffel bag."

"Fergus likely got it from the Buchanans, since they're such a big part of Highland Academy." Paislee could easily imagine a plethora of Highland Academy gear piled up in a garage.

"Possibly. I wish he wouldnae have run away. Oh well . . ." Blaise exhaled. "How is Brody doing these days? Is he ready tae be top dog at Fordythe next year?"

"We'll see if he makes it tae P7," Paislee joked. "Brody's actually been fighting with a friend of his. He tells me the bare minimum so I don't have a lot tae work with. Is Suz like that?"

"She's a chatterbox and willnae stop talking." Blaise glanced at her. "Mibbe girls are different?"

"Aye. Are you going tae have more kids?"

"No . . . Shep and I are both content with one. We want tae travel. You?"

Paislee laughed. "I was already the shameful talk of the shire when I had Brody without a husband. Not something I want tae do again."

They reached Blaise's house and each promised to call if they heard anything—Blaise would ask Shep to talk to Gerard, and Paislee was to let Blaise know what the constables said about Fergus when and if they called her back.

Paislee waved and got into the Juke, which felt small compared to the Range Rover but much more manageable.

★ ★ ★

She passed by the comic book/arcade shop on her way and made the impulsive decision to stop in and talk to Bennett Mclean about their boys.

"Paislee!" Bennett greeted her with a grin when she entered the store. His girlfriend, Alexa, nodded as she stocked magazines at the counter.

A giant sofa had been arranged in the center of the shop with games and video controllers. There was a foosball table, a pool table, and a dartboard. A kid's dream come true. Bennett had endeared himself to Paislee when he'd explained that he'd wanted a business his son could be part of, hence the name, Mclean's.

"Hi, Paislee." Alexa, hair up in a ponytail, applied a box cutter to an empty cardboard box and added it to a neat pile ready for the recycle bin.

"Nice tae see you!" Paislee shouldered her purse.

"What's up?" Bennett rested his hip against the counter. He had shaggy blond hair, jade-green eyes, and a gorgeous smile. "Here tae buy the latest video game Brody has his eye on?"

"Nope." A large selection rose up an entire wall. "I was actually wondering if you'd heard from Headmaster McCall."

His smile faded. "He left a message tae give him a ring, but I havenae done it yet. Why?"

"Well, it seems our two boys have been . . . fighting, at school." She hated to bring it up, since the two were also friends.

"So?" Bennett lifted a shoulder. "Boys will be boys."

Paislee liked his attitude much better than Hamish's. "I have a meeting with the headmaster after school."

"Och, I noticed that you and Hamish arenae as cozy as ye used tae be. Mibbe he just wants tae say hello."

Her cheeks flamed.

"Bennett, really," Alexa sighed. "Excuse him, Paislee, he's got no sense of when tae shut up."

Paislee cleared her throat. "Anyway . . . I wanted tae know if ye'd seen anything odd between them?"

"No." Bennett turned to his girlfriend. "You, Alexa?"

Alexa shifted from one foot to the next. "Wellll . . ."

"What?" Bennett asked.

"What?" Paislee echoed.

"Last Sunday they were pushing each other—nothing major, as ye say, boys will be boys—but they both looked really mad—steam coming from their ears, that mad."

"What did ye do?" Paislee crossed her arms. "Why didn't you say anything?"

"I told them tae calm doon and when I checked on them again, they were back tae being pals. I didnae think anything of it. Why make a big deal, aye?"

Bennett rifled through a magazine in an absent manner. "I dinnae recall seeing anything like that. You know what might be going on, Paislee?"

"Brody's not a big talker but I'll be sure tae ask him about it."

"Could be over a girl," Alexa said. "They're getting tae be that age."

"Aye," Bennett agreed, putting the magazine down. "Edwyn wants his own mobile and I said no."

"Thank heaven. I'm torn about the whole thing, honestly." Paislee jiggled her keys. "But I thought Edwyn had one?"

"I bought him a disposable one tae use when he's away at your house, or another mate's."

"That's brilliant." It was so hard to find the right balance of mothering to smothering. "Oh—I have another question. Do you buy used laptops?"

"No. Not worth the hassle usually. Why?"

She told him about the gaming laptop that had been stolen. "Lydia says it's top of the line."

Alexa nodded. "It is, and worth a pretty penny. I imagine the officers around here have checked all of the game shops?"

"Probably. I just thought I'd ask since I was here. I know nothing about them. Why would somebody need that kind of computer? I have an old PC at the house, and my laptop at work cost less than five hundred."

"Serious gamers make a lot of money, if they're guid, on salary from the game companies, not tae mention prizes. Alexa used tae work for one, right, hon?"

"I was middle of the road." She shrugged, pleased at his compliment. "I still do the occasional test for a new game. We get samples sent tae us here as well. Previews for upcoming games, that sort of thing."

"I had no idea playing games could be so profitable." Still, Paislee was in no hurry to buy such an expensive laptop.

Alexa and Bennett smiled at each other. "Gaming should be fun, right?" Bennett said.

Some older teens came into the shop and browsed the stocked shelves.

"I have to go," Paislee said. "I'll try tae dig a little deeper into the fighting situation and let you know."

Bennett moved around the counter toward the kids. "Same."

In the Juke once more, Paislee listened to a voice message from Grandpa asking where she was at. It was almost time to get Brody and there were no more crisps.

She tried to call him back but there was no answer, so Paislee drove to the market, her thoughts jumping from Fergus to Brody. Would Fergus turn himself in? What had Brody and Edwyn been fighting about? Last week, Brody mentioned that Edwyn had thought Anna, a girl in their class, was cute and liked that she could draw comic figures. Brody didn't understand why they couldn't just play football.

She greeted Colleen, the cashier, and loaded up on snacks—biscuits and crisps, as well as chocolate—then headed to Cashmere Crush, where she parked and went in the back, a cloth grocery bag over her arm.

"I'm here tae save you with supplies," she said.

"Aboot time," Grandpa groused from his seat by the register. "You've been gone all day."

"And what, you're going tae dock my pay?"

He eyed the bag of goodies and took it from her to set on the counter, digging through to find a caramel biscuit. "Thank you. I may have been a wee bit short due tae you starving me. Oh, and the DI stopped by looking for you. Seems he has some questions aboot Fergus Jones."

Chapter 14

Paislee set her purse down on the shelf below the register and reached for her mobile. It figured that she and Detective Inspector Zeffer would just miss each other. "Should I call him?"

The front door opened and the DI strutted in, wearing yet another stylish blue suit. Being a detective meant that he didn't have to wear the Police Scotland uniform. Paislee's thought that he could model for *Detective's Weekly* made her bite her lip to keep from smiling.

"No need, lass," Grandpa said. "He must've been watching for you."

"I saw your Juke pass the station," the DI explained in a huff. "What the blazes were you doing in Elgin? At Fergus Jones's mother's house?"

"His mum passed, and it's his now," Paislee explained, grasping the last comment and answering that first. He always had her on the defensive. "Blaise drove."

He scowled. "How did you know where tae find him?"

"Fergus used tae be a chef for the O'Connors before being hired by the Buchanans. Shep mentioned over lunch today that Fergus would send part of his paycheck tae his mum, and so he had the address."

The DI calmed down, a wee bit like a puffy bluebird relaxing his feathers. "Why did the pair of you decide tae track him down? Why not give the police that information?"

Grandpa looked from the DI to Paislee as if watching a tennis match.

"We weren't sure that he would be there—we thought tae ask his mother where tae find him."

Zeffer spread out his arms. "Why?"

Paislee shuffled her feet. "Well . . . I don't think Fergus is guilty of murdering Kirsten Buchanan."

"And you think this with what proof?"

Him and his proof.

"I saw his expression, I told you that."

The DI brought his arms back in to rest at his hips. The front door opened and a pair of women ambled in. Grandpa reluctantly left her and the detective to welcome them. "Afternoon, ladies."

"I dinnae like you putting yourself in danger." The DI leaned toward her.

"I didn't—Shep O'Connor doesn't believe Fergus is guilty, either, otherwise he wouldn't have let Blaise go tae the house. He's very protective of his family. We had no idea that Fergus's mother was deceased, or that he would be there."

His nostrils flared just the slightest. "Tell me what happened."

"We saw a curtain move when we drove up, otherwise the place seemed deserted. There were muddy footprints on the cement stoop. When we knocked, there was no answer and that's when we realized that something might be up."

He nodded, jaw tight. "So instead of calling for assistance, you did what?"

"We didn't break the law, thank you!"

"Just tell me."

"The wooden fence around the house had a gate that was open." Paislee's cheeks warmed. "We called hello, but didn't hear anything . . . we entered the back garden, and saw Fergus trying tae leap over a fence tae leave the yard."

The DI pressed his fingers to his brow as if in agony. "And?"

Her voice pitched higher. "I called his name but it wasn't until Blaise shouted for him that he stopped and talked tae us. The first thing he said was that he didn't do it."

"Right. A natural response for someone being hunted down."

Zeffer had a point there. "Then we asked why he was running if he was innocent . . . he never did answer that question. But, he did confirm that Kirsten had fired him. He had every expectation of going back tae the Buchanan house and working for the next two weeks. His things are there, which is why he's been hanging around, trying tae get in, but Gerard won't let him."

"Hmm. And all of this took place in the back garden."

"It's true! I suggested we go inside tae get a cup of tea, just tae set him at ease, but he wasn't interested . . . at first. Then he changed his mind."

"Why is your face the color of a brick?"

Paislee hated the redhead curse. "Well, he tricked us. Told us tae go on in, the back door was open. When I turned around tae suggest going tae a tea shop, well, he'd cheeked it over the fence. Quite agile."

The breath escaping his clenched teeth reminded her of air hissing from a balloon. "And then?"

"Well, Blaise was already inside the house—that he'd told us we could go into, by the way."

Grandpa was showing the ladies a shelf with patterns, but half listening, too. He kept scooting closer.

"So, not breaking and entering, is what you're telling me." Zeffer's mouth quirked. "And you went in, too?"

"Blaise was already inside, and I joined her, aye."

"What did you see?" Zeffer pulled his tablet from his pocket.

"There was no power, and a sleeping bag on the couch. Fergus had a duffel bag stuffed with brand-new clothes. It was obvious he was hiding out."

Zeffer raised his head. "And *now* why didnae ye call the police?"

"I did . . . as soon as we got back in the car tae drive tae Blaise's house. She locked up and everything. Oh, but the most important thing is that Fergus has dyed his copper-red hair tae black. I wouldn't have recognized him. There was a box of dye in the bathroom of his house."

"What was he wearing?"

"A black hoodie and jeans. Black runners. Made him look like a teenager rather than a professional chef. He said he needs the money from his rooms at the Buchanans in order tae leave Scotland."

"How can ye think he's not guilty?" The DI sounded incredulous as he added the information she'd given him to his notes. "Anything else?"

"The clothes still had price tags—he probably had tae buy some since Gerard has locked him out."

"When did this happen?"

Paislee checked the time. How could it be quarter past three? She had to pick up Brody and call Hamish for an appointment. "Two? I have tae go."

"I'm not done here."

"Can we finish later? I've got tae pick up Brody."

Zeffer sighed. "I'll call you if I need something. Or you call me if you remember anything more."

"What about Constable Dean?"

"I'm helping with the case."

She didn't want to be critical, but that was probably a good thing as she hadn't heard from the constable at all, nor from Constable Rory, who seemed to be the ones handling the investigation.

"All right." She shooed him toward the front door, called goodbye to Grandpa, and headed out the back to her Juke.

On the way, she dialed Fordythe Primary and asked the receptionist if she could speak with the headmaster.

"He's in a meeting right now," Mrs. Jimenez said.

"Can I schedule something with him tomorrow at three o'clock? Today is busy."

"Sure—let me add it tae his calendar."

"Thank you!"

Paislee hung up and drove around the traffic circles meant to control traffic in growing Nairn. She hated them, but they worked—she was forced to slow down no matter how impatient she got.

She got in the queue behind a brand-new silver van that belonged to her good friend Mary Beth Mulholland. Mary Beth had twin girls who were eight, a year older than Blaise's daughter, Suzannah.

Brody was outside waiting on the curb—no Mrs. Martin, no Headmaster McCall, and no Edwyn.

Paislee breathed a sigh of relief when Brody got in the car and they drove back to Cashmere Crush. "How was school?"

"Guid."

"How did your extra credit go over?"

His nose twisted. "Well, she only gave me half the points."

"What is the lesson here?"

"Keep me homework off the couch."

"You're right." She glanced at him as she drove. "How's Edwyn?"

"Fine. We want tae go campin'."

She played like she didn't know a thing. "Oh?"

"Just the two of us. The parks are open and we'd be careful. Roast marshmallows. Fish for our dinner. It'll be great fun."

Paislee's brain screeched at the idea of unsupervised fire. Two boys in the woods all alone? They'd be bait for predators—human and beast. She was glad she'd been given a warning by Grandpa so that she didn't overreact.

Still, her grip on the wheel tightened.

"I think I'd feel better if you were with an adult. I could take you. Or maybe Bennett, or Grandpa?"

"Mum! We're not weans—lots of kids do it."

She bit the inside of her cheek. "It doesn't matter what other kids are doing. I'm not comfortable with it."

"Why? And don't say 'because.'"

"Because . . . you could be in danger."

"From what?" Brody snorted. "A deer?"

Paislee didn't want to scar the lad by sharing her fears of murderers or molesters or bad people in general. "You know, before we get into a discussion about this, why don't we check the rules on the park website?"

"What rules? Edwyn said we can camp anywhere we want."

While it was true that Scotland's open land allowed for camping in the wild, there were still basic rules. "If you want tae cook, you'll need a campground with proper facilities. Let's check when we get home."

Brody stared at her as if to make sure she wasn't pulling his leg. "Really?"

"It should be easy tae find out, front page, probably."

He nodded. "Edwyn's dad has a tent."

"Well . . . maybe if you want tae we can have a sleepover in the back garden."

"Just the two of us?"

"Let's ask Bennett first. And you'd have tae promise that you'd stay in the yard."

"What aboot a campfire?"

"Definitely not. You might burn the shed down, it's so old." Paislee would keep watch from the upstairs window all night.

They arrived at the shop, where Brody made himself comfy with a snack and a bottle of water, then turned the telly on low.

Grandpa had rung up the two ladies with yarn, patterns, and knitting needles, and was just bagging their items in the paper sack with the interlocking Cs logo. Two more customers were browsing at the front.

"Hiya!" Paislee said with a warm smile. "May I help you?" She made them welcome and answered their questions about local yarn.

The afternoon remained so busy that Paislee was tempted to stay open past six, but Brody and Grandpa grumbled that their bellies were empty.

"It's a smart thing you set us up with a picnic already, Grandpa,"

Paislee said. "I'm done in after today." Searching for Fergus, hoping to find who actually killed Kirsten, worry over Brody and Edwyn.

"A picnic?" Brody asked. "You didnae say that."

"It slipped my mind with the talk about camping. Isn't that a nice surprise? Grandpa made chicken sandwiches for us."

Grandpa busied himself tucking the stools under the high-top tables. "It's a new chicken recipe I wanted tae try."

"Thanks, Grandpa. Mum, can we bring Wallace?"

"Sure."

"I didnae make him a sandwich," Grandpa teased. "He'll have tae have yours."

"I'd share," Brody said loyally.

"I know you would, but he'll be just fine with his dog food." Paislee ushered her family out the back, then locked the door.

They got home in five minutes, changed into shorts and sandals, grabbed Wallace and the picnic basket, then headed to the beach.

Nothing revived her more than fresh salt air, and she was able to push Kirsten a little farther back in her mind.

They set out a plaid picnic blanket and dug into the sandwiches. Thick bread, chicken, onion, celery, mustard. Delicious.

She passed out crisps and apples—not that either Shaw male touched the fruit. Grandpa went for the chocolate bar.

Brody was about to escape to race along the sand when Paislee, having lulled him into relaxing after a full belly, said, "I spoke with Bennett today."

"Aboot camping?" Brody kneeled on the blanket to pet Wallace. "When did ye do that? You were busy all afternoon."

"Not the camping." Paislee held her son's gaze. "About you and Edwyn being physical—pushing, fighting."

"Mum!" He rolled his eyes. "I told you it was nothin'."

"Mrs. Martin warned you both already tae knock it off. Now the headmaster wants tae discuss it." Which meant that it was not "nothing."

Brody groaned. "It's no big deal."

Paislee couldn't let it go, though it would be easier to pretend things were fine. "What are you arguing about, son, so that I know what tae say tae Headmaster McCall?"

"I dinnae want tae tell." He jutted his chin.

"I think you should," Paislee said in a calm voice. "You know you can trust me not tae say anything."

He sat cross-legged on the blanket and gathered Wallace in his lap, his lower lip so far out it could catch rain.

"Is it about the lasses again?"

"Not really." Brody inspected the fur at Wallace's ears.

"Is it about stealing crisps?"

"No." He gently tugged dried grass from the pup's tail.

Paislee lost her patience. "Well?"

"It doesnae matter anymore. He's not doing it. So, I dinnae want tae tell you." Brody popped up like he had a spring in his rear. "Can I go play?"

She shielded her eyes to peer up at him. Getting to the problem would need a different tact. "Aye."

She and Grandpa exchanged a look, then she watched Brody and Wallace leap and play in the sand and surf.

"He's a guid boy, Paislee. Until he breaks your trust, give him the benefit of the doot."

Something Grandpa was trying to prove to his missing son, Craigh. Being a parent had to be the most difficult job in the world. "Why is it that I doubt the headmaster will go so easy on *me* tomorrow?"

Chapter 15

Tuesday morning, Paislee was lost in a project of knitting an infinity scarf with a hidden pocket for keys or a phone, cozy on a padded chair in Cashmere Crush. No customers yet, so it was the perfect time to forge ahead on some new inventory.

According to this morning's news, Fergus Jones was still on the run. She hadn't heard a peep from the DI but that wasn't so unusual—he liked to keep his cards close to his blue-suited chest. There'd been a wonderful spread about the funds raised for the Nairn Food Bank.

Her phone rang and she smiled as she saw that it was Lydia. "Hey!"

"Morning, love." Her best friend lowered her husky voice. "I want tae kidnap you for lunch."

"Naw. I just was out yesterday at Blaise's so I should stay here at the shop with Grandpa."

"So?" Her tongue clicked. "Ye have tae eat."

She suspected that Lydia had an ulterior motive . . . maybe to talk about Corbin. "What do you really want?"

"Ha. Fine. I called Sonya aboot prices for the rooms tae rent for Natalya, and she mentioned that she'd caught video of a man carrying oot the shiny black box for the gaming laptop."

"Who has it?" Paislee set the scarf aside.

"She doesnae know, and she asked me tae come check it oot."

"And you thought of me?" Paislee grinned.

"But of course! I know how you are—you're involved in this now. Then after you're done pestering Sonya, we can get the lunch special at Carousel Café."

"How considerate of you. I'll let Grandpa know."

"I'll pick you up at ten after twelve. Be ready! Gotta run."

Paislee ended the call and exchanged her phone for the scarf. The dove-gray yarn was soft against her skin.

The front door opened and an older woman in an I LOVE NAIRN T-shirt wandered inside, admiring the selection of yarns. "Morning. Is everything cashmere?" she asked.

"No. We carry mostly merino wool." Paislee put the scarf down and joined the lady as she surveyed the selection. "But these shelves here are all cashmere, from local goats. We like tae buy from JoJo's Farm."

"Goats?" Her brow lifted. "Not sheep?"

"Funny misconception that cashmere comes from sheep. Are you visiting here?" The woman's T-shirt and accent placed her as a tourist.

"*Oui*. From France. My husband loves golf and Nairn has been a dream forever." Her smile was friendly. "The kids are off to college, so it's our turn to travel and have fun."

"Congratulations. I was born and raised in Nairn, so I'm probably biased when I say it's lovely." She dreamed that Brody would go to university and be successful. One day she might brag to strangers about it—subtly, of course.

"Oh—can you recommend things to do? I've already been to the castle."

"If you're interested in cashmere, JoJo's offers visits at the farm during special hours tae see the goats—they also have sheep. You'd be able tae see and feel the difference of wool and cashmere for yourself."

The woman clasped her hands together. "That would be something special to share with our friends back home."

Paislee sold the lady two skeins of cashmere—the label had JoJo's information on it—and wished her a happy holiday.

The Frenchwoman left, but a steady trickle of customers kept Paislee on her feet and the scarf neglected.

Grandpa showed up at quarter till noon, a new fishing magazine in hand. "Not that I'll have time tae read, we've been so busy."

"Thank you, tourist season." Paislee rubbed her hands together. "I'll feel better with a cushion in the bank." The pipes were worn, the washer squealed during the spin cycle, and she needed a new bulb for the fridge—that was the easy one. If a major appliance were to go? She shuddered.

Grandpa set the magazine on the counter. "Where are you off tae in such a hurry?"

"The social club with Lydia."

"Arenae you Miss Popular this week?" He hitched his bony hip on a stool—had he lost weight? Was she working him too hard?

"Two days in a row." Paislee immediately felt guilty. "I can stay if it's too much for you."

He took offense and scoffed. "Och, no—go on. I didnae know the club sold food."

"They don't. I mean, they have a kitchen, so they can serve dishes, but they aren't a restaurant." She shrugged. "I guess Sonya—she's the director and owner of the property—wants tae see if Lydia can identify who has the gaming laptop from the security footage."

"What a rat." Grandpa stretched out his legs. "I hope they've caught the crook on video, so that it can be returned. Toss the thief in jail. Why steal a laptop anyway?"

"Don't tell this to Brody or he'll get the wrong idea, but gamers can make a decent salary, Bennett told me. Alexa used to work for one, plus prize money, and free games from the companies."

His brows waggled over his black frames. "Mibbe I should give it a go?"

Paislee reined in his dreams of gaming glory by gesturing to the boxes of inventory in back. "We got some knitting needles in that could be priced if ye have free time."

He shifted on his stool, keeping his back to the stack.

"Anyway, after that, we're stopping for lunch. I'm looking forward tae finding out more about Laird Corbin Smythe. Lydia has been very tight-lipped but I think she really likes him."

"I missed me chance, eh?"

Paislee rolled her eyes. "As if." She grabbed her purse when Lydia texted that she was out front. "Don't let me forget I have the meeting with Hamish today."

A young couple entered the shop. Grandpa rose from the stool. "We might need tae hire someone else tae help oot if we stay this busy."

She winced at the cost and smiled at the browsing customers. "It's only for a few months. I'll be back."

"Cheers!" Grandpa called and Paislee left.

Lydia had the windows down on her sporty red Mercedes. "Hurry, a patrol car has been around twice."

Paislee hopped in the passenger side. "And hello tae you, too. You could just park in the back."

"This is easier. Faster. And more fun tae tweak their noses." Lydia shot her a glance. "So, Blaise told me aboot your little adventure yesterday, driving tae Elgin."

"She did?"

"Over dinner at her house last night when I brought the paperwork for them tae sign. Why didn't I hear aboot it from you? That could've been dangerous, confronting Fergus Jones."

"I didn't mention it because nothing happened, and we were both busy, aye?"

"That's true." Lydia took a right down a side street that led to the main road toward the social club. "Shep raved aboot you, Paislee. He thinks you have a cool head."

"Fooled him, then," she said with a laugh. "He seems like a decent man."

Sky so blue shone through the window and Lydia put her sunglasses on. "I didnae oot you, and aye, he's one of the guid guys.

I wish them every happiness—wait till you see their new place. Much nicer than the rental."

"It was a resort. I worried the whole time that I was going tae drop something. And they don't eat bread. I couldn't live a life without bread."

Lydia chuckled. "I didnae notice at the time, but there was none on the table last night for dinner, either. We had grilled salmon with wild rice. I suppose it's part of Shep's job to be verra fit." She slowed to a stop at a traffic light. "Gotta keep up the right image tae bring in high-paying clients, tae afford the mansion."

"I suppose if I was raised that way, it would be important, but thank heaven Gran was all about warm scones slathered with fresh butter." There wasn't a day that went by that Paislee didn't miss her granny. "Blaise has adapted very well tae it, I think."

"She works her tail off tae make it seem easy—poor dear was under a lot of stress yesterday when I arrived."

"Because of Fergus?" Paislee settled her purse at her feet. It tipped as Lydia floored it when the light turned green.

"Naw. It seems that Christina and Mari are strong-arming Blaise intae one more lunch, in honor of Kirsten. She begged for us both tae come along."

Paislee's stomach immediately tightened as if bracing for bad news. "I'm sure I'm busy."

"I didnae even say when it was!" Lydia maneuvered smoothly into the next lane.

"Fine. When is the lunch?"

"Tomorrow."

Paislee shook her head so hard her braid loosened. "Can't. Grandpa would have a conniption. I might be working him too hard as it is—are their senior labor laws?"

"He's healthy as a horse."

She didn't argue that point but went on to her next objection. "I don't fit with that crowd at all. It would be awkward."

"Me either." Lydia glanced at her, the dark sunglasses hiding her gray eyes. "It's for Blaise."

Who was a client of Lydia's as well as a friend. Duty weighted the cinnamon-scented air in the car.

"Let me think about it." She'd figure out a way to say no later— maybe Wallace could catch the flu and Grandpa would need to stay home with the sickly pup, forcing her to be all alone at the shop.

Lydia scored a slot in the first row before the Social Club and Art Centre. The car park was empty rather than loaded full of vendors and shoppers, or the news van. Or ambulances, or police cars. She swallowed.

"Well, this is night and day," Lydia said. "Compared tae how chaotic it was last weekend."

Paislee climbed from the sporty car into the sunny day that lightened her spirits and banished memories of Kirsten to where Paislee could manage them.

She and Lydia each wore slacks, though Paislee's were khaki while Lydia's were linen. Lydia pulled the glass door open and removed her sunglasses to drop in her purse at her side. "Just as gorgeous as I remembered!"

Paislee followed Lydia into the spacious lobby.

Sonya was at her desk to the right and smiled in greeting. "Hi, Lydia—oh, Paislee, too. What a nice surprise."

"Hello." Paislee lifted her hand.

"I brought her along." Lydia nudged Paislee with her elbow. "She's got a guid eye for faces."

Paislee bit back a laugh. She supposed that was better than saying Paislee had a curious nature, or hey, was downright nosy.

"Come back tae my office, where I have the security footage. I've sent the whole two days' worth on film tae the police—they wanted it tae help with Kirsten's death." Sonya's voice trembled. "But I thought it might be useful for the theft, too, which is not as high a priority for them, considering . . ."

They entered a room in pale blue with green and lavender décor. The furniture was white and Victorian-tropical. Sonya gestured to the chair before the desk where she had everything set up for Lydia to view on a large monitor. Paislee watched over Lydia's shoulder.

"Where am I searching?" Lydia asked.

Sonya cleared her throat and adopted a professional tone as she used a remote control to fast-forward the video. "You'd told me that you'd seen the gaming laptop last at one o'clock on Sunday, so I was able tae narrow the footage down tae the final three hours of the day."

"Inside the conference room?" Paislee asked.

"No, but I installed state-of-the-art security cameras that give us a panoramic scan of the property, including all entrances and exits. For privacy purposes we have cameras in the halls and public areas only."

Lydia smiled up at Sonya. "Smart."

The director shrugged, pleased. "We'll see how smart. If we can nab the thief then it will be proof that the equipment was a worthy investment. Here."

Sonya stopped the film and Paislee realized they were looking at the long, tiled hall leading from the lobby to the conference room.

Lydia sat forward. Paislee had her hand on her friend's shoulder, studying the blur of people—most were carrying bags and boxes as they left the conference room.

"It's three o'clock." Sonya enlarged the image. "See? Is that the gaming box? Shiny black, but I dinnae recall the size."

Lydia squinted and tilted her head, cherry-red waves soft against her cheek. "Aye. I think so. Ye cannae zoom in closer?"

"It just gets more muddled."

"I think that's the box," Paislee said, wishing she could make the image clearer. "Who's carrying it?" The person had a sweatshirt on, with the hood over their face as if to hide. Were they aware of the camera in the hall?

"Nobody I recognized, but Hendrie, the Buchanan chauffer, appears tae be holding the door leading ootside for them." Sonya sighed. "We can agree it was the right box, though?"

"Aye." Paislee studied the monitor screen. The chauffer had a cap over his brown hair, and a navy blue lightweight jacket. "What was Hendrie doing here? He wasn't with Gerard. Lara had taken him home already, remember?"

"I do," Lydia said. "Gerard was hammered. I guess Hendrie could have shown up with a mate tae drive the extra Buchanan car back again."

Paislee nodded, the idea of an "extra car" as ludicrous to her as a nanny and a private chef. "Right. Can you follow the person out tae the car park?"

"Let me switch camera views. It was a madhouse because of the news reporters." Sonya's mouth pinched and Paislee knew she had to be reliving the fiasco of Anders and Kirsten, and Anders telling the newswoman that he thought Gerard had killed his wife.

The camera showed the entire car park. "There's the Bentley. Oh, hey, Hendrie is opening the boot." Her belly clenched when a breeze fluttered and the hoodie showed a man with pale features and black hair. Fergus. He ducked out of sight.

"What is Hendrie doing?" Lydia said. Hendrie came around to the driver's side and got behind the wheel. "The door is still up."

They watched it slam down and then Hendrie cautiously left the lot, avoiding the mayhem as he drove away from the club.

"Go back tae the view of the lot," Paislee said, mouth dry. "I saw Fergus Jones."

"The chef?" Sonya asked. "I know what he looks like and there's been nobody with his red hair. I've been searching, trust me."

Paislee glanced at Sonya. "Fergus dyed his hair tae black."

"Och! I didnae think of that—of course he might change his appearance." Sonya sank backward so she half sat on the edge of her white desk.

Lydia held out her hand for the remote control. "May I?"

"Sure." Sonya sounded defeated. "So, let me get this straight. Fergus Jones stole the gaming laptop."

"And I think Hendrie helped him." Paislee crossed her arms. "But we can't be certain because we don't see what's in the boot or who closes it. Lydia, stop there, where there's a hint of a breeze, that's Fergus's face."

"Got it." Lydia glared at the screen. "Why would Fergus steal the laptop? I'm sure he makes verra good money."

"Gerard won't let him in the house tae get his things," Paislee said. "Maybe he's broke without his severance pay."

"How do you know all this?" Sonya asked incredulously.

"I spoke tae Fergus yesterday. He claims he didn't kill Kirsten but Gerard doesn't believe him. Fergus plans on leaving Scotland, but needs his things. Passport, cash—that kind of stuff."

"What a bastard!" Lydia muttered.

Paislee arched her brow at her indignant friend. "Fergus or Gerard?"

"Fergus. I know you think he's innocent, Paislee, but if he's going tae change his appearance, steal food from children, and try tae skip town, maybe he really did kill Kirsten."

Sonya sucked in a breath and stood.

Lydia turned around to look Paislee in the eye. "You see my point here?"

Sonya nodded. "I think Lydia's right."

How could she deny what she'd seen on tape? Shoulders bowed, Paislee pulled her mobile from her pants' pocket and dialed Detective Inspector Zeffer. He didn't answer, so she left a message saying that Sonya, from the Social Club and Art Centre, had Fergus on video with the gaming laptop in hand.

"He's probably trying tae sell it." Sonya hefted her round chin, her white-blond bob swinging. "For a pittance. And the food bank willnae get any of it."

"That was Sunday, and I saw him yesterday. I bet he already sold it." She told them about being in Fergus's mother's house, the sleeping bag, the new clothes in the Highland Academy duffel bag.

"No way he got four grand," Lydia sputtered. "I'd like tae speak tae the idiot myself."

"I think he's in a desperate place," Paislee said, putting her phone in her pocket.

"They have tae catch him." Sonya paced the floor between the door and her desk. "What if he's so desperate he tries tae harm Gerard, or Maxim?"

Would Fergus hurt someone? Paislee placed her palm over her galloping heart. Though she hadn't sensed anything violent about him, she couldn't be sure. "That would be awful. Listen, make sure tae mark the place on the film where we saw Fergus. I'm certain the DI will drop by, or send someone tae talk tae you."

"I will." Sonya exhaled and blinked. "I'm trying tae keep a positive attitude but it seems like I've worked so hard tae get this building done and now . . . nobody's called tae book any space. They just want tae talk aboot Kirsten's death."

"I'm so sairy." Lydia gently grasped Sonya's wrist. "The Silverstein agency is considering a summer party here. It's a lovely property—dinnae give up."

Sonya's demeanor brightened. "Really? Thank you."

Paislee's phone rang and she answered, recognizing the detective's number. "Hello!"

"It's Zeffer," he said. "I listened tae your message—where are you again?"

"The Social Club . . . Sonya is expecting you, or another officer, tae come by so she can show you where she's found Fergus on video."

"You're sure?"

"Aye. Same hoodie, dyed black hair. Holding the gaming laptop in its shiny black box. It seems like he's in league with Hendrie, the Buchanan chauffer."

"Hmm. I can be there in an hour."

"Lydia and I can't stay, but Sonya will be here. Constable Dean already has the footage for both days tae help with the investigation. Sonya realized that the theft was a lower priority, so she took on searching for Lydia's donation, which she found."

"Got it. Ta." The detective hung up.

Paislee shook her head at the phone. "That man."

The three ladies returned to the white lobby of the club where soothing instrumental music was piped through speakers in the ceiling.

"Thank you for discovering what happened tae the laptop," Lydia said. "Mibbe they should put you in charge of finding who killed Kirsten."

Sonya expelled a puff of air. "I scanned the footage but I have no idea what tae look for."

"I'll call later aboot a firm date for the party." Lydia gave Sonya a quick hug. "It will work oot."

"Take care," Paislee said.

Paislee and Lydia went to the Carousel Café for a quick lunch. Paislee ordered a salad of greens, figs, and goat cheese with a side of crunchy bread. Lydia chose the fish and chips.

They sat across from each other and Lydia pointed her fork at Paislee. "It could have been dangerous going tae Fergus's house. Please promise me you willnae do it again?"

"Promise. I have tae admit that I'm starting tae doubt myself." Paislee went over the events of the day with a shiver—Gerard upsetting the tray, Fergus's mouth wide, as were his eyes. "He was astonished. Dismayed."

"Then why is he running?" Lydia broke off a piece of flaky white fish and dipped it in malt vinegar.

"He wouldn't tell us why he'd gotten fired." Paislee nabbed a golden chip and dunked it in her fig vinaigrette. "Maybe it has something tae do with that. Yum. You should try it."

"I prefer the vinegar, thanks." Lydia added a dash of salt and a squeeze of lemon over her fish. "The simple truth is that he's bolting because he's guilty."

Paislee decided to change the subject to keep the peace. "So, how's Corbin? Did you have a nice time at dinner?"

"Aye." Her friend busied herself with chewing. Swallowing. Repeat.

Avoidance. "That's it?"

"What?" Lydia raised her gaze from her plate.

Paislee smiled—she rarely saw Lydia rattled by a man. "Are you going out with him again?"

Lydia sipped from her water glass. "If he asks, I'll think aboot it."

No commitment but there was something more. "So, you're still in the 'shagging friends' stage."

"I like this stage," Lydia declared. "Lots of exciting sex. Sweet texts and flowers. No need tae hurry oot of it. It's all downhill after this."

Paislee scooted back from the table in exasperation. "Lydia."

"I'm serious." She tapped the table with her fingertip.

She could see that. *Darn it.* "Does Corbin think the same way as you?"

"I hope so." Lydia pointed a wedge of potato soggy with salt and vinegar. "We honestly dinnae talk aboot it. I told him that I like the fun of dating . . . we arenae exclusive."

Paislee watched Lydia raise her guard right before her eyes. "Don't shy away from a guid thing, Lydia."

"So long as it *is* a guid thing." Lydia winked, her long lashes fluttering like a butterfly wing. "Now—enough aboot Corbin."

"And Fergus." Paislee realized she might be wrong about the man. He might have killed Kirsten. "Let's go."

They split the check and Lydia dropped Paislee off at Cashmere Crush.

"Dinnae forget lunch tomorrow—dress fancy!" Lydia said. "I'll try tae find oot where we're going and let you know."

Paislee didn't agree but waved as the red sports car drove off, then stepped toward her shop, stopping to pluck a brown leaf from her front window box of marigolds.

Their row of businesses in the brick single-story building all had flower boxes, from her shop on the corner to the tea shop at the other side. The tea shop had been closed for the past month and Paislee wondered if a new business would move in. It was a prime location on the corner before the park.

"Hi!" she said to Grandpa and the young woman he was

assisting when she went inside. The customer had picked out a lightweight sweater perfect for spring, and now handed over her credit card.

Grandpa asked, "How was lunch?"

"Tasty." Paislee put her purse on the shelf. "Goat cheese and fig salad."

"Sounds perfect." The customer smiled. "I'm hungry."

"Check out the Carousel Café by the wharf. They always have delicious lunch specials."

Grandpa rang up the customer, and Paislee bagged the sweater in tissue paper and passed it to her.

"I'll try oot the café, too. Thanks."

When the customer left, Paislee studied Grandpa closely for signs that he needed to rest. His brown eyes were bright, his wrinkled skin its usual color. "How was it?"

"Busy. Didnae get tae read my magazine, just like I thought." He plunked down on the stool and crossed his arms in a pout.

Guilt made her tone sharp. "Well, I pay you tae work, not read."

"Which I was doing just fine before you got here. What's the matter with you?"

"Sorry—I didn't mean tae snap. You'll tell me if you get tired?"

"Do I look like a Moaning Minnie tae you?"

"No." Grandpa grouched but wasn't a complainer. "Which is why I can't tell if you're working too hard."

Grandpa got up, cheeks now flushed beneath his beard. "I'm fine. I'll let you know if I cannae mind a yarn shop for a few hours. I could do that in me sleep." He snapped his fingers.

He probably could, the stubborn geezer. "I'm sorry."

His shoulders relaxed at her apology, and he tidied a cup of pens by the register. "Did you find oot who stole the laptop?"

"Grandpa, it was Fergus Jones."

He turned toward her with his mouth agape. "The chef on the run?"

"The very same." She brought out the boxes of knitting needles to price and shelve next to the scissors, setting it on the counter as she told him what she'd seen.

"Not only is he wanted for questioning aboot Kirsten's death, they've got him dead tae rights on video stealing the laptop." Grandpa whistled between closed teeth. "Not so smart a move."

"He's looking guilty all around." Paislee slid open the box with a box cutter. She genuinely had believed Fergus to be innocent. What did that say about her judgment? She thought her son to be well-behaved, yet he'd been fighting. "I'm nervous about the meeting with the headmaster today." Brody had kept quiet on why he and Edwyn had argued, so what was she supposed to do? Lock him in his room with bread and water until he confessed all?

Grandpa straightened the skeins of red wool, then the brown. "Dinnae let Hamish McCall get tae you now. Brody promised tae behave, and he's a guid lad."

"I know." Paislee lifted out a variety of knitting needles with a heavy heart. "Most of the time. So far." He was just ten. There were so many ways she could muck it up.

Chapter 16

Paislee arrived at Fordythe and parked in the spot nearest to Hamish's office. She hadn't let her guard down since they'd had a disagreement over a month ago and while she hoped for romantic happiness for Lydia, she had no such desires for herself.

Too busy for one thing, which was why she couldn't believe how close she'd let herself come to thinking that maybe some-day . . . she knew better than that. She was not a dreamer, but a doer.

She pushed through the blue doors of the primary school and waved to Mrs. Jimenez, who sat behind her receptionist's desk, the phone to her ear in her most usual pose.

"Hi—is the headmaster in?"

The secretary lowered the headset. "Aye—go on in. He's expecting you."

School would be out in thirty minutes. Paislee didn't think the meeting would take long. What was there to say? She didn't know why the boys were arguing but Brody had promised to stop fighting.

Paislee knocked on the open door.

"Come in," Hamish called.

She entered his office with a low-level layer of anxiety. "Hello."

He stood, harried, and tugged at his brown tie. He offered his hand to shake and then gestured toward the chair. "Please, sit. How have you been?"

"Busy. Tourist season."

"Ah. Excuse me for one moment." Hamish finished reading a paper on his desk, which gave Paislee the chance to study his face in repose.

Hamish McCall was handsome in a clean-cut way. She guessed his age to be no more than thirty-five and he was young to have such a responsibility.

She reminded herself of that whenever she found him to be a smidge overbearing. Yes, he ran the school fairly but he didn't have kids of his own. He didn't understand how things could go awry at a moment's well-planned notice.

He looked up and caught her staring at him.

She averted her eyes and shifted on the chair.

Hamish scooped the papers into his center drawer to clear his desk. "As you know, I've asked you here tae discuss Brody's behavior."

"Right." Paislee crossed her legs. "I spoke with Bennett Maclean and he said that he hasn't seen the boys fighting at all." She didn't share that Alexa had witnessed them pushing each other, because they'd gotten over whatever it was that bothered them and it sounded like a mended squabble.

"Yes." He held her gaze but she couldn't read his thoughts. "I did contact him as well."

She squirmed, recalling with a wee bit of embarrassment how she'd accused him of needing to be fair.

Hamish cleared his throat. "Mrs. Martin, when I pressed her, mentioned that she'd talked tae you aboot an incident over a girl in their class."

"Yes. But they resolved it. Brody is more into football than the lasses, for now, and didn't understand why Edwyn was distracted."

Hamish half smiled. "It willnae be long. There's a reason I chose primary rather than secondary school. Hormones. Those teachers deserve combat pay," he observed ruefully.

Paislee chuckled before remembering that they weren't friends. "Brody assures me he won't fight with Edwyn anymore."

"All right." Hamish exhaled. "Edwyn has promised the same. Let's hope we can get through the next six weeks before summer holiday without a problem."

She nodded and stopped bobbing her leg. "I agree one hundred percent. Is that all?"

"Yes." He got up.

Paislee rose, too.

Hamish walked her to the door, all five paces. "Have a nice day, Paislee. Thank you for coming in." He peered into her eyes and seemed on the verge of speaking, but then he flattened his full lips and returned to his desk without a word.

Her body warmed but she denied any possible feelings and went outside to wait for Brody in the car. Hamish's blinds were closed. She called Bennett's mobile.

"Hello."

"It's Paislee." She imagined him at his shop with Alexa, confident in his skills as a parent. A business owner. A partner. "I think we're off the hook with Headmaster McCall."

Bennett laughed. "I've never liked being called tae the principal's office. That hasnae changed as an adult."

She teased, "Were you a troublesome lad, Bennett?"

"A perfect angel . . . according to me mum."

"Bennett, what do you know about the boys wanting tae camp on their own?"

A muffled echo sounded as if he adjusted the phone against his shoulder and ear. "Edwyn asked if he could borrow my tent and go tae the park. I said no."

Whew. "I pointed out that they probably had tae be adults tae camp. We were going tae check the website but I don't know what came of it."

"That was smart thinking."

"Why argue over something they aren't allowed tae do? But I did suggest that they could camp in our back garden, if it was okay with you. I'd stay on the back porch or keep an eye out from the upstairs window."

"That's a great idea . . . I would be fine with that. No fire, though."

"And no leaving the yard. By the time I'm done with the rules they might not want tae do it. Maybe it's something we can plan for the summer holiday?"

"I agree. And that gives us a carrot for good grades and decent behavior."

She liked the way Bennett thought. "Say hi tae Alexa for me . . . I'll see you later."

Paislee ended the call just as the bell rang and it was like a tidal wave of children exited the blue doors. Hall monitors and teachers blew whistles to keep order, but the end of the school day meant the end of being quiet.

Edwyn exited first, followed by Brody. The boys didn't speak. Edwyn went to the field with a football and some other kids while Brody practically dragged his backpack to the Juke.

"What's wrong with you?" she asked once he was in.

"Mrs. Martin gave us a terrible assignment." He buckled up.

"Terrible?" The last time he'd told her that they'd had to make a kite that actually flew. "Do we need tae drive by the hardware store?" She'd pick up a bulb for the refrigerator.

"No, it's not a kite. This is awful." He speared her with serious brown eyes filled with horror. "It's *math*."

"You can do math." Paislee turned on the car. The child was being dramatic. Were girls this full of drama?

"Mrs. Martin is going tae have a quiz on Friday and whoever gets all the problems right gets an extra recess on Monday."

He glanced at her from beneath his auburn bangs with such pain that she felt it in her heart. He wanted that extra playtime, but was afraid he'd fail.

"We can practice. I've got flashcards. We'll make it a game, too."

For all that Lydia called Brody a prodigy, the truth was, he had to try hard at his homework and math was especially difficult.

"Edwyn just knows it, like it's nothin'." Brody slammed the toe of his sneaker into his backpack.

"Hey, now. That has tae last until the end of the year." She pulled her attention from the frayed strap. "Maybe Edwyn can quiz you, then?"

"Mum! He called me dumb." He stared out the window and mumbled, "Him and Lucas—they're best mates now."

"Oh . . ." She blinked watery eyes and swallowed over a lump in her throat. "I'm sure this will pass."

"No, it willnae." He wouldn't turn her way.

She forced a light tone. "I talked tae Bennett and he said it would be okay for you two tae camp in our yard this summer."

"Not now, Mum."

If she could take on his hurt, she would. Paislee followed the queue of cars around the traffic circle toward town and Cashmere Crush. "Should we get ice cream after dinner tonight?"

"I dinnae want it."

So not like Brody to say no to ice cream. "Tell you what—we can practice all of the problems so you'll be prepared on Friday, okay? I'll email Mrs. Martin and ask her for a sample test."

"It doesnae matter." His narrow shoulders remained turned away from her.

She parked behind her shop. She would like nothing more than to close up and hang out with Brody to cheer him up, but she couldn't. This was her business and she was the sole provider for her family, though Grandpa more than pulled his weight with cooking and tidying up. Helping her with Brody. He'd fit in with them like he'd always been there.

"Come on, love. We'll figure it out."

When they entered the back of Cashmere Crush, Grandpa was speaking with James from next door.

The very, very wrinkled old man grinned at her—his long, lean limbs and bright eyes reminded her of an aging leprechaun. "Hiya lass, Brody. Why so glum?"

"School sucks," Brody announced.

James laughed. "God's Truth!"

"What's got you so oot of sorts?" Grandpa asked, lightly nudging Brody on the shoulder.

"Math." He dropped his backpack to the floor with a thunk. "You any guid at it?"

Grandpa adjusted his glasses. "I do all right. No whiz, but I can balance me accounts. Why?"

"Edwyn and Lucas said that I'm too dumb to earn an extra recess."

"Well, that ain't true at all," Grandpa spluttered.

"You're a bright kid, Brody. I know that." James crossed his arms, his skin like the leather he worked with. "Should we pay these ex-mates a visit?"

"Uh, no—we don't condone violence." Paislee put herself between Brody and James. "Why don't you get a snack? I'll email your teacher."

Brody nodded and went to the back armchair, large and cozy, and turned on the telly.

"What's going on?" James asked, peeking over her shoulder to Brody.

She explained about the quiz and the coveted prize of extra playing time. "We can study and try tae make it fun for him. It really hurts me that his friends would say that."

"You're thinking like a mum," Grandpa said, shaking his head. "He can stand up for himself. Brush off a few names. Willnae hurt him none."

"He *has* stuck up for himself." Paislee glared at Grandpa. Did the man have no heart? "Maybe that's why the boys have been fighting."

Grandpa smoothed his beard. "How did the meeting go with the headmaster?"

"Fine. I think it was just a warning tae let me know that Brody needs tae walk the straight and narrow for the rest of the school year."

He'd been looking forward to the summer holiday, and

spending time with Edwyn. How could his buddy be so casually heartless?

At ten, he probably wasn't even aware. She couldn't interfere. The only thing in her power was to help Brody study.

"I'll be going, then," James said.

She realized that it was odd for the man to be in her shop for no reason. "Why were you here?"

He put his palm to his heart, eyes dancing. "Blethering with Angus, that's all."

Paislee went around the counter to the high-top table and straightened a pattern book. "You're welcome anytime. That's not what I meant and ye know it."

James brought his finger and thumb together. "Well, I did have just one wee bit of gossip that might interest you."

Just as she'd thought—the two were as bad as she and her friends at Knit and Sip. "What's that?"

"Margot went on a date with Shawn Marcus."

Paislee's mouth dropped open and she snapped it closed. "Our landlord, Shawn? Our Margot? Why on earth would she do that?"

"Och, dunno. I wasnae so bold as tae ask her. She declared he was a perfect gentleman and they're going oot again on Saturday night."

Margot managed the lab a few doors down on their street and hadn't seemed interested in pairing up after her divorce. "But Margot is so smart, and pretty, and she knows what Shawn did tae us." She'd certainly been privy to much of the Leery family's dirty laundry.

"Cannae stop love," James sang.

Paislee briefly covered her eyes, wanting to dispel that image immediately. "I'll pop over tae the lab later this week."

"Dinnae tell her I told you. Let her surprise you." James sauntered out of the shop.

"He's a wild one," Grandpa said admiringly.

"You should go fishing together or something."

"I dinnae need you arranging a playdate, thank ye."

Paislee eyed the ceiling. She couldn't say anything right this afternoon. When a customer walked in, Paislee hurried toward them in greeting. "Hello! Welcome tae Cashmere Crush."

She was glad to be so busy, not wanting to think about Margot and Shawn, or Edwyn, which led to Hamish. And why hadn't the DI called her back? She hoped that he'd be able to use Sonya's video to find Fergus. Which made her think of Kirsten's death just days ago, which brought a pang of regret to her heart.

Paislee swept the floor, dusted the shelves, cleaned the tables, and helped the customers, not allowing herself to slow down.

They closed up at six on the dot, the till full. Brody had eaten two packets of crackers, and one of chocolate.

"I'm still hungry, Mum." He turned off the TV.

Was he growing again? "Why don't we order Chinese? We haven't had that in a long time."

Brody perked at that. "Orange chicken? Extra fortune cookies?"

"You got it." She phoned in their order.

"Tired of me cooking?" Grandpa asked when she hung up the phone.

"Never. But this is tae cheer Brody up."

Grandpa put his hand on his chest. "It's a lang road that's no goat a turnin'."

"What?" Brody asked.

"Gran used tae say that, too . . . just that things may be hard, but they'll get better. They always do."

Chapter 17

The next morning, the headline of the paper unrolled in Paislee's kitchen read in bold print: FERGUS JONES. ARRESTED FOR THE DEATH OF KIRSTEN BUCHANAN.

His hair was jet black, his eyes dark, his skin pale. She scanned the article as she ate her cereal. "Not very informative after the splashy headline."

Grandpa, in his robe and slippers, said, "The earl probably wants tae keep a lid on the crime for tourist season."

Brody slurped milk from his bowl to get the last berry.

"He's all about what's best for Nairn." Paislee finished her cereal and read her text from Lydia reminding her about the lunch date. *Wear the blue dress I picked out for you.*

She blew her bangs back and tapped her grandfather's hand. "Grandpa, I have another lunch date today. Can you show up at eleven thirty instead of noon?"

He took off his glasses to clean them on the soft plaid of his robe. "You're certainly being sociable this week—more lunches oot than you've had since I've been here."

"I don't want tae go." She eyed the text from Lydia. "I'm trying tae get out of it . . . but in case I can't, well . . ."

"Where tae?" He put his glasses back on and blinked like a cat.

"I don't know." She lifted her mobile. "Lydia's driving. We're going tae be moral support for Blaise when she meets her awful friends for lunch—which is going tae be especially sad because Kirsten is dead, and this is tae honor her memory." Paislee refused to let Kirsten's sickly image surface. "Me and Lyd need tae be the good friends against her old mean friends."

"I see why you're eager tae wiggle oot of it."

"It doesnae sound fun, Mum."

"It probably won't be. So, do you mind, Grandpa?"

"I'll be there." Grandpa drank from his cup with a smug expression somehow conveyed via his broad forehead. "Dinnae know how ye managed withoot me."

She didn't either, truth be told. "Any word about Craigh?"

"Naw." He focused on the paper.

Paislee sighed but had no energy to continue the conversation. "Brody, go brush your teeth and hair. Can't be late."

"I already did, before I ate."

"You missed a spot, lad," Grandpa said, ruffling Brody's hair to really mess it up. Brody ducked out of the way and ran up the stairs, Wallace on his heels.

"How can he already need a haircut?" Paislee groaned.

"Growing boy."

"I should let him be a shaggy sheep over the summer."

Grandpa chuckled. "He'd probably like that."

Paislee got up and washed her and Brody's cereal bowls, rinsing them and putting them in the dish drainer. His lunch was packed and on the counter. Grandpa had eaten berries and was munching on toast.

"How would you feel if I got another mobile on my plan? You and Brody could use it when you're out. I'd feel better if you had one, but Brody isn't ready for his own."

Grandpa puffed out his chest. "We're fine. They're dear."

"Not really. It would be worth the peace of mind for you tae have it—for Brody's sake, really." She watched him to see how that went over. "He's too young tae have one for himself."

With a tug on his beard he said, "Let me think on it."

Of course, he couldn't simply agree. "Let me know by next week when the billing cycle starts again for the phone plan. I can get one added tae the monthly payment for cheap."

He nodded and picked up the paper to read the article on Fergus being arrested, effectively blocking the subject. "Think he really did it?"

"No. But I've been wrong before." Paislee hated to admit that her conclusions were not always spot-on.

She headed up the stairs, congratulating herself on planting another seed for the second Shaw family mobile.

Paislee changed from her khakis and tiny-flower print brown-and-cream blouse to a dress Lydia had bought for her for the occasional summer party. It was too good of a sale to pass up, her friend had said.

The blue-and-white dress had cap sleeves and was belted at the waist. Her thin hair never did what she wanted so she dipped her head and fluffed, then spritzed her bangs with hair spray to create volume.

Now, stop staring at yourself in the mirror, and get a move on. She heard Gran say, *A pretty face suits the dish-cloot.* Paislee rarely thought of herself as pretty, but this dress made her feel like it. She swished into the hall and Brody joined her from his room. "Where'd you get that?"

"Lydia."

"It's tidy, Mum. You should let her buy all yer clothes."

"Funny." She gave the linen-like fabric a caress. Linen-like, because who had time to iron?

She and Brody walked down the steps, he holding his backpack, she her bag of knitting and her purse. At the foyer, she gave Wallace a pat and waved to Grandpa. "Don't forget—eleven thirty."

"I'm not daft," Grandpa said from behind the shield of the newspaper.

Brody snickered. They stepped outside, and he raced back in like a bottle rocket. "Me lunch!"

Paislee took a deep breath as they climbed into the Juke.

"Want tae practice some more for your quiz?" She gave Brody credit for really concentrating for a full hour last night after dinner. Mrs. Martin had sent the examples over via email.

"Naw. Me brain aches from too much thinkin'."

Paislee could understand that. She stopped in queue to drop him off and before he jumped out she said, "And no matter what happens, do not fight with anybody—not so much as a push, not even for pretend."

"All right. Can I play football after school today?"

Wednesdays were usually all right for him to stay. "Sure. See you at four thirty."

No Mrs. Martin. No Hamish McCall. Paislee left Fordythe while the gettin' was good.

She arrived at her shop and was ready for customers by nine thirty. Propping the front door open to allow in the fresh May air, she looked out at Market Street, busy with traffic.

This side of the block she wasn't able to see the Firth, but if she stood on her sidewalk, she had a view of the park. She liked to walk around it for exercise when she needed a quick mental break.

To the right of the block on the main strip was the police station. Nairn had a low crime rate but there were growing pains as the town's population increased.

A good thing, in theory, for the businesses that depended on tourism, but she was a small-shire lass at heart and hated to see all the extra traffic lights and car parks, or old buildings torn down for new.

Paislee really admired Sonya's work at the Social Club and Art Centre—she'd kept the Victorian façade in the remodel, while making the interior classically modern. The building had a new start, yet already carried an ugly stain.

Kirsten Buchanan's murder. Would the good accomplished for the Nairn Food Bank overshadow the socialite's death?

Paislee pulled herself from her musing and went inside to complete the last bit on the infinity scarf with the hidden pocket. The morning passed quickly between that and shoppers. She tried very hard to come up with viable reasons to skip lunch. Not wanting to wouldn't cut it for Lydia.

Lydia could handle Mari and Christina.

Two against two were fair fighting odds.

When the door next opened at eleven, Blaise sashayed in. She could have been on her way to high tea with the queen—she even had on a couture hat with a veil.

"Blaise! I thought Lydia was driving."

"Hiya, Paislee . . . you look lovely. Are you ready for lunch?"

"Well . . ." She bit her lip.

"Lydia said you'd have five excuses at the ready for not coming but I was not tae take it personal." Blaise flipped her netted veil to reveal her earnest amber eyes.

Lydia had ratted her out! "Only two, but I was working on my list between customers."

Blaise rested her bag on the table by the pattern book. "I have five reasons for you tae join us—all tae do with me, *personally*."

Paislee was going to cross Lydia off her Christmas list. What best friend?

"First," Blaise announced, putting her hand on the counter where Paislee was working, "we're friends. Second, I trust you. Three, I *need* you tae have my back. Four—"

"Do I not get a say?"

"How can ye argue with any of my points?"

Paislee exhaled so hard she ruffled her hair-sprayed bangs. "Go on."

"Four, I . . ." Blaise's brow scrunched. "I will drive you there and back and pay for the meal. We're going tae the Brick and Ivy."

"No deal." Paislee had never even heard of the restaurant. "I pay my own way."

Blaise fluttered her fingers as if that was the least of the things to worry about.

"Five, we *are* friends. This is a matter of survival. A last meal in Kirsten's memory tae be shared with three snakes. We need equal players."

"You said we're friends twice." Of course she would go.

"It bears repeating," Blaise assured her.

She reached for her knitting. "Who is the third viper?"

"Lara."

"But they were so mean tae Lara—how can she be a part of their posse?"

"Power? Popularity? My guess is that Mari and Christina are duking it out in a genteel way for who will be on top."

"And Lara will just go along with it?"

"I get it." Blaise leaned against the counter. "I used tae be in Lara's position. You do what you must withoot making waves and hope they dinnae find a flaw in your behavior, demeanor, or dress. Otherwise, it will be a miserable two hours."

"*Two* hours?"

"Yes. These were social events with ladies who had nothing else tae fill their day. Me too. Volunteering, fund-raising. Baking the perfect biscuit." She shuddered. "It's embarrassing."

"So why go, with Kirsten gone?"

"It's a lunch in Kirsten's honor and it would seem petty if I didnae attend, but this is my last one. I talked tae Shep aboot it and he supports me. I guess John, Christina's husband, injured his hand so he willnae be playing for a few weeks anyway. Gerard is, understandably, a mess."

"What about Mari's husband?"

"Charlie. He's been traveling a lot for business and hasn't been around as much, which means there willnae be added pressure from the guys."

A couple in their thirties came into Cashmere Crush and Paislee got up to greet them. A hint of the sea air clung to them. They told her they were on holiday from London. She showed them around and then returned to her seat behind the register with Blaise. She didn't believe in the high-pressure sales tactic and had a good feeling that they'd buy something if left to browse.

"Anyway, will you come, please? You're all dressed up."

"Aye." Paislee hoped she wouldn't later regret her decision.

The last time she and Lydia had helped Blaise, Kirsten had ended up dead. "Grandpa will be here at half past eleven."

Blaise clasped her hands together. "Thank you! Lydia is going tae park oot back here if that's all right, and I'll drive the Beast. I dinnae want you tae do anything other than enjoy a fine meal away from the shop." She leaned closer to whisper, "And watch oot for poisoned darts."

"Aren't I supposed tae take a dart for you?"

"Not necessary! Just warn me of the direction it's flying from. I've gotten verra guid at avoiding a direct hit."

Paislee rolled her eyes and smiled at the couple, who'd chosen a gorgeous merino wool blanket in chocolate and espresso.

"Thank you so much for coming in tae Cashmere Crush. I've put my website and business card inside the bag if ye have any questions. Are you in town for long?"

"We return to London tomorrow but it's been a wonderful stay. We'll be back for sure," the woman said.

Her husband nodded.

The pair left and Paislee asked Blaise, "Did you see the paper this morning?"

"Aye. Couldnae believe the headline. Wanted tae shout and call the station tae tell them they've got the wrong man in custody, but I didnae."

"It will get sorted out. Hey, did Shep ask Gerard why they'd fired Fergus?"

Her button nose curled. "Shep didnae want tae tell me, actually. Doesnae like tae share the negative parts of his day . . . as if I'm too fragile tae handle it. Well, I told him that we're partners in this life, and I'm no delicate flower." Blaise nodded resolutely.

Paislee realized that this was touching on a deeper issue in their marriage but didn't comment—just picked up her knitting to listen.

"It turns oot that Gerard and Kirsten were having marriage troubles. She'd gotten that awful message from her agent about no longer being relevant and it really hit her hard. I know Kirsten felt like she'd given up her career for Gerard only tae get burned."

"Kirsten told you that?"

"She was very *candid* during some of our lunches . . . if she thought she could benefit from it." Blaise sat on a stool, baring her knees in the short charcoal dress.

"Oh. Divorce?"

"Therapist, but Gerard thought they were working things oot, according tae Shep."

Paislee started another row and had to look down to remember which project this was . . . the hat. "Maybe Gerard's just saying that now tae get any possible heat off himself as a suspect?"

"Could be." Blaise scanned her mobile, then put it in her purse. "The truth is I'm dreading this lunch, too."

Since it seemed there was no getting out of it, Paislee directed the conversation back to Fergus and Gerard. "Why did they fire Fergus?"

Blaise, who had been such a fountain of information, pursed her mouth.

It must be bad. "Was it drugs?"

"No." Blaise tapped her hand on the counter and peered behind her.

"I won't say anything." If the police thought Fergus was Kirsten's killer, it would be up to Paislee, and Blaise, to prove otherwise.

"All right." *Tap, tap, tap.*

"Blaise!"

Blaise murmured, "Gerard said that they fired Fergus for . . . stealing."

"No!" That matched with what she'd seen for herself with Fergus taking the gaming laptop. It also reiterated criminal behavior.

"Aye. I guess, according tae Gerard, that Kirsten caught Fergus in their home office, rifling through the desk."

"What did he take?"

"Shep didnae say exactly, just that Gerard kept all the keys in the desk."

"Keys tae what?"

"I dinnae ken. Safe? Cars? House?"

"Well, maybe Fergus is guilty, then." Paislee lowered her project, having difficulty accepting that scenario. "But, why would she give him two weeks' notice and allow him tae stay at the house if that's true?"

Blaise straightened on her stool, eyes narrowed. "You're right. That doesnae make sense at all. If Kirsten caught Fergus stealing she would've called the police, not set him up with a severance package."

"One of them is lying." Fergus, or Gerard?

"Let me call Shep." Blaise's lower lip trembled.

"And say what?" Paislee caressed the soft wool of the hat, which calmed her down inside.

"I can ask him tae find the truth. He will."

It must be nice to think of one's husband as a hero. "Gerard has no reason tae lie tae Shep," Paislee said, "unless he's covering up his own crime tae frame the chef. Maybe his hot temper over Anders and Kirsten is just an act, and he planned the shortbread peanut crumble all along."

"Gerard?" Blaise asked, her tone uncertain.

"I didn't think Gerard had the patience tae *plan* murder—from what I've seen he's very impulsive." Paislee looped yarn around her finger, her mind tying the pieces together. "I could be wrong, though."

"You're saying that mibbe Gerard Buchanan set Fergus Jones up tae take the heat for the murder of his wife, that he committed?" Blaise looked scandalized but intrigued. "Not Fergus, even though Fergus is a thief."

"Let's call the DI."

Paislee dialed the detective's number but there was no answer.

It was kind of a letdown to leave a message. "Detective Inspector Zeffer, this is Paislee Shaw. I'm at Cashmere Crush with Blaise O'Connor, and we think you have the wrong man in jail."

Chapter 18

Grandpa arrived at the same time as Lydia, the two laughing companionably as they entered through the back of Cashmere Crush.

"You ladies are dressed fine enough for Buckingham Palace." Grandpa gestured at Lydia, who had a fresh orchid tucked above her ear, then Blaise, with her oval hat and net veil. "Paislee, you need something in your hair."

She didn't have fancy flowers or a hat.

"You dinnae, Paislee—Angus, you're such a tease!" Lydia smacked his arm lightly and the two went off on another gale of laughter.

"You been into the Scotch, Grandpa?" Paislee gave a cautious sniff in his direction.

"No, lass, not yet. I can hold me liquor in any case." He drew himself up and looked down his long nose at her, peering over the black frames of his glasses.

"What's so funny?" Blaise wanted to know.

Lydia smiled. "Och, he was just telling a naughty joke, that's all."

Paislee raised her eyes to the ceiling and Gran. Had he always been such a flirt?

"You can leave the keys if ye want, Paislee," Grandpa offered, "and I'll pick up Brody."

"No need—he wants tae play football after school today, and we'll surely be back by four thirty." Paislee gave their group an admonishing eye. Over four hours of those ladies wasn't fair to ask a saint, which she wasn't.

"And how is my prodigy doing?" Lydia asked.

"Upset about his mate calling him an eejit," Grandpa said.

"Hey now!" Lydia crossed her arms. "What is it with people who are supposed tae be your friends not acting like them?"

"Right?" Blaise seconded.

"It's over math, not his favorite, but we practiced with flash-cards," Paislee said. "Mrs. Martin is offering an extra recess for those that get a hundred percent on Friday's quiz."

"Oh, that's brilliant of her," Lydia said. "Get them tae study what they dinnae want tae give them what they do want."

"I'm verra good at math," Blaise told them all. "I can tutor him if he wants tae be better at it. There are a few tricks." She tapped her temple.

"Tricks?" Grandpa asked. "I thought math was black-and-white. Numbers dinnae lie."

"The first thing is tae fix the belief that many of us tell ourselves—math is hard. Well, it's no different from learning anything else if you put your mind tae it."

"Blaise got a scholarship tae university," Paislee told Grandpa. "A math scholarship."

"Brains and beauty." He whistled.

Blaise blushed.

"Anyway, is what I'm wearing fine for the Brick and Ivy?" Paislee gestured to her blue-and-white dress. "I can stay here if it's not good enough."

"It's perfect," Lydia and Blaise said in unison.

"Ready?" Blaise asked them. "I'm parked across the street by the pub."

"Now there's a guid place tae get lunch." Grandpa smacked his lips. "More my style. Grease and Guinness."

"Will there be multiple forks?" Paislee asked, remembering what her friend Mary Beth Mulholland had once said about finishing school and too much silverware.

"Just copy me," Lydia said. "It'll be no different from our special dinner at Leery Estate."

"There will be three. Salad, entrée, dessert. You'll be fine," Blaise said. "I remember how nervous I was the first time I met Shep's parents and we had a meal—he helped me so that I even knew how tae use the oyster fork."

"Oyster fork?" Paislee repeated.

Lydia burst out laughing. "Dinnae ask me. I slurp them down with a squirt of lemon and horseradish."

Blaise led them out of Cashmere Crush, with Paislee giving a longing look over her shoulder back at her shop as they crossed Market Street. Knitting needles she could discuss all day, but having her manners critiqued by snobby women was not how she wanted to spend her time. Ever.

"So, the Brick and Ivy is a wonderful four-star restaurant near Highland Academy. We used tae meet there after our mornings doing volunteer work tae have a long lunch before getting the kids again at three."

"Sounds nice," Lydia said.

Paislee got into the back, and Lydia climbed in the front of the black-and-silver Range Rover. Paislee spent the fifteen-minute drive looking up the lunch menu so she'd have a head start on what to order and how.

She turned her phone on silent, then switched the volume down instead just in case the school called, or the detective. Both were very important calls she'd take.

When they got there, Paislee smiled to see that the two-story brick building was covered in ivy. So far it was delivering on its promise, which gave her hope for delicious food that wasn't too unrecognizable. Couldn't go wrong with shepherd's pie.

They walked inside and Paislee was pleasantly surprised by the bright and cheery décor—for some reason she'd been expecting dim lighting and an old stale-smoke smell. Mounted heads on the walls.

Instead, there were green landscapes, and the scents of savory herbs and spices. Butter.

Bread?

With these ladies?

Her stomach rumbled.

The hostess—tall, thin, and ruddy-cheeked—smiled politely at them. "Mrs. O'Connor. The other women are already seated. We werenae expecting three of you—let us go reset the table."

Blaise checked the time and said, "Five till noon. I guess we're all early."

The hostess laughed politely and led them to a private room with a fireplace, and a light oak round table. The woman whispered into a waiter's ear and the round table set for four was set for six in the blink of an eye. Two waitstaff remained in attendance.

The three seated seemed surprised to see Blaise with Paislee and Lydia. Paislee thought the women resembled crows in their black dresses. Lara's brown hair was held back in a bun, Mari's darker brown hair curled to her shoulders, and Christina's blond tresses were in a loose braid.

Mari rose—if possible the woman had lost even more weight. "Blaise! Darling, you didnae say you'd be bringing guests."

"You all remember Paislee Shaw, and Lydia Barron?" Blaise made the rounds of cheek-kissing and hugging, Lydia and Paislee also played along.

Lara gave Blaise's arm an extra squeeze. "So glad you could make this lunch, in memory of Kirsten." The assistant bowed her head and sniffed.

"Stop already, Lara," Christina begged. "You've been crying all week. I can have John prescribe ye something that will ease all of our pain."

"I might take you up on that," Mari interjected. "Just when I think I'm moving on, I remember something Kirsten said, or did, and it brings all the grief shooting back through me again."

"How's Gerard? And Maxim?" Blaise perched on the edge of her seat as daintily as a butterfly to a rose petal. "We sent a basket of food tae the house."

"I've offered Gerard the use of our chef," Christina said, "but he declined. Somebody must be helping, though—you know how he feels aboot assigned jobs. Kirsten, as his wife, and Fergus, as the chef, had the kitchen as their domain. Hendrie the chauffer, the nanny, the gardener—everybody must stick tae their roles." She sighed and said in a droll tone directed to Lydia and Paislee, "His was king of the castle."

"I have tae do all the cooking at our house," Mari explained to them. "My digestive system is very fragile. That's why I like tae eat here—I know and trust the food."

Paislee, who had the constitution of a healthy horse, commiserated with a polite smile.

"I can eat anything," Lydia said.

"Tall, which helps keep the weight off, too," Christina observed.

"Christina!" Mari chided.

"What?" She smoothed her braid. "It's a compliment."

Mari shook her head and murmured, "Someone's been hitting the sauce again."

Christina straightened and folded her hands in her lap—was there a tremble in her fingers? Booze, or nerves?

Blaise arched her brow at Lydia and Paislee as if to say, *See?* Paislee checked the time on her phone. Quarter past noon, verbal shots already fired.

The sommelier came around first with wine suggestions. Despite her caustic remark to Christina, Mari ordered a glass of chardonnay. "Shall we get a bottle for the table?"

"At least one," Lara said. "For six of us. Is white okay with everybody?"

Blaise and Lydia nodded, so Paislee did, too.

Breadbaskets were brought out as their wineglasses were filled.

"Gluten free," Mari said, "so I can have just one piece. But it's so good you'd never know it."

"And the butter is fat free," Lara said. "They add herbs tae create terrific flavor."

She glanced at Lydia. Was everything to be diet?

It seemed a shame to dine at such a fancy restaurant and worry about calories—then again, if this was a weekly treat, she could understand being careful.

Maybe. Her mouth watered at all of the tempting smells.

"There is no rush," the waiter said. "Just let us know when you're ready tae order."

"Thank you," Lara said, as did Mari. "Shall we start with salads or a vegetable plate? I skipped breakfast. Maxim is having such a difficult time." Her voice turned husky.

Christina lifted her upper lip.

"Have another roll," Mari said. "I dinnae want tae be rushed."

Lara reached for a piece of bread, her hand shaking.

The waitstaff melted back from the room.

Mari leaned across the table to Lara. "Are you staying at the house? Overnight?"

"In the guest room, Mari." Lara slicked her dark hair over her ear. "Tae be there for Maxim. The cherub just lost his mum. He's devastated."

Mari lifted her glass. "Let's have a toast. Tae Kirsten."

"Tae Kirsten," they chorused. The name stuck in Paislee's throat as Kirsten's panicked face as she fought to breathe landed in her head.

"I miss her," Lara said. "She was so dynamic that her loss leaves a void in the house. Maxim cries and cries, and I cry with him."

"And Gerard?" Christina asked in a snarky tone.

Lara didn't catch it and answered sincerely, "He's upset, but he tries tae hide it, thanks tae that whole Anders debacle. What was Kirsten thinking?"

"She wasnae in her right mind, obviously," Mari said loyally.

"She had that awful news from her agent. She and Gerard were arguing over her going back tae work as a model . . . and when she finally got him tae reluctantly agree, her agent turned her doon."

"Oh, no. That's terrible," Paislee said.

"Verra." Mari sighed. "Sure, she wasnae eighteen anymore, but she didnae have a jiggle or a wrinkle. And her bone structure! It wasnae fair of him tae be so brutal. Nearly forty is not the same as *being* forty."

Christina sipped her wine. "Did everyone see that they've arrested Fergus?"

"I've been racking my brain wondering when Fergus added the crumble topping. Kirsten has no peanuts in her house, and she said that they wrapped the shortbread that morning." Lara bowed her head. "What a gamble he was taking in order tae kill her. What if she hadnae tasted the shortbread cookie?"

"Hers from home had a dusting of brown sugar and they looked the same as what Fergus brought oot for judging. I wonder if he toasted the peanuts at the club?" Mari asked.

Paislee could ask Sonya if the cooker had been used. The memory of how fast Kirsten had reacted to the cookie made her throat dry. She pressed her fingers to her jugular. "She licked the topping but barely took a bite."

"Her allergy was severe." Lara finished her roll and eyed the basket with longing.

"Lara, just have another one!" Blaise encouraged. "I will, too."

"Oh, stop pouting, Lara." Mari waved to the waiter. "We'd like tae order now."

"Soup or salad?"

Mari spoke for the group. "A raw vegetable platter and a Caesar salad, dressing and croutons on the side."

Christina gestured to Paislee and Lydia. "Sairy—this is our normal way of doing it. Do ye mind? You'll order your own entrée, of course."

"Not at all," Lydia said. "But there will be croutons? That's my favorite part of the Caesar salad. Extra anchovy for me."

Paislee bit her lip at Mari and Christina's matching dismay. She didn't care for anchovies at all but she was tempted to get extra, too.

Blaise grinned. "The croutons here are delicious. Nice and buttery."

Lara started to smile, then ducked her face before she was caught consorting with the enemy.

"What are the lunch options?" Lydia asked.

The waiter kept a professional expression but his eyes twinkled. "We have grilled grouper over a bed of brown rice and veg, lamb chops with creamy mashed turnips, or a shepherd's pie with chicken in golden gravy."

"We'll need a few minutes," Mari said.

It was clear to Paislee that Mari was the leader of the trio. Christina didn't seem the kind to want to be in charge, content to let Mari make the rules, even as she didn't want to let Lara get too full of herself. Happy in the middle.

Blaise had said that Christina suffered from anxiety. Maybe she'd realize how happy she could be with Kirsten gone and choose nicer friends. Paislee smiled at Christina. "Whatever happened with your trip tae the station on Sunday? I hope Constable Dean apologized for not returning your phone calls."

"Ha! He had the nerve tae request my mobile records." Christina sipped her wine. "John hired a solicitor and by the time we're done, that constable will regret being so rude. And all because my fingerprints were on that blasted EpiPen. I never should have picked it up." She raised her brow at Blaise.

"I'm sairy tae hear that," Blaise said.

"I had no idea," Lara commiserated.

"John is taking care of it." Mari patted Christina's hand.

The salads arrived. Paislee skipped the anchovy dressing but added extra Parmesan, capers, oil, and croutons. She knew the others watched her, but didn't let that stop her from popping a crunchy crouton in her mouth. Garlic and butter exploded over her tongue. "These are spectacular."

"The best, right?" Blaise added some to her plate too.

"So," Lydia said, slicing into her salad, "Christina, Blaise, and Mari, and Kirsten—you're not married, are you, Lara?"

"No." Lara chewed delicately.

"The four of you all knew each other because of golf . . . or was it the kids at the academy that brought you together?"

"Lara is the odd woman oot," Mari said. "But Kirsten hired her tae be a tutor, and her personal assistant."

"Mari!" Lara said.

"It's true. Kirsten knew aboot your little crush on Gerard and thought it was cute. She and Gerard used tae laugh aboot it."

Paislee gulped her swallow of iceberg lettuce and Parmesan. They had?

Lara's cheeks were so red it seemed painful. "She told him that?"

"Aye." Mari nibbled a single lettuce leaf, her gaze on Lara.

"Is it true, Christina?" Lara asked. "Did you all laugh?"

"Yes. Sairy. Dinnae fash aboot it now. Kirsten . . . she's gone." Christina finished her wine and gestured for the waiter. "Can you bring me a vodka tonic, please?"

"You should at least get through lunch." Mari sipped from her wineglass, which was still half full.

"It's none of your business what I drink." Christina's brave words were belied by a faint warble in her tone.

"I think we're shocking Paislee," Lara said faintly.

Paislee drank some water to hide any facial reaction she might have. "I'm fine."

"It's no surprise tae those of us who knew her best," Mari said. "Kirsten had a way of finding things oot aboot people." She eyed Blaise. "Right?"

Blaise paled beneath her perfect makeup.

Mari nibbled another lettuce leaf. "Blaise, I still remember meeting you and Suzannah the first year of primary. You were so bubbly, your daughter an angel."

Blaise cut into her salad, her expression unchanging but it was like waiting for the ax to fall to hear what Mari would say. At last she said, "And Kirsten marked you right away as someone special."

Blaise swallowed and cleared her throat. "How sweet."

"Then she found oot somehow aboot you not really being one of us. Raised in an orphanage." Mari's slender nostrils flared.

Lara refilled her wine from the bottle in the center of the table. "Shall we order our entrées?" Paislee had to give the woman points for effort in trying to change the subject.

"This is all water under the bridge now," Christina said, accepting her vodka from the waiter. "Blaise and Suzannah are leaving. Just stop it."

"Should we share your secret with your new friends?" Mari asked Christina.

"Only after we share yours, Miss I Was Fat as a Kid," Christina snapped.

Mari winced and dropped her lettuce leaf to her plate.

Lara waved a menu frantically at the waiter by the door.

Two came around and took their food orders. Paislee chose the lamb chop, Blaise and Lydia the shepherd's pie, and the other three chose the grilled fish.

The waiters left and Paislee hoped to help keep the conversation on nice things. Warm, loving memories of a woman killed. Unfortunately, it was easy to see that Kirsten had a wake of people behind her that she'd manipulated and treated cruelly.

The ladies discussed the school, and how privileged their children were to go to Highland Academy . . . that is, Mari and Christina discussed it, as if to rub the superior ratings in Blaise's nose since she was leaving. Lara was semi-included as Maxim's tutor. Mari's daughter, Mia, already had a new set of friends.

"Since when?" Blaise asked, hurt.

"I suggested that she not play with Suzannah." Mari shrugged her bony shoulder.

Blaise's nose flared. "Why would you do that?"

"It wasnae my idea," Mari said. "It was Kirsten's. She told Maxim not tae play with Suz, either."

"Is that true? What aboot Robby, Christina?"

Christina drank her vodka. "I'm sairy, but yes, I told him. Kirsten was a terrible bitch. This lunch was a bad idea."

Paislee couldn't agree more.

"Going tae call John?" Mari asked. "Nobody knows her as well as he does." She made sure to make eye contact with them all. "He's been her psychiatrist since she was *sixteen*."

Patient-client, underage—that broke all kinds of rules.

"Mari!" Christina dropped her napkin. "How could you? Of all people . . . I could—"

Lara patted Christina's shoulder. "It's all right. I already knew."

"Kirsten told you?" Christina asked in tears.

"Kirsten told everybody everything." Mari shrugged. The woman narrowed her gaze to somehow make it even sharper. "Gerard said Fergus stole from them, but I don't think so. I wonder if Kirsten found oot something aboot Fergus that made him snap?"

Chapter 19

Paislee immediately wondered the same. Kirsten knew how to get under everyone's skin, and it wasn't a stretch to think that someone, namely the fired chef, might decide to retaliate. Fergus didn't seem like a killer, but what if he'd meant to scare her and it had gone too far?

Blaise pushed her half-finished meal away. "I agree that it seems strange for Kirsten to have offered Fergus a severance package if he'd stolen something. Fergus liked tae party. What if she found oot, and that's why he was let go?"

"How would you know that aboot him?" Lara wiped a tear from her eye.

"He used tae work for us," Blaise said in a soft voice.

"That's right!" Mari snapped her fingers. "Kirsten and Gerard snatched him from you guys—she was quite proud."

"They stole your chef, Blaise?" Lara blew out a breath. "That's low."

Blaise scooted to the edge of her chair. "They offered him a substantial raise. It was a better fit for Fergus."

Mari laughed. "What does that mean?"

"I think it means that the Buchanans liked tae party a little more than the O'Connors. Is that right?" Christina asked.

"Shep has an image tae protect in the community." Blaise raised her chin without apology.

"So." Lara allowed a smile at that. "Not Kirsten's win but yours, Blaise. That's brilliant."

"Except that Fergus is a killer," Mari said.

Blaise glumly nodded. "We never saw that side of him, if it's true."

"*If* it's true? Why do ye say it like that?" Mari put her sharp elbow on the table.

"I never thought she'd fire him so something must have gone on that we dinnae know aboot." Christina sipped daintily from her cut-glass tumbler and kept it in her hand like a security blanket.

"You never really know people," Lydia said. She finished her meal with gusto and sighed at the empty plate. "This was verra guid. I'll be back for sure. It's just right for some of our upper-echelon clientele."

"What do you do?" Lara asked.

"I'm an estate agent at Silverstein's."

"She's my agent," Blaise said proudly.

"Why did you have tae move?" Mari asked with a heavy tone. "I thought that we'd all be together until the children graduated."

Blaise took a deep breath before answering, "Shep wanted tae expand his career. Being the head golf pro in Nairn is better than being one of many at Inverness—you know how that is."

"But you didnae have tae sell your house in Inverness. You could have commuted." Mari sighed.

Christina nodded, blue eyes big.

"I wanted a change as well." Blaise finished her wine. "We've decided tae make Nairn our home."

Paislee knew that getting away from the ladies who lunched had been a big part of the move from Inverness. It was less than a thirty-minute commute and they could have done it but just didn't want to.

They planned on putting down roots.

She understood that and happened to think that Nairn was perfect for making a home.

"John misses Shep terribly." Christina gave the clear liquid in her tumbler a gentle swirl and explained to the rest of the table, "John, Gerard, and Shep used tae meet for a game and drinks twice a week. Then Gerard had tae go and get that job for Shep in Nairn."

"Hey! Shep earned that job." Blaise seemed to realize how that sounded and calmed down. "I know that Gerard put in a good word, but Shep is very talented in his own right."

"I know, I know." Christina raised her hand and smiled at Mari. "Be grateful that Charlie's been traveling more and hasnae been part of the group."

Mari flinched.

What was it with these women that they had to put each other down all the time? Exclude other people in order to feel good? Maybe Christina should be discussing *that* with her doctor husband.

Lara spoke to Paislee, who had done her best to be quiet and polite and part of the furniture. If Blaise needed her she was here, but she had no intention of exchanging phone numbers.

". . . so what do you think of Nairn's new social club? I'm sure the renovation of an eyesore in the community will help bring up home values."

"I like it . . . I especially appreciate the connection Sonya has tae the place—her great-grandparents holidayed there. Was it an *eyesore*?" Lydia asked.

Lara lifted a shoulder, embarrassed. "I'm sairy. I'm just repeating what Kirsten had said aboot the place. I never saw it before we were there for the Nairn Food Bank event."

Paislee shifted toward Lara. "Did you know Anders?" Since his splash in the news on Sunday accusing Gerard of murder he'd been out of sight.

"No. I mean, he was welcomed in the Buchanan house tae discuss the plans for the event. Anders needed Gerard tae sign off tae be a premier member of the club. Gerard was excited tae help," Lara said. "He likes tae tackle 'big' projects."

"That makes him look like a hero," Christina butted in. Her words had a hint of a slur. "He especially likes that."

Lara blushed as if not used to the airing of dirty laundry over a meal. She scooped her rice into a bite-size pile. "I didnae know aboot Anders and Kirsten."

Paislee dabbed her lips with a napkin. "How many of these lunches have you been at?"

"This is my fourth," Lara said. "Once Blaise kept cancelling, Kirsten wanted me tae tag along."

"Where did you meet Kirsten?" Paislee smashed a pea into some potato, swirled it in the lamb chop juice, then popped it in her mouth. Each ingredient on her plate had been superbly flavored.

"At Highland Academy. I was a substitute teacher in the kids' first year and we hit it off. Maxim is verra bright and doesnae really need special tutoring but she and Gerard want him tae be the best in class."

"Like they were, the best?"

She shrugged. Paislee got the feeling that Lara was not solely on board with the whole number-one thing.

But would Lara fight Gerard on it?

Paislee didn't sense that much of a backbone in Lara—especially if she had romantic feelings for Gerard, who she'd seen for herself had a short fuse.

"What are you two whispering aboot?" Mari leaned over her full plate of grilled fish to see down the table.

Paislee smiled and shook her head. "No whispering." She turned back to Lara. "Do you still sub at the school?"

"Aye, occasionally. Teaching positions at HA are verra sought after. This is one way tae get your foot in."

"Go HA!" Christina cheered, in a much happier mood after her second vodka.

The waitstaff arrived to clear their plates. Mari hadn't touched more than two bites. "Would you like a box?"

"Yes, please."

"Anybody else?" The waiter glanced at the other empty plates. "How aboot dessert?"

"None for me," Paislee said, checking the time on her mobile. Was this awful lunch finally over?

Lydia nudged Paislee's leg with the toe of her shoe, mouth twitching. Too obvious?

"Thank you for letting us intrude on your lunch in Kirsten's honor," Lydia announced, knowing good and well that Blaise hadn't given the others an option.

It took another ten minutes to say goodbye, and chatter about getting together again, mostly from an intoxicated Christina. Lara escaped first, bless her, then Mari. Paislee discreetly read up on mobile sharing plans until it was finally time to go.

They followed Christina to the lobby, past the hostess stand.

"I forgot me purse," the blonde said. "Dinnae wait. I'm riding with Mari." She hurried back to their private dining room.

"Coming?" Lydia asked Paislee.

She pointed to the women's restroom sign. "I'd like tae wash up real quick."

"We'll bring the Beast around," Blaise said. "I *have* tae get fresh air."

Lydia and Blaise rushed out to the car and Paislee went inside the gorgeous washroom with scented soap and warm towels to dry her hands on. She was grateful that the ordeal was over, and from now on Blaise could stand on her own.

When she was patting her fingers, she heard a flush, then a tiny whimper from behind one of the stalls.

Paislee hadn't realized anybody else was in the room. Alarmed, she bent down to check for shoes and saw the heels on super-skinny legs, as if someone was being sick.

Mari had disappeared right after Lara. The last thing she wanted was to embarrass the woman, but it didn't feel right to leave her there, either.

Christina! She'd said she was getting a ride with Mari. Paislee hurried out to find her, and luckily Christina was already waiting on a leather love seat in the lobby.

"I think Mari is ill."

Christina tucked her purse beneath her arm and stood. "Naw, that's her after-eating ritual. She's fine."

At Paislee's lifted brow, Christina snickered. "Not fine, obviously, but this is her normal behavior. Bulimia. It's worse now, caused by the stress of Kirsten's death."

"Oh. She's getting help?"

"Aye." Christina stepped to the side as the sound of the toilet flushing reached them. "You should go."

"All right." Paislee studied the blond woman in concern, then admitted to herself that she was concerned for all of them. None of the three would appreciate it. She dashed outside.

Blaise, behind the wheel of the Beast, had pulled up in front of the door of the Brick and Ivy. Lydia was in back this time and so Paislee climbed in front.

"Full chauffeur service, as promised," Blaise said.

"Thank you." She buckled up, eager to leave this place. "Did you know that Mari has bulimia?"

"I'd heard that but she doesnae talk aboot it. Oh, no. Did you see something?"

Paislee shared what had happened. "I'm glad she's getting help, but those women are a tidy mess. You were brilliant to break away. I hope Lara can, too."

"How long has Mari had it?" Lydia poked her head between the seats up front from the middle back bench.

"I dinnae know. Kirsten would tease her aboot being fat as a kid. She called me Little Orphan Annie, and you heard the caustic remarks she made tae Christina aboot marrying her doctor."

"She wasn't nice," Paislee said.

"No."

"Paislee, I can see your curiosity now, wanting tae know the why of her bad behavior," Lydia said in a somber tone. "But sometimes people are just . . . mean. They dinnae need a reason."

Blaise drove toward downtown Nairn. "Kirsten was born with a platinum spoon in her mouth. She had everything."

"And still not happy?" Paislee sighed. "She was spoiled."

"Rotten," Lydia agreed.

"Maybe being born into all of that wealth ruined them." Paislee patted Blaise's arm. "Being raised in an orphanage saved you from being just like them. It was a blessing."

Blaise's diamond on her wedding ring sparkled in the sunlight as she held the steering wheel. "How so?"

"Christina has a drinking problem, and has been seeing her husband, who was her psychiatrist, from the age of sixteen. That is all kinds of wrong, by the way."

"Improper. Immoral, illegal." Lydia folded down a finger with each word. "No wonder Christina hated Kirsten teasing her aboot it."

Paislee continued, "Mari has bulimia. Kirsten was spoiled rotten tae the core. You, Blaise, know how tae appreciate the beautiful things in life because they didn't come easy. Are the men like that? Their husbands?"

Blaise tapped her thumb to the leather casing. "Gerard can be entitled. John thinks very highly of himself and his doctor's license. Mari's husband, Charlie, is nice enough, but he's a wee bit jealous that he's not a celebrity like Shep. He's not as good a golfer. Charlie travels for business so was always a little apart from the weekly rounds of golf and drinks."

"Mari seemed tae be upset about that," Paislee said. "Christina made sure to get in that dig."

Blaise giggled. "Shep thought he was gay at first. Bleached white teeth, longish hair, and I admit he seems on the effeminate side, but these days, who knows? Anything goes. He and Mari have a beautiful daughter. That she told not to play with my Suz." Her mirth fled.

Lydia did a quick scan on Charlie Gilmore and oohed aloud. "He's gorgeous—look, Paislee."

Paislee accepted the mobile Lydia thrust at her. "He *is* handsome." And she could understand why Shep might have thought him gay. His features were slightly feminine and in almost all his photos, he had his arm slung around another guy. The pictures with Mari and his daughter, Mia, were beautiful, but posed.

She handed the phone back to Lydia. "Mari is smiling. Makes her very pretty instead of brittle and fragile. He must know about the bulimia?"

Blaise scrunched her nose as she drove. "You would think, right? I cannae imagine you'd be able tae keep hurling on the daily a secret."

Paislee's phone rang, the sound so low she could hardly hear it. She brought it from her purse and read the screen. "The detective," she told her friends before she answered, "Hello!"

"Paislee, are you still at lunch?" The DI's voice had become familiar over the last few months and she caught an urgency in his words.

"We're on our way back. Is everything all right?" She felt Lydia and Blaise stare at her.

"Can you stop by the station?"

"Now?" She pulled her phone back to see the time. Three. Paislee didn't have to pick up Brody until four thirty. "Sure."

"It shouldnae take long but I want tae discuss your phone message aboot Fergus."

Perhaps they'd been too exuberant in their message about the detective jailing the wrong man. "You want Blaise tae come, too?"

"Nope. Let's start with you."

"I should be there in ten minutes."

"See you then."

Paislee ended the call and raised the volume now that they were out of the fancy restaurant. "He wants tae talk about why we don't think Fergus is guilty of killing Kirsten, even though he was a thief."

Blaise looked slightly disappointed that she wasn't being asked to the station, too.

"You have tae tell us everything as soon as you're done," Lydia said. "But text, though, because I have a client from three thirty until five."

"You both have busy lives. I have nothing." Blaise scowled.

"That's not true," Lydia said. "You have a grand house tae manage—just wait, and appreciate any free time you have because it will be gone before you know it."

Blaise exhaled. "I suppose you're right."

Paislee was glad that she hadn't been born with a platinum spoon. Not even a silver spoon. And while she might make *many* mistakes in the motherhood department, spoiling Brody rotten wasn't going to be one of them.

Chapter 20

Paislee entered the Nairn Police Station and greeted the receptionist, Amelia Henry, her friend and fellow knitter who'd started knitting two years ago when she quit smoking as a way to keep her hands busy.

Big, dark blue eyes glimmered from an elfin face; Amelia's dark brown hair was in a short shag. "Afternoon, Paislee! What are you doing here?"

"Stopping in tae see the detective," Paislee said. "Is he in?"

"Aye." Amelia pressed a button and spoke into an intercom. "Paislee Shaw here, DI Zeffer."

A buzz sounded, then, "Send her back, please."

Paislee knew her way through the station, which wasn't grand but a simple two-story building that abutted to the park. Behind that was the beach, though you couldn't see it from here. There was a tree that offered shade over a lone picnic table.

"Want me tae walk with you?" Amelia asked in her normal voice. She mouthed, "Everything okay?"

"I'm fine," she said aloud, then whispered back, "I'll text you later."

The new DI didn't do things the same way Inspector Shinner had, and had put his designer boot down on sharing information about cases in the station. They tended to leak to the public, which was against protocol, and Zeffer wouldn't have it.

She reached his back office and knocked, though the door was partially open.

"Come in."

"You wanted tae see me?"

"Aye, have a seat."

Paislee couldn't help but note the differences between Zeffer's and Hamish McCall's offices. The headmaster's was browns and woods with framed certificates on the wall. Nothing personal of nature. Purely a professional space.

The DI had finally allowed his staff to finish painting after the inspector left. He'd chosen pale blue on the walls, which was actually quite calming. However, his desk and the furniture were black, right down to the black metal folding chairs before his desk, as if he didn't want anyone to get too comfy sitting there.

State your business and move on was the unspoken message. The only pictures up were ones of Nairn that somebody else had probably hung. Again, nothing personal at all—as if both men poured their personalities into their business persona.

The chair squeaked as she sat and her belly fluttered. What did he want to discuss? She bit the inside of her lip to keep from babbling.

Zeffer's sharp cheekbones seemed even more protruding today as his sea-glass green eyes scrutinized her beneath trimmed russet brows—her own weren't as nice.

Hamish's were thick and natural. If she had to guess, she'd say that Hamish was a few years older than Zeffer, at thirty-five or thirty-six, compared to Zeffer, in his early thirties.

Zeffer continued to stare at her.

She stared back.

Both men were young for their positions. Each was slightly arrogant. Both flustered her, for different reasons. Hamish she found attractive but they couldn't even be friends while Brody was in primary school. Hamish was their boss.

Zeffer was coldly handsome and he flustered her with his rules and unspoken expectations. His keen wit.

He'd told her once that she would never be a good police officer because even though she had a gift for observation, she thought with her heart and not her head, which would make her a liability on the task force.

Burning building with a baby/kitten/human inside? She'd run in to save them, no argument. It didn't bother her any as she had zero interest in the law, other than helping her friend Amelia study if she decided to take the officer test.

She got the teensiest bit of joy from knowing that Zeffer hated asking for her assistance, and yet, sometimes he did. Like now. And it was burning him up inside.

Paislee smiled with a wee bit more confidence. "How have ye been? Enjoying the braw weather in our seaside town? You know that Nairn has the most sunshine in all of Scotland."

He steepled his fingers together, elbows on his desk. "Just because I'm new tae Nairn doesnae mean I'm unaware of the town's draw."

She pointed to the tree visible from his window. "When was the last time you walked on the beach for fun?"

"I dinnae do that. Especially when there's a murderer on the loose."

Loose? "But I thought you had Fergus in custody? The paper said you'd arrested him."

"The paper was mistaken—and I'd already let him go by the time I heard your message. I dinnae want you thinking that I released him because you didnae think he was guilty."

She sat back in the chair. Somebody was extra growly today. "I'm glad you let him go, even though he stole the laptop."

"A ticket offense. Not jail." Zeffer rubbed his jaw. "Just out of curiosity, why didnae you think he was guilty?"

"I saw his face that day. Fergus was truly alarmed when Kirsten collapsed. But then I doubted myself."

"Why is that?"

Paislee shrugged. "At lunch today, Mari wondered aloud if Kirsten had discovered something about Fergus tae make him snap. Kirsten used people's weaknesses tae make them feel bad."

"Who all was at this lunch?" He opened his tablet to take notes.

"Mari Gilmore, Christina Baird, and Lara Fisk. Blaise O'Connor used tae be part of the clique, too. With the exception of Lara, they're moms at Highland Academy. Blaise asked Lydia and I to go with her so that we could protect her from any barbed comments."

"If you knew it was going tae be a roast, why go?"

"It was a lunch tae honor Kirsten . . . but she wasn't kind. No surprise things took a darker turn."

"Kirsten and Gerard sponsored the Nairn Food Bank drive." He lowered his fingers to lay his palms flat on the desk. It was a statement, not a question.

"Aye, that's true . . . but for selfish reasons. Does that count in the 'good' column, I wonder? Gerard Buchanan, according tae Lara and Christina, took on projects that allowed him tae be larger than life."

"I know people like that," the DI said.

"I don't know many, thank heaven. Anyway, before Blaise and I went tae lunch, we got tae chatting. What if Gerard was the one tae set Fergus up? Have the chef, who had been fired that morning, take the blame for killing Kirsten, while he did the deed."

His russet brow arched. "Why?"

It was like knowing you had the right answer in class but being challenged to explain it. Her mouth dried and she swallowed. "Because Gerard is *very* smart. What if he found out about the affair between Kirsten and Anders sooner than Saturday afternoon? Do you think he's the kind tae take that quietly? Kirsten, once a top model, was his trophy. Her agent let her go for being too old. They were in marriage counseling."

Zeffer sat back, hands on his flat stomach, twirling his thumbs.

Paislee sighed. "But the truth is, Gerard's temper also crosses him off the list, at least tae my way of thinking."

"Oh?" He remained in his relaxed pose.

"Well, according tae the ladies, he's not a man who will be found in the kitchen—that was his wife's domain, and Fergus's. He didn't cook. The crumble would have taken time tae plan, and tae do such a good job tae fool Kirsten . . ."

"He wouldnae have made the peanut and brown sugar topping."

"Exactly."

Zeffer crossed one leg over the other in thought. "While I released Fergus I also told him not tae leave town."

"He needs tae get into his room at the Buchanan house tae get his things."

"I had Officer Payne take him. Mr. Buchanan was there tae supervise and make sure Fergus only collected what was his."

She nodded. "Smart. Fergus seems tae have real sticky fingers. Not only did he steal the gaming laptop, but Blaise found out through Shep, who got it from Gerard, that Kirsten had fired Fergus for theft after she caught him rummaging around in their office. The women don't believe it." Paislee tilted her head. "Why wouldn't Kirsten report him stealing? Why let him work at the house for two weeks? Gerard could be lying, except there is proof that Fergus is a thief. I don't know how you do it. There are too many possibilities."

He chuckled, his gaze out the window. "You have tae follow each lead."

"Do you know what happened tae the laptop?"

Zeffer straightened and focused on Paislee. "After watching the video, I tracked down the chauffeur, Hendrie Stewart. He started babbling as soon as I got out of the SUV." Grinning, the detective said, "It's how we nabbed Fergus, thanks tae Hendrie turning over on his mate."

Paislee sat forward. She'd wondered if they were working together. "How so?"

"Hendrie drove Fergus tae Highland Academy, where Fergus sold it tae one of the older kids—sixteen, with a trust fund. Talked it up, brand-new system, nothing like it around. He had the money in hours."

"Oh!" She thought of the duffel bag with the school initials. Paislee had assumed Fergus had taken it from the Buchanans but maybe it had come from this kid.

"Cash," Zeffer clarified.

"Why was Fergus broke? Blaise said that chefs make very good money, and Fergus got a raise when he was hired on from the O'Connors tae the Buchanans."

"He likes tae party." Zeffer shrugged as if it were all just another day. "Girls, drugs, alcohol. That lifestyle isnae cheap. I'm surprised he still had his mother's house, actually. Fergus was in over his head."

That would explain why he was so thin, too, despite his talent for creating wonderful meals. "Will you get the console back?"

Zeffer raised his brow.

"What? It was stolen property. The Silverstein Real Estate Agency donated it for a good cause—the food bank."

"I'm not at liberty tae discuss that." Zeffer tapped the tablet on his desk. "What else did you learn at lunch today?"

She considered acting like she'd learned nothing but that would only hinder finding Kirsten's killer. Kirsten's pleading gaze arose in Paislee's mind and she tamped it back down. "Well, Christina Baird likes her vodka, Mari Gilmore suffers from bulimia, Lara Fisk has a crush on Gerard Buchanan. John usually golfs with Shep O'Connor but he hurt his hand and can't. Mari's husband, Charlie, travels a lot and isn't as tight with the other guys."

His nostrils flared slightly—but he'd asked. "Anything else?"

"Blaise is ready tae pull her daughter from the school. Do you know that Kirsten made sure that the parents told their kids not tae play with Suzannah?"

"It's a cutthroat world," he said, grinding his back teeth. "Let's keep it aboot the adults."

Paislee went through what she hadn't already shared that might matter. "Anders loved Kirsten but she didn't love him. She was rejected by her agent and was feeling restless, which is why she had the affair. Oh—whatever happened tae that note?"

"You were right. It was a love note from Kirsten. You said that the Buchanans were in therapy?" He lifted his tablet. "Gerard did-nae mention that during his interview."

"See? Keeping secrets makes him look guilty."

Zeffer jotted something down. "I might have tae stop in and ask him a few more questions."

"Gerard was really mad when he showed up at the club on Sunday, blitzed and ready tae fight. He threatened Anders. Said he was going tae kill him."

"That's what Sonya said." His voice softened as he spoke her name.

Interesting. Not "Ms. Marshal." The director-owner had made an impression. "Sonya also has a reason tae hate Kirsten—disrupting her and Anders's open relationship with the affair."

His upper lip twitched. "Kirsten was still murdered even if she was terrible. Just makes it more challenging tae find her killer."

Paislee checked the time on her mobile and swallowed a gasp. Quarter past four.

"Someplace more important tae be?" Zeffer had sarcasm down to an art.

Her ears steamed with embarrassment but she held her ground. "Yes, actually. Brody needs tae be picked up from school. I told you I couldn't stay long. Is that all?"

"What time did you first see Fergus at the club on Saturday?"

She thought back. "I don't recall really seeing him until he presented the cookies. That would have been after four."

"Aye. Hendrie said that he didnae know Fergus had been fired until after everything happened. Fergus had shown up in the Fiat tae assist Kirsten with her shortbread presentation at half past two. Not only were there three plates for the judges, but they'd planned tae offer whisky with cookies for everyone after the contest."

"Gerard made a speech that first day—he loved center stage. It seemed a foregone conclusion that Kirsten would win. It turns out that she cheated, even at the Highland Academy bake sales. Blaise confronted the principal, who admitted tae accepting two weeks every summer at the Buchanan seaside cottage."

Zeffer propped his elbow on his desk. "That is verra low . . . but we're straying off topic. The *fact* is we were able tae corroborate what Hendrie told us with the footage from Sonya's state-of-the-art security cameras. Fergus arrived at two thirty to prepare the biscuits for the judges. He is seen going into the kitchen of the club, and the conference room. The hall is congested because of the influx of shoppers so it's hard tae tell folks apart, except for Fergus's copper hair." Exhaling, he said, "Sonya's thinking of getting people's permission and adding cameras in the private rooms."

" 'Sonya,' huh?"

Zeffer arched his brow. "What?"

"It took you months before you'd call me Paislee." She looked over her nose at him. "You still revert tae 'Ms. Shaw.' "

"You're Ms. Shaw when you're part of a murder investigation." He held his hands to his sides.

She started to laugh. "Fine." Her phone rang and she recognized the Fordythe number, but when she answered there was a dial tone. "I really do have tae go." There were ten minutes before she had to be there and now she might even be late.

"I willnae keep you." He actually smiled at her. "I appreciate you stopping by."

"As if I had a choice?"

Zeffer waved his hand for her to go. "And dinnae tell your friends all we talked aboot."

"You know I will. It's not against the law."

"Guid day, *Ms. Shaw.*"

Chapter 21

Paislee jogged to Cashmere Crush, going around the back to get the Juke. She had no time to even offer a quick hello to Grandpa as she had to race to Fordythe to pick up Brody from school. Whoever had called from there hadn't left a message. Maybe it was Brody reminding her?

During the thankfully short drive she went over what she'd learned from the enigmatic detective. The man kept things close to his chest.

She arrived to a mostly empty car park, as the teachers had already gone home except . . . Hamish McCall was on the walkway with Brody between the queue for pickup and the school itself. Aye, it was 4:33, but for heaven's sake!

Then Brody raised his head and she saw that he had a paper towel to his nose—bloody—and an ice pack.

Alarmed, she parked in the drop-off lane—nobody was behind her as school was officially out—and visually scanned Brody for further injuries. Dirt, bruises, but no bones poking out that she could see.

"What happened?"

Hamish winced at her accusatory tone.

Brody shuffled his feet, his backpack over one arm, a tear in his school pants.

"Did you fall?"

"No." His voice was low and she could tell he was on the verge of tears that he wouldn't want to shed in front of anybody.

She glanced at the headmaster and then her son.

Brody said not a word as he pressed the towel and ice to his poor face.

Hamish rocked back on his loafers. "I didnae see this, and Mr. Peters is still on the field with the others, but according to his mates, Brody fell after blocking the ball with his face."

Paislee peered at her child. He wasn't afraid to play rough. "On purpose?"

"Everyone, including Brody, has said it was an accident." Hamish shrugged behind Brody and gave a head shake.

"I see." She patted Brody on the arm, and smoothed a lock of auburn hair back from his brow. How to handle this? *Don't overreact to the blood or dirt or the fact that he might have been bullied.* Paislee knelt down to look Brody in the eye. "Should we go see Doc Whyte tae check you out?"

"No!"

She stood and asked Hamish, "What if his nose is broken?"

Hamish squeezed her shoulder in a compassionate manner meant to calm her down. "It doesnae appear so tae me but if it makes ye feel better, of course."

"We dinnae need the doc, Mum."

"And you're a doctor now?" She opened the passenger side and helped Brody into the Juke.

Hamish murmured, "I really dinnae think it is, but if the bridge turns blue and swollen, or he's in pain, or has trouble breathing, then yes, call Doc Whyte."

"I will." She closed the door and stepped away from the Juke to ask, "Who was Brody playing with?"

"Edwyn, Lucas, and Samuel all had a part, but I'm not sure what exactly happened. They've all agreed it was an accident, but . . ."

She bit her lip and looked from the car and her son to the head-master. "I will tell you this in confidence . . . just so you know.

Brody and Edwyn had a falling out over the math quiz on Friday and getting a possible free recess with Mrs. Martin, if you get them all correct. Brody struggles with math, but he's really trying because I guess there was something said about him . . ." Paislee couldn't bring herself to repeat the insult. ". . . not being able to get them all."

Hamish rubbed his jaw. "I see."

"He'll do his best, which is all anybody can do. We have flashcards and we're trying tae make it fun. I'm not one of those mums that think competition isn't healthy, just so you know." She raised her chin.

He only nodded, which she took as a win.

Paislee palmed her keys. "Well, we'll see you tomorrow."

"Keep the ice on his nose," Hamish said kindly. "He'll be all right."

She got into the car, wiping her eyes with a tea-stained napkin on the console without Brody's noticing.

Brody radiated angst as they drove away. Once they left the school lot he tossed the ice pack down to his feet. "I hate football. I'm never playing again."

"Hey now . . . what happened? The truth, if ye please." Paislee automatically drove down toward the water and the pier to take the long way back to the shop. This would need more than five minutes to sort.

Thanks to her grandfather, she knew Cashmere Crush was in good hands.

"Lucas lined up the ball and aimed it at my face! Edwyn laughed. Samuel pushed him back and then . . ."

"Where was Mr. Peters during all of this?"

"Talking tae some of the other kids."

"Oh." Even with supervision these things happened. "I won't stand by for you tae be bullied at school, Brody. Let's drive right back tae Fordythe and get tae the bottom of this right now. It's not okay."

"Mum!" He glared at her, then at his backpack. "No—ye cannae do that."

"Why not?"

"I'm not going tae grass up me mates."

"They aren't your mates if they broke your nose, Brody."

"They didnae, the headmaster said so." He peeked at her. "It hurts, though." His eyes shimmered with unshed tears.

The tip of her nose stung and she dabbed at her welling eyes with the napkin. He couldn't go to work with her like this. He was ten. A kid. But not a baby. "Let's get you home and set up comfy. You can watch telly there, just until me and Grandpa get home."

"By myself?"

Paislee felt caught between a rock and a hard place. She had to get Grandpa and close the shop but Brody didn't need to be yanked around. He should be comfortable at home with Wallace.

It would only be for an hour.

"Just this one time, and only if you have Wallace with you, and you stay on the couch. Keep the door locked. No phone. No computer."

She'd run out of rules by the time they reached the house.

He perked up as they walked in. Wallace greeted them with exuberant tail wags, sniffing the bloody towel with interest, before settling down to give Brody a bark.

"He knows something's wrong," Brody said. "Don'tchya, boy?"

Paislee looked at the time on the mobile. Five! "Your Grandpa is gonna want another raise at this rate and I might just have tae give it tae him."

She went over the rules one last time. "We will be back as soon as possible. No later than six ten. Call if you need anything or if you get scared, and I'll have Grandpa come right home."

Paislee left with trepidation and said a prayer to Gran to watch over him.

She heard him cheer when she locked the door.

Before she got too annoyed, she remembered the first time

she'd been home alone—there was a grown-up-ness about it that made you feel as if you were finally to be trusted.

And she also recalled getting into the sweets as soon as her mum's back was turned.

If that was the worst thing that happened? She could handle that.

She arrived at the shop from the back and went inside as Grandpa rang up a customer.

"There you are!" He turned toward her. "I was getting worried."

The customer left, and she joined Grandpa by the register. "Take a break, Grandpa. I'll get these next folks." She squeezed his hand. "Thank you."

He sank down on the stool and opened a bottle of fizzy water. "Business has been steady."

"Too much?" She checked him for signs of overwork. His complexion was flushed but he was breathing all right.

"I'm fine, lass, just fine, but I hope you dinnae plan on taking any more four-hour lunches for a while."

"No, no. I promise." She'd had it with going out and planned on bringing a sandwich for the rest of the week.

"Where's the lad?"

"Brody got into a scuffle with Edwyn and his mates—ended up with a ball tae the nose. Blood and everything. I thought he might rest better at home."

"Sure." Grandpa half rose. "Should I leave now?"

She held up her hand to motion him back down. "You aren't walking anywhere." Paislee checked her phone. Quarter past five. "I told him he could be alone for an hour. This is his first time. I hope he doesn't get into any trouble. He really wanted tae stay home. Do you think I made a mistake?"

Her pulse raced.

"Naw." Grandpa didn't sound convinced.

"We should go. I'll lock up." She stepped toward the browsing shoppers up front to ask them to hurry.

"Wait a minute, now," Grandpa suggested. "Mibbe we can be home at five thirty. Give him a little freedom."

She faced him, hands clasped. "It's just that he might be in pain."

"Or nicking the secret stash of biscuits in the pantry."

Paislee laughed at the image. "That's what I did the first time I was alone by myself."

"He's a guid kid. Mibbe we should see how he does."

It was wonderful to have an ally—unexpected and sometimes cranky, but an ally nonetheless.

"Can you tell me about this yarn here?" A woman with her friend pointed to the bright shelves. "What's the difference between cashmere and merino?"

Paislee sauntered forward. "Well . . . one comes from a goat, and the other a sheep . . ."

After dinner, and a special trip to the pier for ice cream, she and Grandpa were on the back porch watching Brody play fetch with Wallace. He was still sore, poor sweetie, and taking a break from the flashcards.

Wallace flew across the yard on short, fringed legs, tail high, orange ball in his mouth, eyes dancing. A boy needed a dog, and Wallace was the perfect fit for their family. Loving and energetic, smart and loyal. Wallace would always pick Brody first, darn Edwyn.

Paislee opened her knitting bag at her feet. "Why do people have tae be so mean?"

"Whatchya talking aboot?"

"Well, Blaise's *supposed* friends. Brody's *supposed* friends."

"You didnae have particular kids you didnae get along with at school?"

Paislee glanced at Grandpa and grinned. "Well, sure, but Dana

Madison never kicked a ball in my face. She just told everyone when I liked Stephan."

"Mibbe that's a girl thing. I got pounded plenty from the bigger boys in school. Probably did my share of pounding, too, not that I'm proud of it." He sipped from a mug of tea.

"Times have changed, Grandpa."

"Not arguing that fair point. Brody sounded pretty certain the lad hammered him on purpose when he was telling us aboot it over dinner."

"It's not right." Paislee settled the shawl she was working on over her lap. The order had come in earlier and the sunshine yellow color offered a balance to her dark mood. "But it isn't as hurtful as Edwyn laughing."

Grandpa scratched his beard and stretched his legs out, relaxing after a long day.

"Brody never said why the boy did it, though."

"He might not know why, Paislee. Edwyn, now, I'm disappointed in him but mibbe they'll work it oot."

"Should I call Bennett?" Paislee lowered her knitting needles. "I'd want him tae call me if the situation was reversed, but that doesn't mean the same thing. Ignorance is bliss, could be."

"Bennett's a guid man . . . but, if you really want my opinion, I'd wait for a few days tae see how things fall oot *after* the math test."

"Why is that?"

"Well, if our Brody aces the thing, then it's proof that he's not the eejit that Lucas boy called him."

She frowned, her hands automatically creating the shell lace pattern.

"Not saying it's right, I'm just suggesting that it might work itself oot and then if you've got Bennett involved it could turn into something that the boys willnae be able tae fix on their own, ye see?"

That was actually fairly wise advice. Sage.

"I do. Thanks." Paislee changed the subject to something in her control. "Did you see the paper on the table? Fordythe is collecting canned goods. I just can't believe that *any* child might go hungry during the summer holiday."

"Should teach 'em all to fish and forage and they'd be fine." Grandpa raised his silvery brows. "Scotland is the land of plenty."

Paislee knitted the next row. "That might have worked for you while you were on your own, but that was only two weeks, and you're a grown man. Children require actual sustenance to be healthy."

"Och, lass, I was just gettin' yer goat." Grandpa sat up and gestured his mug at her. "No child should miss a meal."

The thought made her sad. "I'll call Sonya tomorrow morning and ask what else I can do. This cause is dear tae her and she might have some ideas."

"And you're going tae take it on? Ye barely have time for yourself as it is."

"I can't not know about the problem now, Grandpa. I'll plan tae buy extra when we pick up our messages tae donate tae the food bank. We might get groceries on sale, but we don't go hungry."

Grandpa nodded and got to his feet. "This conversation calls for a wee nip. Can I get you one?"

"Aye, please."

Her mobile rang and she looked down to see who it was. Lydia was at dinner with Corbin—she'd actually called it a date. At a fancy restaurant and dancing after. She'd sounded very happy.

"It's Blaise." Paislee set aside her knitting to answer. "Hiya!"

"Paislee?" Blaise had a thick voice as if she was upset.

"It's me. What's wrong?"

Paislee considered putting it on speaker but decided to wait in case what Blaise had to say was personal.

"It . . . it's . . ." Blaise took a deep breath. "That two-faced Lara just called me."

Uh-oh. "And?"

"I answered instead of letting it go tae voice mail because I thought this might be aboot Maxim, or school. Anyway, I answered and . . ." Blaise exhaled.

Paislee nodded encouragingly though Blaise couldn't see her.

"And that awful woman said that she, Mari, and Christina had talked aboot our get-together today. I am no longer invited tae the lunches."

"Isn't that what you wanted?"

"Well, sure," Blaise said, "but on my terms."

Paislee sucked in her lower lip to keep from laughing. "Hmm. All right. Just so I understand. You didn't want tae do the lunches, and now you don't have tae. And you're upset because . . ."

Blaise groaned. "That sounds very immature, eh? I was upset because they had Lara call. Not Mari. Not Christina. Lara. They sent the newbie." She chuckled in self-deprecation. "Anyway, that part of my life is officially over. Thanks for coming tae lunch. How are you?"

"I'm all right. Brody hurt his nose today playing football, though, so we're taking it easy on the porch." She made a mental note of the bullying similarities. How to teach Brody to stand up for himself, without him pushing back? It made her head spin.

"Poor sweetie!" Blaise crooned.

"He's fine." Paislee smoothed the soft yellow yarn. "We went out for ice cream."

"That fixes everything—at least in this house. What did the detective want?"

"I should have texted, sorry! DI Zeffer had already released Fergus, but he still wanted to know why we thought the chef wasn't guilty. He likes tae hear my thoughts on things and then he usually mocks me for not having proof tae back up my guesses."

"He's a bit of a hard-ass. Cute, though."

"In a frost-bite kind of way. When did you meet him?" Paislee was brought back to the awful day when Kirsten died. "Stupid question. Sorry."

"He reminds me of someone but I can't place it. I will, though. What's his first name?"

"Mack. Detective Inspector Mack Zeffer."

"So, I knew Fergus had been released," Blaise said. "He stopped by."

Paislee felt her jaw drop. "What did he want?"

"Fergus asked Shep for a recommendation, tae get a new job. Said he was ashamed of how he'd been acting."

Paislee straightened. Where was Grandpa with her drink? She'd need a double at this rate. "Shep knows he stole the gaming laptop? What did Fergus say about being fired for stealing?"

"Fergus didnae say for what, just that when Kirsten fired him Saturday morning, he demanded two weeks' notice and severance pay or he'd go tae Gerard aboot her affair with Anders. He sounded sincerely sorry for everything. And this is why I adore my husband."

"What did he do?"

"Shep took Fergus oot tae the green tae play nine holes and talk. He pointed oot that Fergus has lost two jobs now due tae partying, and he's stolen the laptop, which is a crime. He'll have tae go tae court and pay a fine. Shep really tried tae get him tae examine his life. He offered tae mentor him, if Fergus would go tae rehab."

Paislee glanced behind her to the kitchen door, thirsty. "That is nice—once he pays for his crimes."

"Aye. I feel the same. No getting off without paying the price, but after that, then yes. I think we should help."

They shared a laugh. "Where is Fergus now?"

Blaise shifted the phone. "His mum's house in Elgin."

"You know who's done a complete disappearing act? Anders Campbell." Paislee watched her son and dog in the grass.

"Sonya kicked him oot that day," Blaise said. "He was a liability tae the club, accusing Gerard like that. I mean, mibbe Gerard did it, but still."

"I'm curious where he went. What if Kirsten had tried tae break things off with him, and he went crazy? Decided that if he couldn't have her, nobody could?"

"That's terrible!"

Brody lobbed the ball and in a freak accident it bounced off the clothesline pole, then ricocheted back into his face. "Ow!" His nose spurted blood like a geyser.

"Oh no—I gotta go."

"Everything okay?"

"Fine!"

Paislee hung up and grabbed the first thing close at hand, the bright yellow shawl she was working on, but quickly exchanged that for an old towel draped over the chair.

"Brody, love, you've got tae be careful. If it doesn't stop bleeding, we're going tae call Doc Whyte." She pressed the towel to his nose, trying not to share her alarm.

Grandpa put their fortified tea mugs down on the small table on the porch. He descended the few steps and studied the bloody mess on her son's face. "It's just a scratch," he pronounced. "Mibbe we should pack it with mud, like Georgie did fer his cheek?"

Paislee began to wonder if there was something in the male DNA that rebelled against visiting a doctor.

Chapter 22

"Got your lunch? Your homework?" Paislee waited at the front door, keys in hand. They had ten minutes to get to Fordythe. Nervous perspiration broke out on her forehead like a fever. She'd had that awful dream again where she and Brody were late. Kirsten had made another nightly appearance, demanding justice. Was it any wonder she'd slept through her alarm?

"Aye." Brody lifted his backpack.

Wallace barked at the back door to be let out for the day. "I'll get it." Grandpa walked down the hall, dressed for work. Today was going to be a full day for all of them.

"It's a good thing Wallace remembered." Paislee eyed Brody's nose in the light shining into the foyer from the small window. A slight bluish-purple mark could be seen if she tilted her son's head just right. "Otherwise there might be a mess for us when we came home."

The dog was house-trained but he'd gotten used to Grandpa being here part of the day. Wallace would be fine no matter the weather. If it rained there was a covered back porch, but with these blue skies it wasn't likely.

Grandpa rubbed his hands as he joined them. "Ready."

They all trooped out and down the stairs to the Juke beneath the carport.

Paislee got behind the wheel, Brody in the back and Grandpa
riding shotgun, the rolled paper from breakfast under his arm.
They hadn't had a chance to read more than the first page—which
was an advertisement for the Nairn fresh market on Sunday.

"I think we should go," Paislee said.

"I want tae take you fly-fishing!" Brody countered.

"We can't do both. Can we?" She had no idea how long fishing
would take but was keen on checking out the market.

Grandpa buckled in. "Why not? Market in the morning, and
fish in the afternoon. I'll ask Georgie if there's a bad time for fly-
fishing."

"The market will be dumb." Brody tipped his backpack over.

"Why do ye think that?" She looked back at him.

He pursed his lips. "Who wants veggies?"

Grandpa scowled. "The lad has a point. My vote is for a day
on the river."

"Grandpa, your neep-and-tattie casserole is delicious. It would
be perfect with whatever fish we catch." She shivered at the idea
of fishing. It was not her idea of fun, but she'd made a promise to
herself to try new things for Brody's sake.

She had to set a good example.

"Aye, that's true, too." He nodded. "I'll call Georgie from the
shop."

"Can I help with the knife again, Grandpa?"

He turned and gave Brody the eye. "Ye mean the potato
peeler?"

Brody gulped. "Oh. Yeah."

"We'll see." Grandpa glanced at Paislee and scratched his beard
as if hiding a smile.

They were on a mission to get Brody a pocketknife, but she
was holding out till he was twelve.

They dropped Brody off at school as the bell rang, but before
Paislee let him out she reminded him to behave. "If there is trouble, like someone trying tae kick another ball tae your face, then

let Mrs. Martin or Headmaster McCall know. I won't stand for you being hurt at school, Brody."

"I'm not telling." His lip curled.

"Stand up for yourself, that's all, lad," Grandpa advised. "Dinnae fight back, but dinnae run scared, either." He shook a wrinkled fist. "I can show you a few self-defense moves."

Paislee bowed her head. "No. No fighting."

"He's got tae protect his face now." Grandpa humphed.

Brody scooted out of the vehicle. "Bye. See you right after school gets oot."

"That means he doesn't want to play football," she said to Grandpa as the door slammed.

Grandpa shrugged. "He'll be awright. Give it time."

"You're not tae encourage him tae be violent—I mean it."

"I can show him how tae block a few direct moves." Grandpa adjusted the seat belt over his shoulder. "It's different."

She sighed. Her mobile rang and she used her Bluetooth to answer, hands free. "Hello, this is Paislee."

"Hiya, Paislee. It's Sonya, from the club, returning your call aboot the next food drive."

That was fast. "Hi. A notice came home from the school about getting in more canned goods, and I remembered what you'd said about kids going hungry over the summer. I just want tae help."

"Why dinnae you stop by this morning and pick up some pamphlets?"

She noted the time. Cashmere Crush officially didn't open until ten. "You're there now? I can just pop in."

"Wonderful. I'll get it all together for you and then you can let me know if you have any questions."

Paislee ended the call.

"She sounds nice," Grandpa said. "I'd like tae see the property—there was a loch behind it once chock full of trout."

Leaving the school, she drove toward the club. "I have a confession about fishing this Sunday." His ears perked and he leaned close. "I just . . . between you and me, I just don't want tae put a worm on a hook. I know you think it's being a priss but . . . I just can't do it."

"Lucky for you, Georgie makes our flies—they're gorgeous things made tae resemble insects but are feathers. Your secret will be safe," he said with a chuckle.

She breathed out in relief. "And cleaning the fish?"

"I got you." Grandpa removed his glasses to wipe a smudge and put them back on. "Though I bet Brody would be chuffed tae do it for ye, too, and think it a game."

"That's smart thinking." Paislee tapped the wheel—her grandfather was a wily old man. "Hope you don't mind a quick stop before work? I can just run in if you want."

"Naw, I'm eager tae see the place since it's been refurbished."

Not four minutes later, Paislee parked before the Victorian brick building.

"It's like how it used tae be in its glory days," Grandpa said as they got out and walked toward the front door. "All brick and glass."

Paislee swallowed down a spurt of apprehension as Kirsten bubbled up to the surface. *No time for this right now.* By sheer force of will, Paislee pasted a smile on her face as she and Grandpa entered the spacious lobby of white marble and glass. Potted palms added to the soothing aesthetic.

Sonya waited at the front desk—she had a thin paper bag ready as promised. "Guid morning, Paislee. And who is this?"

"My grandfather, Angus Shaw."

"Sonya Marshal." Sonya, in an eggshell-colored pantsuit that Lydia would approve of, walked around the desk with her hand out to shake. "Pleased tae meet you."

"And you. I'll be joining some old fishing mates here for a party next month," he said, turning around admiringly. "This is well done."

"That's wonderful." Sonya clasped her hands. "Since the incident with Kirsten, well, we've had folks cancel their reservations."

"I'm sorry tae hear that." Paislee accepted the offered bag of information. "We'll be sure tae spread the word of your services. People will come around. The property is too beautiful tae be ignored for long."

"Your words tae God's ear," a masculine voice said, then Anders appeared from Sonya's private office. His brownish-blond hair was slicked back with gel, and his beige lightweight suit had not a wrinkle.

Paislee blinked with surprise and Sonya's cheeks tinted pink with embarrassment.

Oh, so she'd taken him back. Had he been laying low with Sonya this whole time?

It was none of her business, unless he was guilty, but she felt that it was too bad for Sonya, who deserved someone who loved her totally. Paislee could never share in a relationship.

"Hi, Paislee." Anders shook Grandpa's hand. "I'm Anders Campbell—co-director of the club."

"Anders! Nice tae see you again." Paislee swallowed down the polite lie. She had no desire to be friendly with this man who had cheated on Sonya, and with Kirsten, hurting Gerard and their little boy, Maxim.

"If ye have any questions, let me know." Anders brushed his hands together. "Paislee, as a business owner, perhaps you'd be interested in one of our sponsorship levels."

He and Kirsten had used Gerard to reach a premier level as if that brought prestige. Paislee stepped toward the door to leave rather than engage in conversation with a man she had no respect for, but Anders had his hand out to Grandpa. "Let me give you the tour."

"Anders, they're in a hurry," Sonya said, not looking at Paislee.

Grandpa, however, was already walking down the hall, leaving the ladies no choice but to follow.

"I'm . . ." Sonya tried to explain.

Paislee inched ahead to make it clear that she wasn't judging the woman, but she didn't want to talk about it, either. Since she was here, she recalled wondering about the cooking facilities. "I'd actually like tae see the kitchen . . . is it down this way?"

"At the very end of the hall."

They dutifully admired all of the conference spaces between the lobby and the end of the building.

"Just our office and the studio suite by the front there," Anders said. "And this is the big conference room, where the Nairn Food Bank event was held."

Without the tables and the dais, the space was enormous. "You could have five parties in here," Grandpa said.

"Angus, the fisherman's party you'll be at is next tae this one," Sonya said. "There's a theater here, too."

Grandpa smoothed back a strand of silver-gray hair. "I was here as a younger man and this is quite the turnaround from what was old, tae modern. I like it."

Sonya's eyes glowed with pleasure.

"Why the kitchen, Paislee?" Anders opened a door to a space that was double the size of hers—but still not huge. She had a moment of longing for the brand-new silver refrigerator but let it go.

Did Anders have a reason to want Kirsten out of the way? If he loved her, and they were planning on running away together, it didn't make sense for him to kill her. Mari had said Kirsten wasn't serious about Anders, though.

She cleared her throat when he stared at her expectantly. "Oh, I was just wondering that day of the cookie contest if the kitchen had been used for any baking."

Sonya and Anders exchanged a look, then Sonya shook her head. "As you can see, no cooker. We have an electric kettle, a coffee machine, and a microwave to reheat things. The refrigerator. We didn't want the hassle of needing a food-and-liquor license."

"Not even a toaster oven," Paislee said.

"We have cling wrap and foil." Anders pulled out a drawer. "Fergus arranged the plates for the judges at Kirsten's request tae make sure that they were all the same. He'd also prepped sixty dishes with shortbread for the vendors."

Paislee realized that whoever had added the new topping to Kirsten's shortbread would have had to have baked it off this property and brought it in.

Fergus had every opportunity to add it in private. He had means, and motive.

As if he'd read her mind, Anders said, "I hear they arrested Fergus for stealing the gaming laptop, and also for Kirsten's murder."

Paislee didn't say that the man was free but asked, "You think he did it?"

Anders set his jaw. "He was the only person back here."

"Surely not the only one," Paislee persisted. "Gerard, or her friends . . . what about her assistant, Lara . . . ?"

"I dinnae like or respect Gerard Buchanan." Anders raised his chin.

"I know. You accused him of murder," Paislee reminded him, and Sonya.

Sonya gulped. "Well, we went through all of the footage, Paislee. Gerard is in full sight at all times. If he added the crumble, he didnae do it here."

"The man didn't cook. Too guid for that. You should have heard him drone on about archaic gender roles." Anders shut the kitchen door and started back down the long hall.

"Did Gerard and Kirsten arrive that morning together?" she asked.

Anders nodded. "Hendrie drove them."

"Hendrie and Fergus were friends, I think," Sonya said. "Why else would Hendrie have helped Fergus steal the laptop?"

"They were," Paislee said.

Sonya continued, "There's a status among the staff of wealthy families, did you know that?"

"No." Paislee put her hand in her khaki pocket as they walked.

"How so?" Grandpa asked.

"Well," Sonya explained in a teacher-ish tone, "the chauffer for the Buchanans might not have as much social clout as, say, the prime minister's driver. The chef for the earl will have more clout than your average millionaire's cook."

Paislee smiled—this was not her reality. "Where would it gain them prestige?"

"Parties. Invites tae private houses."

Parties? It was possible that the subsocial scene was where Fergus had gotten in over his head, wanting to live the glittery life among his peers. "I had no idea."

"Well, you're rather naïve," Anders pointed out.

"Anders!"

"It's true, Sonya." He raised his hands. "God, dinnae shoot the messenger, love. It's cute."

Fergus had referred to Hendrie as a mate of sorts. Hendrie had held the door open for Fergus, and then driven Fergus to Highland Academy, where Fergus had sold the gaming laptop. For a chunk of the money? Out of the goodness of his heart?

Paislee schooled her features before facing Anders. "Did you get the console back?"

"Naw—but the parents paid us four thousand for it, so that we wouldnae press charges. All turned oot all right in the end. Money in the coffers for the food bank, aye?" Anders had the slick tone of a salesman.

Was that all right? Where was the responsibility for the child to learn not to buy stolen goods . . . wait, the charges had been dropped? Was that why Zeffer had released Fergus? And him not saying anything . . . och!

Paislee breathed a sigh of relief when they reached the gorgeous lobby. She lifted the bag. "Well, thank you for the tour. I'll call you, Sonya, once I read through this."

Sonya smiled. "You can do as much or as little as ye like. It would be simple tae put a box for food donations in your shop. Or you might want tae commit tae a monthly cash donation."

"I'll think on it," Paislee said as they left the club.

Grandpa climbed in the passenger side and Paislee behind the wheel. They each wore that polite fake smile you wear when you think someone is watching.

Once they reached the end of the car park, Grandpa's shoulders sagged. "What on earth was that all aboot? What is that lovely woman doing with that dunderhead?"

"I don't know, Grandpa. Anders was the one having the affair with Kirsten, while he and Sonya had an open relationship. She didn't like it and kicked him out when she found out but he's wormed his way back into her life."

"Some women cannae function withoot a man."

"I appreciate wanting a partner, but it's easier tae do things for yourself than be stuck with someone ye can't trust."

"You've been raised right, lass. Agnes would be verra proud."

Chapter 23

Paislee kept busy all day and sent Grandpa to pick up Brody so they could go home and have dinner, just the two of them. Any spare minute she had between customers and setting up for the Thursday night Knit and Sip, she got in a few rows on her knitting projects. She was currently juggling three.

Lydia and Blaise arrived at quarter till six, each carrying appetizers. Amelia walked in from the station, her black leather backpack filled with her knitting over her shoulder. "I heard the DI cursing up a storm this week. Sometimes I hear your name, Paislee," Amelia said with a laugh.

"*Mine?*" Paislee asked innocently. She was still a trifle annoyed that Zeffer hadn't shared the real reason he'd let Fergus free. Dropped charges.

"Hi, Lydia, Blaise. Mm. What did you create for us this week, Lydia?"

Lydia lifted the lid off a ceramic dish of something cheesy and gooey. "Artichoke and fennel dip with homemade tortilla strips."

Amelia pulled a tin of chocolate-covered almonds from her bag and set them on the counter. "Here's my contribution, since I dinnae cook."

"Chocolate is always perfect. Whisky?" Lydia asked.

"Of course!" Amelia took a seat. Paislee had set the chairs and stools in a loose circle near the high-top tables Lydia used as a serving counter and bar.

Lydia uncovered the bowl of cut fruit from Blaise as Elspeth Booth, tall and slender with a stylish silver bob, came in. She carried her knitting in a cloth bag and was currently working on a new afghan for her couch. She shared a house with her blind sister, Susan.

Mary Beth was the last to arrive, out of breath. "Sairy! I was just finishing up dinner for the family. Arran should be able tae put dishes into the washer, but no. You'd think I was asking him and the girls tae walk into the middle of a busy street blindfolded. Do I look like the maid?"

Her husband, Arran Mulholland, was a talented solicitor and their twin girls were eight and quite lovely—all of them plump due to Mary Beth's fabulous cooking.

"Why did you ask Arran tae do it instead of the maid?" Blaise asked.

"Oh, love, we dinnae really have a maid. I was being verra sarcastic. No, normally it is my delight tae take care of the house and raise the girls and Arran earns for our family, but on Thursday nights he can pitch in. The girls, too. Is that so wrong?"

"Not at all," Amelia agreed.

"Sounds very traditional," Elspeth said.

"You all know how important my Thursday evenings with you are." Mary Beth sank as daintily as a large woman could onto a wooden chair.

Paislee chuckled. "I'm glad tae see you." She sat in another chair, and brought the yellow shawl she was working on to her lap.

"What's the conversation tae be aboot tonight?" Elspeth asked.

"The murder, of course," Blaise said. She was on her second coin purse so that her daughter, Suzannah, could give one to a friend.

Mary Beth's cornflower-blue eyes twinkled. "As it should be—I saw the paper. Paislee, what did we talk aboot before DI Zeffer came tae town?"

"I remember," Lydia said with a laugh. "Widower Mann and his stream of loves at the retirement home."

"He's still at it." Elspeth pursed her lips even as her slender shoulders shook.

"Well, I dinnae ken aboot the murder part but Kirsten's funeral will be Saturday at the church, and then an open house at the Buchanans." Blaise glanced up from her project. "They just decided today on the time."

"Why the delay?" Mary Beth asked.

"Shep said that Gerard was having difficulty accepting what happened, but they were finally able tae reach him with reason." She sighed. "He's been heavily into the bottle all week, poor man."

"No answers tae be found there." Mary Beth used to drink whisky herself but now she stuck to iced tea or fizzy waters—she'd lost some weight by doing so and claimed to be all around healthier.

"I suppose not," Elspeth said. "Speaking of, Lydia, may I have a glass of white wine?"

Lydia poured a healthy glass and delivered it to Elspeth. "There ye are."

Blaise smiled at Lydia, then Paislee. "You both are invited tae the funeral and afterward, tae the Buchanans."

Paislee's smile slipped. "I can't go tae a funeral on Saturday, Blaise. It's our busiest day."

"It's at eleven," Blaise pleaded. "We're having our chef send over a big casserole, and a roasted lamb."

Lydia nodded, but didn't commit when she saw Paislee shake her head.

"I really want you and Lydia tae come." Blaise shrugged. "I mean, it would be strange if you didnae."

Strange? Paislee kept knitting with her head down as she said, "We only know her through you. We weren't personal friends." She looked at Blaise directly. "Not strange at all."

"But you were vendors at the fund-raiser," Blaise countered as if it was only good manners to show up at the funeral even if you barely knew the person.

"It's been very hard this week already!" Paislee spoke to Lydia, and the group, ignoring Blaise's pouting lip. "I've turned into a lady who lunches and I don't recommend it. I'm behind on my custom orders and Grandpa is going tae demand either a raise, or that we hire another person, which I can't afford tae do. Sorry."

Amelia raised her hand as if they were in school. "I'll help you, Paislee. I can work on Saturdays through tourist season, if you like. I'm not doing anything else."

"Really? I mean, not this Saturday, but through summer?" That would be a relief.

Her friend nodded and sipped amber liquid from her tumbler.

Paislee trusted Amelia and liked her—Amelia was good with visitors at the police station. So, why not? "Let's try it out. I can pay a wee bit more than minimum wage."

"Fine. Or if you're strapped, I'll work for store credit."

"How sweet!" Mary Beth said.

"I can pay her," Paislee told them all.

"I think that's a great idea." Lydia hugged Amelia's shoulders. Amelia blushed.

"So, you can come tae the funeral," Blaise announced, without a question. "I'll need moral support. Go ahead, Paislee, tell them how it was at the Brick and Ivy."

"You went there?" Mary Beth asked, impressed. "The lamb chops are melt in your mouth."

"We did," Paislee said. "It was terrific, but . . ."

"What?" Elspeth asked, forgoing her afghan for wine and gossip.

"The company almost ruined the meal," Paislee said.

"I've eaten there," said Mary Beth. "The company would have tae be really, really bad."

Mary Beth and Elspeth laughed.

"It was. Toxic." Lydia scooped dip onto a small paper plate and put an assortment of dried tortilla strips along it. "Who wants tae nibble?"

"Me!" Amelia said, rising to get the dish.

Lydia handed the knitters each one while they worked. She

loved Thursday nights and was their official hostess even though she didn't knit.

"Who was the ringleader?" Mary Beth asked. "Now that Kirsten is gone?"

"I think they're jockeying for position." Lydia held her wine-glass. "Mari, Christina, or Lara."

"I've heard of the other two, but who is Lara?" Mary Beth asked.

Paislee explained, "Lara was Kirsten's personal assistant, and Maxim's tutor, who got promoted tae lunch partner when Blaise 'couldn't' make all the lunches after moving tae Nairn."

"I've never had tae creatively get oot of more social events . . ." Blaise slid a tortilla through the dip and put it in her mouth. "Oh, yum, Lydia."

"Thanks. Paislee, how is Brody's nose today?"

"There's a wee bit of a bruise but it wasn't broken. What rotten luck tae smack himself in the face a second time." Paislee shook her head.

"Poor lad." Elspeth clucked her tongue to her teeth. "Wait, a second time?"

"Aye." Paislee ate a chocolate-covered almond, then wiped her fingers on a paper napkin to make sure the yarn stayed clean. "I just don't understand bullies."

Blaise looked up from her coin purse. "What? I didnae realize that the first time was deliberate. You said a ball tae the face?"

"Schools have zero tolerance for that kind of behavior," Mary Beth said immediately.

"Hamish met me at the curb with Brody at his side tae explain that all of the boys said it was an accident. He didn't believe them but what else could he do? I mean, Brody told me in the car that a lad had done it on purpose but he wouldn't be telling and grassing up his mates, thank you very much."

"Of course not," Amelia said. "Then it would be worse for him later. He'll need tae stand up for himself."

"You sound like Grandpa, Amelia. We don't condone violence."

"If ye haven't noticed, it's a violent world. Murders here in Nairn, even." Amelia shrugged.

"I hate that you're right. But still." Paislee told her empathetic friends what had happened and the hurt feelings being worse than the ball to the face. "How am I supposed tae raise a good man in this kind of world?"

"Brody is a sweet lad," Lydia said. "He's cute and smart and funny."

"Can ye tell she's biased?" Paislee looked to the ceiling even as she smiled. "Lydia, this all started because your prodigy was more interested in building sugar bridges tae watch the ants than his math problems."

Mary Beth and Blaise both burst into laughter. "Thank heaven I have girls," Mary Beth said.

"I was just thinking the same! Suzannah is a daydreamer, though." Blaise pointed her knitting needle at Paislee. "And I told you I'd help tutor Brody if he needs it."

"I appreciate it, Blaise. Right now, Grandpa and I have decided tae see how things shake out tomorrow—after the quiz."

"It's smart tae not make a big deal of it, I suppose," Amelia said.

"That is what I hope." Paislee sipped her wine, which had appeared at her side like magic. "This is sweet—I like it."

"A moscato," Lydia said. "I knew you would."

"Oh! I spoke tae Sonya today—she's back with Anders." Paislee quickly filled the other ladies in on what was going on, including that the crumble would have had to have been baked somewhere else.

"Sonya is too smart tae take back a dog like that," Lydia said. "I was telling Corbin about her and—"

"Corbin?" Amelia asked.

Lydia fanned her suddenly pink face. "Well. He's been pestering me, so I agreed tae go on another date."

"This makes three," Paislee said with a grin.

"Awesome!" Blaise clapped. The other women all cheered—
Lydia deserved someone wonderful. Everybody did.

"Anyway," Lydia said, "I told him aboot the brilliant work
she's done at the social club and he's agreed tae have one of his
business functions there."

"Nairn Social Cub. Who knew?" Elspeth paused to get a sip of
wine and then start another row.

"It's a lovely building with such history," Blaise said. "I hope
it's a huge success."

"When Grandpa and I were there this morning tae pick up
information about the food bank we got a tour. Sonya said some of
the reservations were cancelled, so that will be good news for her."

"What information?" Mary Beth asked. "Does this have tae
do with the letter that came home from Fordythe aboot another
canned food drive?"

Paislee nodded. "I can't imagine a child going hungry just because school isn't in session."

"It's shameful," Elspeth said. "Father Dixon always kept a box
oot for donations, but it never seemed tae be enough."

"Did he take the items to the food pantry, or hand them out to
parishioners himself?" Paislee glanced up at Elspeth.

"I used tae handle that as part of my job. We kept the closet
open for families in need. Some accepted the help—others took
too much, and others not enough." Elspeth smiled. "I loved being
able to drop off goodies as a surprise. They needed not just food
but clothes. Blankets."

They all looked at the blanket she was making.

"We could do blankets," Amelia said. "For winter. Caps,
scarves."

"Definitely!" Paislee agreed. "I love the idea of assisting those
in our neighborhood."

"That is so doable." Lydia whisked out a pad of paper by the
register and grabbed a pen. "What's the most urgent need?"

Paislee said, "I think Sonya's raised enough money to get things that are important for Nairn and the surrounding areas they support. People don't come into my shop carrying cans of food, so maybe I can do a donation jar for people's change tae donate for Fordythe Primary, specifically."

"Surely there are programs through the school," Lydia suggested.

Mary Beth jumped in, "That's where kids in poorer families get their meals. There is funding for that, but when class is not in session . . . well, not all of the bairns eat."

"What aboot their parents?" Lydia asked. "Dinnae they work?"

Amelia shrugged. "Times can be hard. My folks didnae have much money when they raised us. Dad fished, my brothers hunt even now. Mom has a small garden."

"Did you go tae the church, or food bank?" Elspeth asked. "When things were tight?"

"Naw."

"Why not?" Paislee turned to Amelia.

"Scots Pride." Amelia lifted her tumbler.

"That's fine if you're an adult, and make that choice," Mary Beth said. "But surely not for the weans."

"There were not many nights we went tae bed hungry," Amelia said defensively. "Now, it might have been venison jerky and water, but it was what we had."

"I wish I'd known when you were younger," Elspeth said. "I would've stopped at your house like a fairy godmother. What did you want?"

Amelia grinned. "I was the weird kid that wanted salad." She sipped her whisky. "I have a guid job now but I learned how tae survive at a young age."

"If you have kids of your own?" Blaise asked.

"Och, I'll not have bairns. I cannae even commit tae a pup."

Paislee reached over to pat Amelia on the knee. "I admire the person you are. I'm glad tae have you saving my life on Saturdays."

Amelia half smiled.

There was something to be said for the character earned by not being born with that silver spoon.

What would Gran think of all this? Maybe the lesson would be that no matter how you enter this life, it's full of things to learn in order to grow into your best self.

She thought of that until Lydia pushed her arm. "What?"

"What are you thinking?" Lydia lifted the wine bottle to top her glass off.

She shook her head—between Grandpa and Amelia her emotions were on the raw side and wine wouldn't make it better. "Nothing important. What am I going tae do about Brody and the mean kids?"

"I thought you were going tae wait." Lydia brought the bottle back to the high-top table.

"Kids that bully grow up into adults that bully—I've seen it for myself." Blaise offered her opinion hesitantly as if not wanting to offend any of them.

"You're right." Mary Beth jabbed her needle into a ball of yarn. "I have never been thin and my weight has made me a target. I fear for my girls. I'm trying tae teach them tae be confident and kind, and healthy, too. It's not easy."

"No . . ." Blaise commiserated. "It's not. Do you realize that Kirsten was so awful she told her son not tae play with my Suzannah? And for the other kids in the clique, too. I had no idea. Just found that oot yesterday."

Mary Beth sighed. "What did Suzannah say?"

"Well, I asked her right away. She hadnae noticed—she's playing with a new girl. I'm making an extra coin purse so that Suzannah can bring her a present."

"Bribing kids tae be your friend isnae healthy, either," Amelia said.

"I'm no—oh, am I?" Blaise sat back in surprise. "I just thought it would be nice!"

"Are you making them for all kids in class?" Mary Beth asked.

"No." Blaise paled.

"Well, then . . ." Mary Beth shrugged. "Maybe wait and invite her over for a special one-on-one playdate and give it tae her then."

"That's a better idea," Elspeth chimed in. Paislee also agreed.

"I should just pull her from Highland Academy," Blaise said in a miserable tone.

"The year is almost over." Lydia gave Blaise more chips with dip. "You can make it. If you want tae."

Blaise exhaled and looked at Paislee. "Aboot Brody . . . I think you should talk tae the teacher and the headmaster. Kids shouldnae be allowed tae get away with being mean."

How to protect your child without making them a target? "We'll know more tomorrow, after the quiz."

"I love the idea of helping those in our neighborhood, Paislee." Lydia changed the subject to something positive and raised her sheet of paper. "I'm going tae devise a brilliant plan."

"We'll help, too," the ladies all said.

Paislee was grateful to be surrounded by true friends.

The more the idea settled, the more she was also grateful to go to Kirsten's funeral Saturday, a week to the day of the socialite's death. It would give her a chance to see who actually mourned Kirsten Buchanan, and who rejoiced that the witch was dead.

Chapter 24

Bully on the playground. Brody was at Fordythe with Edwyn, arguing over a bloody football, then the scene changed and the kids were gone. She and Lydia were behind the social club, beneath the beech tree. *Bully in designer clothes.* Paislee watched the rise and fall of Kirsten Buchanan's chest as she kneeled by her body. Her lips stung from pressing down on Kirsten's mouth.

Fergus, Gerard, Christina, Hendrie. Anders. Sonya. Mari. Lara. Blaise. Hendrie, opening the door for her and Lydia that morning with a friendly smile under his chauffer's cap. Hendrie, supposedly napping on the job. Fergus calling Hendrie a mate. Hendrie helping Fergus unload the stolen gaming laptop at the private school.

Paislee tossed her head on her pillow. Anxiety and trepidation filled her as she realized that despite her efforts, Kirsten was dying on the grass behind the club. Fallen shortbread at Fergus's shoes. The pulse at her neck thrummed. Perspiration soaked her sheets as she curled her fingers into them to find an anchor.

In her dream, Kirsten's eyes flung open, death gleaming from the brown orbs. Paislee gasped and sucked in air as she sat straight up in her bed with a chilling fright.

You are not my friend! She reached over and flicked on the bedside lamp to illuminate her bedroom with ghost-banishing light.

Her heart thudded as she scanned her room for anything out of the ordinary.

No ghosts. Kirsten, whose memory she'd denied daytime examination in order to cope with what had happened, and her part in it by failing to save her, was now taking over her dreams.

Paislee, mouth dry, shoved the comforter back and left her room to use the bathroom across the hall.

Wallace joined her, watching her as she splashed water on her face. His tail wagged back and forth, his head cocked, ears up, then he placed one paw on her shin.

She scratched his head. "Good boy. I'm all right. We are all right. No ghosts. Oh, what a nightmare, Wallace."

Paislee got a glimpse of her image, wide light blue eyes with shadows beneath them, cheeks sunken, reminding her of a skull. Death.

She bent down and splashed more water to clear the image.

Paislee grabbed her mobile then quietly went down the stairs to the kitchen, missing the third and fifth steps so they wouldn't creak. Wallace padded behind her and she let him out—it was so early, the sky was still dark.

Filling the electric kettle, she pressed the on lever and stepped back, hands around her waist.

How utterly terrifying. During this past week, Paislee had managed to somehow push the memory of what happened away but Kirsten wasn't waiting anymore.

Pouring hot water over a Brodies tea ball in a mug, she shuffled out the back door to the screened porch and sat on the step. Wallace lay next to her and they surveyed the back garden.

Shed, clothesline, Gran's flowerpots. She patted her pup and gradually the fear receded.

"What does it mean, boy? What was Kirsten trying tae tell me?"

Wallace wagged his tail. She thought back to Saturday afternoon and how things had happened. Hendrie had been there, in the background, all along.

She sent a text to Blaise to have her call her later. Blaise might know more about the Buchanan chauffer. Smiling, affable. He would have seen everything going on and watched in silence. What if he had a grudge against Kirsten Buchanan?

Her phone rang right away and she jumped, staring at the device in her palm. It was nearing half past five in the morning, and she hadn't thought Blaise would be awake.

"Oh, I'm sorry—I hope I didn't wake you."

"No." Blaise's voice was a near whisper. "The police just left. They're searching for Fergus."

"Again? But he didn't do it!"

Blaise started to cry. "Hendrie is dead, Paislee. And they think Fergus did it."

A dart of fear shot through her chest and she scrambled to her feet, looking around the yard. For what? A thin figure in a hoodie?

"They don't know where he is?"

"No."

"How did Hendrie die?"

"The constable wouldnae say. Paislee, what did ye want tae talk aboot?"

"Hendrie."

"What?" Blaise's question seemed loud though it was her normal voice.

Paislee leaned against the wicker armchair, one hand at her stomach. "I had the worst dream about Hendrie, and Kirsten, and Fergus." She told Blaise about it in a rush, goose bumps prickling her skin. "I'm on my back porch, still frightened. That's never happened tae me before."

"What does it mean?"

"Maybe my subconscious had picked up that Hendrie knew something about Kirsten's death."

"You're not wrong—someone else put that together, too," Blaise said. "And killed him."

"Before he could tell the police what he knew." Paislee paced the natural wood boards rather than sit. Lighter gray colored the horizon from charcoal. Dawn was coming, if she could just hold on. Morning would chase the last of her fears away. "I think it was Gerard. Gerard killed Hendrie, and Kirsten."

"I told Constable Dean that we didnae think it was Fergus. This is terrible."

"I know." Overwhelmed, Paislee sank down in the wicker chair and made room for Wallace on her lap. The pup jumped up and gave her hand a lick.

"What should we do?"

"What can we do? If I tell the DI that I had a bad dream about Hendrie he will never speak tae me about a case again." She pushed hair from her face. "And that would be *after* he got over his fit of laughter."

Blaise sighed. In the background she could hear a phone ring. "Hang on," Blaise said as she muffled the speaker on her phone. Then, "The police have Fergus."

"Can Shep go talk tae him? Ask him about Gerard?"

"I'm sure he'll try. He really wants tae help the guy. I have tae go . . . we'll talk later, okay? And tell Brody guid luck on his math quiz today."

That had fallen off her radar. "Thanks, Blaise."

Paislee gazed out over the lightening sky. Birds chirped and the world woke up. Wallace was warm on her lap.

But did they have the right man in jail? *Enough*. It was time to get Kirsten out of mind again and put on her Mum hat. She went inside to make Lorne sausage and eggs for breakfast—it was not a cereal kind of day.

"What's all this?" Brody said when he, sleepy-eyed, joined her and Grandpa at the table.

"It's a special day—you'll need extra energy for your quiz."

His nose scrunched and Paislee tried not to focus on the slight bruising from the bridge to his left eye. It made her very angry that the act had been deliberate. She and Grandpa fired math questions at him while they ate and he aced every one.

He finally said, "No more!" Paislee didn't miss his confidence in himself, which mattered to her more than his getting an extra recess.

They were all ready to leave for the day by half past eight and it felt good to spend an extra five minutes with Wallace outside before loading into the Juke. The sky was bonny blue and the shadows of her nightmare banished as she'd hoped.

They arrived at Fordythe and Paislee turned to Brody when it was their turn to drop off in queue at the curb. He was in the backseat and opened the door to hop out. "You know those answers upside down and backward," she assured him. "Maybe you can get extra credit if you stand on your head and get them all right?"

He slung his backpack over his arm and grinned, waving.

"You got this!" Grandpa shouted with his window rolled down.

The kids all entered the building to go to their classrooms. No Hamish, no Mrs. Martin. Brody didn't want her to talk to the headmaster or his teacher and said if she did he wouldn't tell her things in the future.

She felt as if her hands were tied—but just until after today.

They drove toward Cashmere Crush. "So," Grandpa said, "what's botherin' ye, lass?"

"What? Nothing." She checked her mirrors and glanced at him with a shrug.

He removed his glasses to give her a good staring at.

"I had a nightmare last night, that's all."

"Aboot?" he pressed.

She blew out a breath. Maybe if she told him about it, it would go away. "Kirsten. I was with her at the end, and I guess I can't just get over it."

He nodded to show he was listening.

"Kirsten was a bully and had no real friends. My dream started with Brody and Edwyn on the field at Fordythe, but then changed tae the social club."

"I'm not surprised that you dreamed aboot what happened. Her killer hasnae been caught, and you're verra smart when it comes tae figuring oot these things."

"I don't know about that," she said with a snort. "My mind decided that Hendrie, the Buchanan chauffer, might be a good witness. He's always around in the background. So I talked tae Blaise—"

"This morning?" His voice resonated with surprise.

"Aye." Paislee looked over at him. "She was already up when I texted her—the police were at her house searching for Fergus."

"But they'd released him."

"Because the charges were dropped for the theft of the gaming laptop. The DI probably didn't have evidence tae hold him for Kirsten's murder, because he didn't do it. Now they think he killed Hendrie."

Grandpa reached across the console to pat her shoulder. "Hendrie's dead? How?"

"I don't know."

"Oh, lass." He straightened. "So, Fergus is on the loose?"

"Naw, they've got him now. Shep is going tae try and talk tae him." She turned right. "I'd love tae know what Hendrie meant about something he said to the police that day—about nobody being around that wasn't supposed tae be."

"You can't go yourself?"

"Naw." She considered Constable Dean's or the DI's reaction if she just showed up at the jail—she'd be escorted right back out.

"I suppose being curious isnae a guid enough reason," he chuckled.

She parked behind the shop. James waved from his back stoop. "I have tae go tae the Buchanan funeral tomorrow."

"What? Paislee, I—"

"Hang on. I'd like you tae train Amelia Henry—she's going tae be there the whole day so you can have assistance."

"From the police station?"

"Yep. She's going tae help us out on Saturdays for a while. I think you'd do a wonderful job showing her the ropes."

"Oh . . ." He rubbed his beard.

"And of course, I'll be giving you a slight raise."

At that he smiled wide.

"Also, I've decided tae order another mobile. We can pick it up later tonight. It will be for the house, but you and Brody will probably share it."

"You're making all kinds of decisions."

She nodded—if she didn't, who would? "Grandpa, I know you can't commit tae staying with us, but I would like you tae. No matter what happens with Craigh."

"Oh." His eyes widened behind his glasses and he unbuckled his seat belt, looking away. "We'll see. I cannae promise anything."

"Yeah. I know." They each got out, and she locked the doors of the Juke. They walked up the back steps and into Cashmere Crush together.

"We have a yarn delivery today," she said. "Do you mind clearing space on the shelf next to the beige skeins from JoJo's?"

They went about their morning in companionable silence, in the routine of setting up the shop for the day. She put music on low, counted the till, and then checked for online custom sweater orders.

She hoped to get her three projects down to two today, finishing up the yellow shawl. The instant she sat down to begin work, Kirsten's memory surfaced. Knowing she stood to make a fool of herself, she called the DI and left a message for him to call her back.

When her mobile rang, it was Blaise, not the detective. "They willnae let Shep talk with Fergus. Fergus hasnae been officially charged with anything—they're just holding him for questioning. Shep threatened to get a solicitor if needed."

"Mary Beth's husband, Arran, might be able tae help. Fergus is lucky tae have a champion."

"Shep is all aboot the underdog." Blaise's tone was filled with love for her partner. "So, I'm calling tae invite you, your grandfather, and Brody over tonight for fish and chips on the green. We can let them all hit buckets of balls—unless you have other plans? This is last minute."

A Friday night? Of course they were free. "I'll ask."

"It'll be fun, I promise. I invited Lydia but she's having dinner with Corbin again."

"She's smitten and I couldn't be happier." Paislee adjusted the phone against her ear. "What will we be doing while they are hitting the balls?"

"I'm glad you caught that. *We* will make our own list of who might have access tae the Buchanan car. Who Hendrie might have seen. I called Sonya tae have a peek at her security footage. She wasnae sure if she should send it, but I promised a hefty contribution tae the food bank."

As they ended the call, Paislee realized that Gran and Lydia were right—a person caught a lot more flies with honey. Especially the green kind.

Chapter 25

The DI still hadn't returned Paislee's call by the time she left the shop to pick up Brody from school at half past three. She'd spent all afternoon worrying over how he'd done on his test like a tiny knot in an otherwise perfect sweater.

She parked ten minutes early to go inside. Mrs. Jimenez greeted her with a broad smile. "Hi, Paislee!"

"Afternoon . . . how are you?" She slung her purse over her shoulder.

"Just fine." She'd been typing on her computer keyboard but lifted her fingers from the *tap, tap, tap.* "Here tae see the headmaster? He's actually in with Mrs. Martin's class."

Oh no. "Is everything all right?"

"They're celebrating! I hear the occasional shout. Go on doon. After you sign in, of course." Mrs. Jimenez returned to typing.

Paislee scrawled her name on the sheet, then hurried down the linoleum hall. She could hear cheers from the very end, which was Mrs. Martin's classroom. Was there a birthday going on?

She knocked and Hamish opened the door for her—he looked rather smug in his brown suit with the plaid tie in the blue and red school colors.

"What's going on?"

Brody saw her and grinned with two thumbs-up.

"All of the students got a hundred percent." Hamish crossed his arms, pleased as any proud parent. "Mrs. Martin and I got tae talking after what happened on the field the other day"—he didn't name names, but she knew he was referring to Brody and Edwyn—"and while competition is vital tae reaching new heights, we decided tae make it inclusive of all the students."

"What does that mean?" Paislee shook her head, confused.

"Brody had shown marked improvement and when Mrs. Martin asked how he'd been doing it, he shared your strategy of flashcards and pop quizzes at home." He nodded at her with approval.

"We just wanted tae help."

"So, we did that here, too. Well, Mrs. Martin did it. Every student who got them all right was given flashcards tae assist the ones that were straggling, making it a group activity, all working toward the same goal—extra recess for everybody, but earned."

Paislee noticed that Brody and Edwyn seemed to be getting along. "Who is the other boy with Brody?"

"Samuel."

"Ah." She recognized Lucas from a few days ago. How she'd love to give the boy a good talking to. "And things have been better there, too?"

"I think so."

"That's great, then." They shared a smile, on the same side for once in a long time. She'd missed that feeling.

Clearing her throat, she pushed away from the wall to join Mrs. Martin. "Success," she said overly brightly.

"Ms. Shaw." The middle-aged teacher clasped her hand. "Brody really improved this week. I hear you engaged with him at home?"

"We did. Being prepared helped his confidence."

"Well, he earned the extra recess and helped the other kids, too. You should be proud of him."

She smiled her thanks. "I am. If he starts tae build any more sugar ant bridges just let me know and we'll try tae nip the problem in the bud."

"Kids will be kids." Mrs. Martin leaned her head toward Paislee. "I wasnae too concerned. Tae a ten-year-old, ants are much more interesting than math."

Paislee appreciated the woman's down-to-earth philosophy.

"And how are things with you at home? Grandpa settling in?"

"He is. It's been nice tae have the help, tae be honest."

"Well . . ." She winked and gestured to her family photo on her desk with her kids and grandkids. "When you're ready tae date just let me know. I still have one son single. I just know you'd get on."

It was the second time the teacher had tried to set Paislee up, but Paislee was not ready for that. "I actually had a question for you about the food drive. I'd love tae help local families over the summer holiday. I don't have a lot extra, but if you know of anyone, no names needed, I'll do what I can."

Mrs. Martin adjusted the glasses that had been sliding down her nose. "Let me think aboot that. Cans are always welcome. Oatmeal is easy. Cereal."

"I feel like I've had a blindfold removed, after working at the social club this last weekend for the Nairn Food Bank. I guess I didn't realize how close tae home we have hungry kids. I'd like tae do my part."

"You've been working hard tae provide a home for your son. There is no shame in that." Mrs. Martin squeezed Paislee's forearm.

"Thanks. You'll let me know? It can be an anonymous donation."

"All right. I've got tae get back tae the class . . . I'll be sending home information about the end-of-year party, too. You've signed on tae chaperone."

"Looking forward tae it." Paislee stepped back. The party was going to be at the golf course. Maybe it was time to learn the game.

When she glanced back to the door, Hamish was gone.

She and Brody left the school in high spirits. "Congratulations! I'm really proud of you, love."

"Thanks, Mum."

"I saw you and Edwyn hanging out."

"Yeah. Samuel, too. Lucas said he was sairy for kicking the ball at me."

"He did? That's great." All of her worrying and it had worked out on its own. Grandpa had the right of it. "What did ye say? 'Get lost'?" She smiled at him.

Brody laughed. "Thought aboot it, but then changed my mind. I asked myself what you would say."

"Ah, Brody . . ." She reached across the console to touch his arm.

"Edwyn felt bad aboot calling me an eejit, but that was kinda my fault for goofin' off in class. I didnae like it."

"So you changed it." Paislee's heart was so full it might burst.

"Yep. Can we get ice cream? Or Chinese?"

"Actually, we've been invited for fish and chips at Blaise O'Connor's house. She said you can hit a bucket of balls, whatever that means."

He scowled. "But Suzannah is a girl, and younger than me."

"Hey! Manners, please. Grandpa's coming, too. And I'll have ye know that Shep O'Connor is the golf pro in Nairn, and you'd best be polite."

Brody went back to pouting all the way to Cashmere Crush. Grandpa's congratulations lifted his spirits, and when Grandpa explained how fun it would be to hit the golf balls into a net as hard as you could, that saved the evening ahead.

And who didn't love fish and chips?

"Did ye tell him aboot the new mobile?"

Brody bounced off the armchair in back and Paislee grabbed him by the shoulders. "This is for you and Grandpa when I'm not there. You can use it tae take pictures, but it is *not yours*. It is mine . . . tae be borrowed with my permission by other members of the family."

Her very clear instructions didn't wipe the smile from his face. She shook her head and hoped she wasn't making a mistake.

She dropped the guys off at home, then went to pick up the

phone. While she was in the shopping center, she got the bulb for the fridge, and bought a large chocolate cake for dessert.

At the last second, she texted Blaise. *Any food allergies? I'm picking up chocolate cake.*

None! Will go perfect with homemade vanilla ice cream. Can't wait to see you guys.

Paislee drove home, leaving the cake in the car while she ran inside the house. Brody met her at the door, still bouncing. "Can I see it?"

She'd gotten a durable black case for the phone. "Aye. But leave it here, please. It needs tae charge."

Paislee gave him the supplies and he and Grandpa set it up next to the home phone. She placed the bulb on the counter.

"I'll put that in tomorrow, lass."

"Thanks. Has Wallace been fed?" The dog jumped up on the back door to greet her. She let him in and he went straight to his water dish.

"Yep," Brody said. He'd changed from his school uniform to shorts and a T-shirt with the cartoon Batman on it.

"Feels strange tae be going oot." Grandpa slicked back his silver-gray hair that he'd dampened down. He'd changed into a clean polo shirt.

"It does, doesn't it?" Friday nights were usually spent at home with a movie and popcorn. And while Grandpa and Brody had fun, she and Blaise could hopefully track down who really killed Kirsten, and who killed Hendrie to keep their secret.

Paislee petted Wallace. "In or out, boy?"

Wallace tilted his head, then raced to the couch where he plopped down, expectantly waiting for Brody.

"We'll be back." Brody tossed the orange rubber ball to the pup, who caught it and wagged his tail.

The Shaw family got back in the Juke.

"Is this chocolate, Mum?" Brody asked when he saw the cake box in the back seat.

"Yes—make sure it doesn't spill."

"Should I taste it first?"

"I will know if there is one finger swipe out of that frosting, young man."

Grandpa snickered.

They arrived at the O'Connor rental home on the golf course. The sun was still bright, as it didn't set until nine and it was only seven.

Blaise, Suzannah, and Shep ushered them inside as if they were special guests.

"Drinks?" Shep asked. "We've got wine, beer, whisky."

"I'll have a beer," Brody said. "I aced me quiz today."

Shep and Blaise laughed while Paislee wished she could sink through the floor. "Congratulations," Shep said. "How about root beer instead? Is it okay if you have soda?"

"Just one," Paislee answered for her son.

"Brilliant!"

Suzannah smiled shyly at Brody. She was in shorts as well, her reddish-gold hair in a ponytail. "Da says we can go tae the putting green on the golf cart. I sometimes get tae drive it."

Brody looked at Paislee with excitement. Paislee said, "I'm sure with supervision." The last thing she needed was for Brody to drive a cart into one of those lake things.

"That would be correct." Shep gestured for them to follow him. "Come on back tae the pool. The heater is broken, otherwise we would have had you bring your swimsuits."

A heated pool sounded amazing.

"We'll invite you tae our new house." Blaise winked. "It even has a hot tub."

They all went to a covered and screened area where a turquoise pool was surrounded with green foliage and comfortable lounge chairs. There was a full bar, and a variety of tables. A television with cartoons on.

"I thought we'd have appetizers, then they can go hit balls while we catch up," Blaise murmured to Paislee. "Then when they get back, we can eat. Is that all right?"

"Sure." Paislee felt like she was at a holiday resort.

"I texted Lydia that chocolate cake and ice cream would be served around nine thirty if she wanted tae stop by with Corbin. I havenae met him yet."

Paislee smiled at her enthusiasm. "What did Lydia say?"

"Mibbe."

Paislee laughed. "I've only met Corbin once. She's keeping him tae herself."

Grandpa sat at the bar counter and ordered a whisky neat. Paislee sat next to him and chose a white wine. Blaise asked for a martini.

Shep ran the bar like a professional. Paislee could tell that he liked to be the host.

Brody and Suzannah each had a root beer and a bowl of pretzels with a side of soft cheese to dip in as they watched cartoons. On the counter for the adults were cold shrimp, Caprese salad on a crustini, pretzels and cheese sauce, and tiny spinach quiche.

Blaise centered her martini on a cocktail napkin. "Shep, tell Paislee and Angus what you found oot aboot Hendrie and Fergus."

"Were you able tae talk tae him?" Paislee asked in surprise.

"Och, no." Shep poured a light beer into a glass for himself. "I called around tae find oot what was going on."

Grandpa leaned in to hear.

Shep held the foaming glass. "Seems Mari phoned Lara when Hendrie didnae pick up Maxim from school yesterday afternoon."

"Mari contacted Lara?" How odd, Paislee thought. "Why didn't she call Gerard?"

"Gerard's been hitting the bottle pretty hard, from what John told me—Christina's husband. It's possible Mari did call and he didnae hear the phone ring."

"Oh. Lara is staying at the Buchanan house tae help with Maxim." Paislee turned to Grandpa. "She's his tutor but is trying tae fill in more."

"If you ask Mari and Christina," Blaise said, "Lara wants tae be the next Mrs. Buchanan."

"She's already sleeping over. Sounds like she has her foot in the door." Grandpa munched down on a tomato mozzarella toast.

"Is that true?" Shep asked. "What a mess. Well, Lara went tae pick up Maxim and asked around aboot Hendrie. She was worried for him as he took his job seriously. The last time Hendrie and the Bentley SUV were seen was when he had dropped Maxim off at the school that morning."

Blaise stirred an olive through her gin. "I would call Lara, but she was so awful tae me that I cannae bring meself tae do it."

Paislee explained to Grandpa, "Lara told Blaise she wouldn't be welcome at any more lady lunches."

Blaise sipped, then set her glass down on the napkin. "They might have been my only supposed friends at Highland Academy, but I knew one of the other mothers tae speak with . . . so I called Kerry and asked how Maxim was doing. She was happy tae fill me in. Said her heart just went out tae him—normally such a friendly boy, but now Maxim just wants tae sit alone. This morning he came tae school verra upset, in tears, and she saw him talking tae the teacher, Mr. Francis."

"Poor boy," Paislee said, heart aching for his loss of security. "What about?"

"They tried tae find oot what was wrong but Maxim just said he wanted his mum. I asked Suz, but she was oblivious."

"She's seven," Shep said in defense of their daughter.

Paislee wiped her eyes.

"I just meant that Suz has a new friend and they're inseparable. Anyway, Kerry tracked doon Christina outside, blethering with Mari, and told them aboot Maxim—she said they were verra snooty, but that they'd keep an eye on him. For Kirsten's sake."

"What aboot Hendrie?" Grandpa asked.

"That afternoon when Hendrie never showed tae pick up Maxim, Kerry immediately went tae Mari and Christina, and they called Lara, right in front of her. Lara was shocked that Maxim was still at the school." Blaise glanced at her husband.

"The police found the Bentley in a ditch, Hendrie's neck broken," Shep said.

"That's tragic." Paislee placed her hand over her thumping heart. "But how can that be traced tae Fergus?"

"Exactly what I thought. The police want tae use him as a scapegoat." Blaise sipped her martini.

"We dinnae know that, Blaise. The officer I talked tae said the SUV was sideswiped, and there were skid marks on the road. They're treating it as a murder in relation tae Kirsten's death."

The kids shuffled over, empty root beer glasses on the table. "Can we go play now, Da?" Suzannah asked. She had her pink golf clubs, just her size, at her side. "I told Brody you'd let him drive the golf cart."

"As I recall, there are no seat belts." Grandpa drained his whisky.

"Have fun!" Paislee fluttered her fingers as they left.

Once they were gone, Blaise refilled her martini glass and topped off Paislee's wine. "Are you feeling any better, after this morning?"

Paislee's dream rushed back at her, and the fear. Gerard so drunk he didn't hear the school call . . . "Maybe Gerard is drinking himself silly out of guilt for what he's done."

Blaise brought out a slip of paper and a pen. "Gerard. Hmm. Why kill Hendrie? Why not keep him employed and pay him extra for his silence?"

"Maybe Hendrie wanted more. Fergus alluded tae him and Hendrie being friends from work who partied together—they would both be privy tae Buchanan family secrets." Paislee drank her wine, savoring the pear flavors. "Maybe Hendrie was saying that Gerard was the only other person who'd been in the Bentley that day. Gerard knew the location of the EpiPen, and took it."

"But why try tae frame me?" Blaise patted her chest.

"He knew that you and Kirsten were no longer friends."

"And what, it was just bad luck that Christina picked it up first, accusing me?" Blaise's brow lifted.

"*Her* bad luck. It worked out for you."

"He also framed Fergus? I dinnae ken, Paislee. We've shared dinners at each other's houses. Our kids are in the same class." Blaise put the pen down on the paper, not having written a thing.

"Ma'am?" The maid entered the pool area, followed by Lydia and Corbin.

"We decided tae crash your dinner, too—how are you?" Lydia exclaimed, hugging first Blaise, then Paislee.

Friday night passed in a whirl of fun and friendship. Corbin got on with everyone like he'd known them all forever and he treated Lydia like a queen. It was such a grand time that Paislee almost completely put Kirsten's death from her mind.

But not quite.

Chapter 26

Saturday morning was a wee bit more frantic than the last Saturday mornings since Grandpa's arrival. Paislee had gotten used to letting Brody and Grandpa take their time and meet her for a few hours before they dashed off back home or to the beach with Wallace.

It wasn't even eight and she had a splitting headache. Brody was taking his sweet time in the bathroom, Grandpa was extra *crabbit* over his tea and late morning paper, and Wallace wanted in and out, in and out, to chase some bird hatchlings in the back garden.

Paislee pressed her fingers to her brow. She'd gotten but four hours of sleep last night, thanks to the ghostly Kirsten haunting her dreams.

I don't have to be your friend to mourn your death, or find your killer, Paislee wanted to say—but to whom, exactly, without looking completely mental?

"Out then," she told Wallace as he scratched at the back door . . . again. She let him out and brought a full mug of dark tea to the round table.

"That paper man needs tae be fired. I'd say 'lad' but I got a guid look at him, and he's retirement age. Should know how tae get the paper delivered on time."

"What's the matter with you?" Paislee asked crossly. "Did ye stay up too late last night, and need a nap?"

"Not amusing, lass, not today." He dunked a cinnamon scone in his mug.

"I didn't sleep well, either," she admitted. "Are you upset about training Amelia? She'll be there at ten, and I don't leave until noon. This is a help tae us, not meant tae be stressful. I'll return as soon as I can, politely."

He slurped his tea.

"It's not like I want tae go tae this service."

"Aye, I ken." He shrugged. "It's been a busy week, is all."

"Tomorrow, if ye like, we can sleep in and not go anywhere if we don't feel like it—how's that?"

His shoulders lifted. "Could be a nice relaxing day."

It occurred to Paislee that before he'd come to live with her he probably had lots of time to himself and maybe missed it. "If Brody really wants tae go out, I'll take him. You rest."

"I'm not an auld man that cannae keep up. Dinnae coddle me."

"I never suggested that!" Paislee sipped her tea and listened as the bath upstairs drained. "Finally. My turn for a quick shower." Paislee got up and squeezed his shoulder. "Thank you, Grandpa."

"Welcome." He pulled a bottle of pain reliever from his robe pocket. "I tweaked me back while hitting the golf balls last night, and just waiting for me aspirin to kick in. Sairy for whinging, lass."

Nodding with understanding, she went upstairs and got her things, then headed into the bathroom. Brody's wet towel on the floor was his attempt to mop up the mess he'd made when getting out of the tub.

Not a battle she was willing to take on this morning. Paislee knocked on his door. "Get dressed, love, and go have some cereal."

"I am!" he called through his closed door. Squeaking sounds emanated from the bed as he jumped up and down.

She shook her head. Fifteen minutes later, Paislee was out and dressed herself, choosing black slacks and a soft black blouse for the service. She wore low heels and had a matching black jacket. Kirsten weighted her thoughts. Who would be there today? Would the killer show?

Finger-fluffing her hair, Paislee added powder for her face, eyeliner, and lip gloss, pinching her cheeks for pink. Good enough.

She grabbed her purse and headed downstairs, mentally telling Kirsten that after the funeral, the ghost needed to get out of her bedroom, and her head. This would be goodbye.

Brody brought a dripping spoonful of Weetabix to his mouth, chewed, swallowed and said, "Why are ye dressed up, Mum?"

"I'm going tae a funeral today for Kirsten Buchanan, remember? Make sure you have a book and your video game—otherwise Grandpa can put you tae work."

Grandpa shuffled out of his bedroom, silver hair combed, a smile on his face. "I like the sound of that. What is the labor law anyway? Six?"

"I want tae stay home, like I did before." His heel kicked back against the chair.

"Stop doing that. You were injured, and it was an hour." She pointed to his shoe. "Don't give me any sass now."

Paislee topped off her mug with hot water and snagged a piece of toast from the center of the table. Grandpa must've made a stack.

"No butter? No jam?" Brody scrunched his nose. "Gross."

"Did I ask you?" She took another bite. "What did you think about golf yesterday?"

"I liked hitting the ball really hard but Suzannah said that you dinnae have tae whack it. It's where ye hit the ball that makes it go far."

"That sounds pretty smart tae me."

"She's all right, for a girl."

Paislee raised her brow. "I won't hear that again, thank you."

Grandpa snickered and ducked into the bathroom to brush his teeth.

"Well, she is." Brody, about to kick back again, stopped at her expression. "Anyway, I liked it. She said her da is famous for teaching people how tae golf and she's been doing it since she was a wean."

"Are you interested in lessons?"

He tilted his head. "I'd rather play football."

"Well, the end-of-year party is going tae be at the golf course and maybe you can try something more challenging than the bucket of balls."

Grandpa joined them at the table, his back ache better. "I'd like to take lessons to stay limber. Now that I'm getting a raise, I'll be in clover."

"Ha." Paislee hid her smile in her mug.

Brody finished his cereal and darted outside to play fetch with Wallace for a few minutes. Before Grandpa, Brody used to go every Saturday with Paislee to Cashmere Crush. The last two months had been a break for them all.

What would she do if they found Craigh and he wanted Grandpa back?

Paislee didn't want him to go. Gran was either cheering them on from Heaven or shaking her angelic fist at them. "Time tae go."

She parked behind the shop and they spilled out like sand from a shoe. The sky was so bright a blue she blinked at the surreal color. "Another bonny day," she said.

"And we have tae be inside," Brody groused. "I'm old enough tae go tae the park meself."

"No, you're not." Even if he was, she wasn't ready.

"In my day—" Grandpa started to say.

"If you want that raise . . ." Paislee said, climbing the stairs.

"You've got yer game, lad. You'll be fine."

"Amelia will be here, Brody." She opened the back and they filed in. "She's going tae start working on Saturdays."

"Amelia's pretty cool." He dropped his things on the armchair before the small telly in the back. "She likes video games."

"I'd like for you tae make her feel welcome, all right?"

"Aye." Brody stuck his hands in his jeans pockets.

"Why don't you go unlock the front door?" Paislee shelved her purse beneath the register and opened the safe to set up the cash in the till. She'd just finished when Amelia walked in, followed by Detective Inspector Zeffer.

"Hi, Amelia!" Brody said. "Hello, sir. Are you going tae work for us today, too?"

Grandpa chuckled and rubbed Brody's hair. "That I'd like tae see."

Amelia grinned while the DI's nose flared. "I'm here tae speak tae your mum," he said, then turned to Amelia. "You're working here?"

"First day is today." Amelia crossed her arms to face Zeffer, who was much taller than she. "Just Saturdays when they need extra help, DI. Willnae affect me other job at all."

He scowled but couldn't say anything regarding what Amelia did on her free time, so long as it was legal. "Paislee, might I have a word?"

"Certainly." She bit the inside of her cheek to keep from laughing as she stayed by the register. The day was looking up.

"In private."

"Why don't we take a walk down tae the park?" she suggested. "But I can only be a few minutes. I have tae train Amelia and get ready for Kirsten's funeral."

His jaw clenched. "It's aboot your message. Is it still relevant, now that we have Fergus in jail?"

"Aye. I think so." The DI had the wrong man—that seemed relevant.

Paislee could see he still had questions but didn't want to talk in front of her whole crew.

"I'll be just a minute." She ushered the DI toward the door and they walked out into the brilliant sunshine. It was so lovely she sighed.

"I'm sairy I didnae get back tae you yesterday." He stuffed his hands into the pockets of his blue slacks. Italian loafers. The man

exuded style. "I assumed you wanted tae tell me that you still dinnae think Fergus is guilty."

"I don't." Paislee didn't say anything about her bad dreams
with Kirsten's accusatory remarks, or the guilt she felt at not being
able to save her.

"Listen, Paislee. Kirsten fired Fergus for stealing."

"That's what Shep found out . . . from Gerard. Gerard might
be covering up his own crime."

"I followed the lead to its logical conclusion." Zeffer slowed
and untucked his hands. "Fergus stole two of Kirsten's rings and
pawned them."

"Oh." That was more specific than just rooting around a desk
searching for keys.

"The only reason she found oot was because the jeweler recognized the design of one of the rings . . . Gerard had it made for
Kirsten especially after Maxim was born."

They stared at each other on the sidewalk, his eyes intense.

"What do you want me tae say?"

"That you can see how he might be guilty!" Zeffer's arms flew
outward, his palms up.

Paislee lowered her gaze, realizing she had to try another way.
"I had a nightmare last night. I feel like Hendrie—"

"Who is dead."

"I know that!" She cleared her throat. "He said that he didn't
see anybody going tae their car, the Bentley, that shouldn't have
been there. That, tae me, means Gerard. And what if Gerard wants
tae frame Fergus for stealing?"

Zeffer was so frustrated with her that he ground his back teeth.
"Here's another hard fact, Paislee . . . the Bentley was sideswiped
down a steep hill. Hendrie's neck, broken. Chances were very
good at that angle of a fall that it would be fatal—especially if the
driver, Hendrie, wasn't wearing a seat belt."

"Why wouldn't he have a belt on?"

"It was sabotaged. Somebody slashed it. And that same someone, my money is on Fergus, took the extra Buchanan family Fiat and drove Hendrie off the road in that precise spot tae stop him from sharing what he'd witnessed with the police. Hendrie saw Fergus add the crumble."

"You don't know that."

"We have CCTV footage of a man in a hoodie, like you told me Fergus wore, behind the wheel of the Fiat. The Fiat has matching paint chips on the side. Those are facts, not feelings."

She exhaled, trying not to let the DI ruin the beautiful day but it was too late. "Has he confessed?"

"No."

"Why would Fergus kill his mate? Hendrie helped him."

"No such thing as loyalty when it comes tae prison." Zeffer patted her shoulder. "It's right that Fergus is in jail for the funeral service. It will provide closure for Gerard, and Maxim."

She stiffened. "Unless Gerard is the real killer. He had access tae the Fiat—he drove it tae the club that Sunday when he threatened tae kill Anders. He could have decided that Hendrie was a liability. Staff know the dirty secrets that go on in a big house."

He briefly closed his eyes. "Just, *och*. You can trust me tae do my job, which is tae find a murderer. Not only Kirsten's but now Hendrie's."

She straightened. "This isn't personal, DI."

"How aboot you get back tae work and I'll let you know when we get that full confession. That should set your nightmares at ease. I really thought that you and I were making progress, but I realize now that was wishful thinking on my part."

Paislee squashed the urge to tell him he was right, and that she did trust him—it wasn't that. "It's not a matter of trust, Detective."

He raised his hand and strode away from her.

Why did she feel so bad?

She went back inside, disturbed by how the conversation had gone. She held up both palms against all three expectant faces. "I can't talk about it. Fergus is in jail." Paislee walked briskly toward the register. "Now, Amelia, what do you know about counting out money?"

Two hours passed quickly and Lydia sauntered in to get her. "Hello!" Lydia wrapped Brody in a hug and gave him a bag from a popular gaming store. "This is a prezzie for my prodigy getting a hundred percent on his math quiz."

Brody's eyes rounded in delight as he pulled out a new game. "Thanks, Aunt Lydia. This is pure barry—wait till I show Samuel."

"I thought Edwyn was your best mate?" she said, hand on her hip. She was ready for the funeral in a black dress with short sleeves.

"I like Samuel, too." Brody shrugged and hurried back to the armchair and out of sight as he opened the gift.

"Thanks for that," Paislee said. "He'll not bother Grandpa and Amelia for hours."

"I owe you one." Grandpa wiped his forehead as if making a narrow escape.

He and Lydia laughed and Paislee rolled her eyes at Amelia.

"I'm gonna like workin' here," Amelia said. "I saw a deck of cards?"

"If it's slow, I like a game of solitaire," Grandpa said. "Not that it has been, much, this last month."

Amelia grinned. "I'm pretty good at poker." She smoothed a short wave behind her ear. "But dinnae complain tae the boss if ye lose your shirt."

"On that note," Lydia said, "we should get going, Paislee."

"I'd say have fun, but yer going tae a funeral. Got a hankie?" Grandpa asked.

"I doot I'll be crying," Lydia said. "There will probably be cheers instead."

"I have tissues in my purse." Paislee lifted her bag, then kissed Brody on the forehead. "Be good."

★ ★ ★

She and Lydia drove to Inverness, Lydia chattering nonstop about Corbin.

"What did ye think of him? It was his idea tae cancel our date tae crash Blaise's dinner party. Do you think that was rude?"

"I think it's fantastic. He wants tae fit in with your close friends. And Blaise did invite you first."

"That's what I figured, too. Paislee, he's so amazing. Funny. The man can kiss tae curl me toes. I think I might be in trouble."

"Trouble trouble?" Paislee rested her hand on her stomach.

"Naw—not that. Sairy." Lydia patted her heart. "I meant, here. I've never felt like this before and it really blows me away."

"Let yourself be in love, Lydia."

Her friend practically glowed as she talked about Corbin. Paislee discovered that he was one of four boys, the third in line and so considered himself the most useless of the Smythe children. "They have the heir, the spare, and the baby." He'd been wild in his youth but now wanted to settle down.

"He wants a family." Lydia peered at Paislee over her sunglasses.

"You don't have tae sound so horrified." Paislee laughed.

Lydia nibbled her lower lip, concentrating on the road. "I want a career."

"These days you can have both," Paislee assured her. "Times have changed, even in Nairn."

They neared Inverness and traffic thickened. "I wish we didnae have tae do this, but it's for Blaise." Lydia glanced at Paislee. "If it was anybody else, I'd say let's skip it and get a glass of wine on the loch."

"That's very tempting." Paislee gave a little smile. "The DI really believes Fergus is guilty—they have a picture of a man in a hoodie driving the Buchanan Fiat that forced the Bentley off the road."

"But you don't?"

"I think it's Gerard. I really do."

"Well, this is a guid time tae watch him, and see if he makes a mistake. Gives himself away. Tears. No tears."

"Only a full confession will do," Paislee told Lydia as she found a parking spot across from Saint Mary's church.

Saint Mary's was known for its grand architecture and stained glass windows. While she'd never been there for a mass, she had toured the inside. It was gorgeous. And packed. They were lucky to score a spot.

"I can't believe how crowded this is."

Lydia removed her sunglasses and climbed out of her Mercedes. "Even if you dinnae agree with the DI aboot who killed her, this will be a media circus. Kirsten Buchanan, Scots Socialite, was *murdered.*"

Chapter 27

Paislee and Lydia entered Saint Mary's, which retained an ancient feel although parts of the church had been refurbished. "1837," Lydia read from a plaque on the wall. "Almost as old as your shop."

"Give or take twenty years." Her home was over a hundred years old, but her business on Market Street was two hundred and change. "This is stunning, though."

Lydia found them seats in a pew toward the back. "In case we need tae escape," she whispered. "There's Blaise, up in the fifth row with Shep and Suzannah." They sat and Lydia sent a text to their friend that they were there.

Paislee studied the packed church. Cameras flashed from media photographers. A man in a black robe marched the reporter out. "Have some decency, if ye please. The family is laying a loved one tae rest."

The priest closed the doors and told two ushers that only family or friends were to be allowed in. The men took up position, hands clasped before them, elbows out.

"Blaise says she's saved us seats but I'd rather stay here. You?"

"Definitely." Paislee rubbed her arms. "Is it too late tae get that glass of wine you suggested?"

Music from an organ began to play and the best friends quieted. Paislee studied the mourners up front. Mari, with her daughter, Mia. Christina, John, and their son, Robby. Gerard, Maxim. And Lara with them. Interesting. Gerard was stoic as he kept his arm around his son. No tears, but sorrow etched lines in his face.

Blaise, Shep, Suzannah. Sonya was there, without Anders. It hit her suddenly that though this funeral was for Kirsten, Hendrie was also dead. Would his funeral command as many mourners? He'd barely made the paper that morning.

She and Lydia were teary eyed when Maxim was mentioned by the priest, mourning his mother. Whoever had taken that boy's mum from him deserved prison. She just wasn't sure it was Fergus. At last it was over, and she rose, with Lydia right behind her.

When they got outside they each dragged in a breath. "It's so sad," Paislee said.

"I know. C'mon. There will be refreshments of the whisky sort at the Buchanan estate and I could use a dram or two." Lydia leaned close as they walked. "Now, I realize this is in poor taste, but this house is superb. It's worth almost two million, on ten acres, a kilometer on the Nairn River. One of the older houses in Inverness, it's been completely redone—I saw pictures online."

Her friend was an amazing estate agent and it was no surprise that such a promising property would make her gray eyes shine.

They took their time and drove around the neighborhood before going to the house. Lydia passed through a black gate in a brick fence around the property and waited on the gravel lot for Blaise and Shep to arrive so they could walk in together.

While they waited in the Mercedes, Lydia pointed out features of the house. "That would be the maid's quarters, and the chauffer's, and the chef's. On the opposite side is the greenhouse that provides fresh vegetables for the family. You can get trout and salmon from the river, and they've got sheep for mutton. All inclusive. People who can afford it are going back tae that lifestyle."

Paislee admired the long stone building trimmed in white. "I can't imagine needing a private wing for staff. Grandpa was lucky we hadn't ever repurposed Gran's rooms."

"I like Angus." Lydia removed her sunglasses and tossed them on the dashboard. "Someday I want tae know what happened between your grandparents that Gran couldnae get past."

Paislee wondered, too. But now, if it put her grandfather in a bad light, would she still want to know? Probably not, if she had to be honest. "I think they loved each other deeply."

"How love should be," Lydia said dreamily. "Oh, look. Here's another lovely couple . . . Shep and Blaise in the Range Rover. Hurry. I've got tae see this foyer up close. Italian marble. Would it be rude tae leave a business card on his counter? In case he ever wants tae sell?"

Paislee didn't require finishing school to know that answer. "Very."

They got out and joined the O'Connors and the other people now walking toward the house. Gerard stood at the wide-open front door.

"Welcome," he said. He'd lost his glamorous movie-star looks. His dark hair was mussed, and he'd missed some black stubble on his chin when he'd shaved. His eyes were bloodshot.

Maxim stood next to him, then Lara on the other side. Maxim's hand was clasped in each of theirs as if he couldn't let go. He had beautiful brown eyes that held shadows. Too young, she thought, to know such pain as losing a parent.

She'd been sixteen when she'd lost her da and it had rocked her world. Nothing had been safe again.

Find my killer, Kirsten said from inside her head. Paislee blinked and swallowed.

"How d'ya do, Maxim?" Paislee knelt down to hug the boy. He took it in good graces and she straightened, facing Gerard. "I have a son, ten, and my heart aches for your loss."

Gerard dragged her into a hug as well, his lower lip quivering. Her skin goose-bumped at this show of grief. What if he hadn't killed his wife?

Who, then?

Lara was next to hug Paislee. "We thank you for coming."

Her tone was much kinder than it had been at lunch just a few days ago. "I'm sorry for your loss." Although "losing" Kirsten might just be to Lara's gain.

Paislee and Lydia then followed the path of people headed to the back of the home where a giant buffet had been spread out. There was a bar area, and food, and tables set up for folks to sit at. The windows were long and showcased a green lawn as lush as a golf course.

A sickly pale woman in a black uniform with an apron gestured people toward the buffet line, where three servers offered to dish out food.

Was that the maid who had access to the Fiat? How did the DI know it wasn't her, in a hoodie? She was the same slight build as Fergus.

"I want the bar first," Lydia said. "Any chance we can sneak away tae see the rest of the place?"

"Christina is there, in line with a man who must be John, and their son, Robby. Let's join them." Paislee glanced back at the maid. The girl had the shakes. Why was she so upset?

"All right." Lydia tugged her away from the maid.

They reached the small queue at the bar. "Christina," Lydia spoke in a low, compassionate voice. "How are you? You must miss your dear friend terribly."

Christina's blue eyes spilled over with tears and John put his arm around her, while her son took her hand, her family uniting around her. "I do."

Dear friend.

Not a friend.

Not Gerard. Not Fergus. Maybe not the maid. Christina—she'd had the EpiPen. She'd had it in her possession and tried to set up Blaise. The police had requested her phone records.

Paislee gasped and pressed her hand to her stomach as if sucker-punched.

She had to be wrong.

"Vodka neat, please," Christina ordered from the bartender.

"Are you sure that's wise, dear? With your medication?" The last was meant to be a whisper though they all heard.

Christina pushed her husband away. He was at least fifteen years older. "Just one tae calm my nerves. I've been a wreck and you know it, John."

"I'm sairy, hon. I'll take a Scotch and soda." John ordered, then handed the vodka to Christina and noticed Paislee when he glanced up from his wife. "Have we met?"

"I'm Paislee Shaw, and this is Lydia Barron." John shook their hands. "We know Kirsten and the other ladies through Blaise."

"Did I hear my name?" Blaise, Shep, and Suzannah joined them. Suzannah and Robby ran off to greet Mari's daughter, Mia. Mari stepped behind them in line to order a drink.

"Hi, Mari," Paislee said. "Your daughter has your beautiful smile." All she could think of was how she'd heard Mari retching after lunch so she quickly looked away.

"She's my mini." Mari clasped Blaise in a hug, then Christina. "I'm so sairy for any mean things I may have said tae any of you. Kirsten's funeral today has revealed light on my own unkind actions."

"Oh!" Christina squeezed Mari's hand. "Me too."

"Really?" Blaise asked. "I'd hate tae leave Highland Academy with hard feelings. I'm sairy, too."

The men stepped back from the outpouring of emotion.

Paislee and Lydia shared a smile, but Paislee couldn't stop watching Christina. The DI always said to get proof. First, she'd cross the maid off her list.

"I'm sairy we had Lara call you aboot those lunches," Mari said. "That was pure stupidity. And now Lara isnae letting Gerard oot of her sight. It's disrespectful. Our Kirsten's only been dead a week."

Christina leaned discreetly around Blaise and Mari to where Lara stood next to Gerard, who had finally left the front door. The two adults had young Maxim between them like a family.

Lara had wanted Kirsten's life. Lara, as her assistant, knew of her allergies. Had access to Kirsten's shortbread. Hendrie might not have batted an eye at Lara getting in the Bentley to retrieve the EpiPen. Lara could have put it on Blaise's chair, hoping to earn her place in the clique while firmly getting rid of Blaise.

Paislee looked away from the trio. If only Hendrie were still alive to tell her who he'd seen that day.

The group remained in a comfortable knot conversing over the shock of Kirsten's murderer being the chef, Fergus, who'd also killed loyal Hendrie. They gathered around two tall tables with high-top stools. The kids raced by them, playing their own game. A formal breathtaking portrait of Kirsten hung on the wall, overseeing them all.

The maid collected dirty plates and took them to what must be the kitchen. Paislee followed her. This would be Kirsten's domain as well as Fergus's. Also the waitstaff's, but not Gerard's, who ran the home.

"Excuse me," Paislee said as she caught the girl in the hall, hands empty after her return from the kitchen.

"Ma'am?" She hooked her thumbs inside the long pocket of her apron.

Paislee smiled in a friendly manner. "I was wondering how well you know Fergus Jones?"

She froze in place. Her hair was scraped back into a tight bun. "We worked together, that's all. I wasnae part of their crowd."

"'Their'?" Paislee tilted her head. "I don't believe Fergus drove Hendrie off the road. Do you think he would do that to his friend?"

The girl burst into sobs. "It wasnae me—I cannae afford tae get sacked because of those two, and I'm barely hangin' on with missing work tae take care of me mum. I told the police I saw someone in a hoodie, and I did."

"But you didn't see Fergus."

The maid raised her gaze. "I cannae say for sure. I just know it wasnae me." She raced away from Paislee to a dark corridor and slipped down it. Was this where the private staff rooms were? Lydia had pointed out that they'd be next to the kitchen.

Lydia waved for her to join them and Paislee made a note to come back. The high-strung maid would surely cave with just a few more questions.

"Time tae eat," Lydia said. They filled plates of lamb, trout, and various side dishes, and then sat in the middle of the ladies' gang and their husbands—the children had their own table in another section of the rooms chaperoned by staff.

Paislee drank a cup of tea and watched the clique interact. They were friends, Kirsten's and Gerard's. Lara fluttered her hands and giggled a lot. Mari, on the other side of Gerard, had her shoulders bowed as she stuffed another piece of buttered potato in her mouth.

"And where is your husband, Mari?" Christina asked. "I just now realized Charlie wasnae with you. I've gotten used tae seeing you on your own."

She stiffened. "Oh, he's traveling."

Gerard inched his chair away from her.

Lara, who hadn't been part of the make-up session, said, "Now, you're among mates here, Mari. You can tell the truth."

"What do you mean?" Mari put her fork down.

"Kirsten told me that you and Charlie are separated. He hasnae been at a school meeting since before the winter holiday."

"You . . ." Mari spluttered, eyes filled with hurt.

Lara's mouth thinned. "You shouldnae sit so close tae Gerard."

Mari twisted her napkin at her lap. "How dare you speak like that tae me! Why are you even sitting here with us—shouldnae you be watching Maxim?"

Shep cleared his throat to draw attention to himself. "Are you entering the Gold Cup this year, John?"

Gerard straightened in his seat, but almost toppled from too much to drink. "*I* am. Need tae keep tae my routine."

"You do, Gerard," Lara said soothingly. "You're number one."

It was obvious to everyone at the table what was going on. Was Gerard too drunk and overwrought to see the truth? Lara wanted him. Lara would do whatever it took to keep him.

Had she been the one to get Kirsten out of her way?

Shep finished his meal in quick bites and stood. "How aboot a cigar, gentlemen?"

Quick thinking, Shep. For the first time in her life, Paislee wished she smoked cigars to listen in on their conversation. She and Lydia looked at each other and shrugged. It would be too obvious to tag along with the guys.

Besides, she was pretty sure that it was one of the women here at this very table who'd killed Kirsten Buchanan.

She reached for her purse and pulled her phone from the side pocket.

She'd missed a call from the DI.

He'd sent a text.

Be careful. Fergus not the murderer.

Chapter 28

Paislee tried to get up from the table on the pretext to follow Mari, who'd hastily gotten up and excused herself, but Christina called her back.

Mari probably had gone to the bathroom to throw up after Lara's attack. Talk about stressful, having your secret outed at the table like that. Paislee needed to phone the DI.

"Let's not ruin the day," Christina said. "Lara, that was terrible and mean. Please tell me you're not planning on stepping into Kirsten's shoes."

Paislee remained seated but passed her phone beneath the table to Lydia, who read the message with wide eyes. She nodded, understanding that Paislee had to return his call.

"Paislee, I'm sairy if we're keeping you," Lara snapped. "I dinnae ken why Blaise insisted on the two of you being here. You dinnae belong."

Lara stared at her with watery eyes. Could she be the murderer? Blaise was so angry that her cheeks were red and her voice shook. "What is the matter with you, Lara?"

Lydia put her hand on Paislee's shoulder. "Paislee has tae call the shop for her grandfather. There's a problem that requires her assistance."

"Please dinnae go," Blaise said, sucking in her lip.

Christina's jaw clenched. The blonde had been questioned by the constable and released, they'd requested her phone records, and they'd still arrested Fergus. Not Christina. However, Lara had access to Kirsten's daily life.

The maid cleared the plates, making a point to not look at Paislee. "May I bring anything else?"

"No thank you," Christina said. "This is a funeral, not a damn party."

The maid scooted back, her bun quivering. "Sairy, ma'am."

Paislee held her phone under the table and texted the DI to let him know that she was with Lydia inside the Buchanans' house. The men were outside smoking cigars but she was sure it was one of the women. Lara. *Had all the cookies been topped with peanut, or just the judges'?* She kept the ringer off.

It had to be Lara. She'd been caught by Hendrie and ran him off the road to save her new little life with Gerard and Maxim.

Mari returned from the kitchen, followed by a tall server with a tray and six glasses for wine. "Phones down, ladies," she trilled. "I'd like your attention, please."

She had the server pour from a gorgeous black bottle with a shimmery label that you knew was expensive just by its presentation.

"I miss Kirsten so much," Mari said in a thick voice. "I brought this bottle for her last week and now she'll never get tae drink it. It was her favorite, Red Velvet."

"I know it was her favorite." Lara began to cry. "You all hate me. I care for Maxim. I care for Gerard."

"They belong tae Kirsten," Christina said, swirling the wine in her glass. "Not you!"

Mari tapped the glass with a spoon. "Since we didnae get tae open it last week, I thought I'd share it with all of you, in her memory."

"Kirsten is dead." Lara wiped her eyes and glanced guiltily at Kirsten's portrait. "She groomed me tae take her place."

"She wanted you tae tutor her son, not take over her marriage bed," Christina said heatedly.

Mari cleared her throat with impatience. "Can we focus on the toast tae Kirsten, please? This is for her. There will be time for reminiscing afterward."

The red liquid smelled of black cherry and Paislee brought it to her nose. The bouquet, as Lydia would say, was deep and floral. Plum, currant. Decadent. Like these women's lives. She nodded at Lydia—this would be delicious.

"Before we drink . . ." Mari paused to gaze at each of them as she kept her glass before her. "I'd like tae say a few words tae help me move on. We all know that Kirsten could be cutting. I used tae think she didnae mean tae be so harsh, but I learned that she actually liked it."

Christina bowed her head and set down the glass she'd been about to sip from. "This wine is a couple hundred a bottle, so let's not get too sappy or I willnae be able tae enjoy it."

Paislee couldn't imagine spending so much on wine. Was Christina exaggerating?

Mari's mouth twisted. "Christina, when you asked aboot my husband, did you already know he was sleeping around with other men?"

Paislee sucked in a breath, as did Blaise, Lydia, and Christina. Lara did not appear surprised.

"I'll take that as a no." Mari's thin arm quaked, the wine sloshing inside the crystal glass. "Kirsten showed me pictures Friday night when I'd gone tae her, upset aboot Charlie leaving me. My best friend in the world said that he preferred a man tae me—that his lover had more curves." Her face crumpled like a dried apple. "She told me that it was my fault he hadn't stayed."

Paislee gripped the wine stem, sick.

Christina glared at Kirsten's portrait. "Her cruelty was how she kept us in line."

"That's beyond cruel," Blaise whispered. "Mari, darling, please don't hurt yourself further by going on aboot this. You did nothing wrong."

Mari raised her glass. "Blaise, you were the nicest friend we had—and you left us. I dinnae blame you." She skewered Lara with a glare. "You knew aboot Charlie," she said raspily.

"Aye." Lara brought her glass to the table, her voice thick. "Kirsten told me everything aboot Charlie on Saturday as I helped her get the table set up. I'm sairy I said anything. I just saw you sitting so close tae Gerard and I got jealous."

"With friends like you all, who needs enemies? To friendship." Mari drained her wine.

"To friendship." Lara, desperate to be included, followed suit.

That was no proper toast. Friday night? Had what Kirsten done to Mari been the final straw? Paislee remembered back to Saturday, when Gerard had asked for a ride to the hospital to be with Kirsten, already dead. Mari had said, "I rode with you, Ger." She'd been there all along. That's what Hendrie *could* have told.

Mari poured more wine from the bottle to her glass. "Drink, my friends!"

Not my friend.

Paislee noticed a granular residue along the edge of her glass from where she'd swirled it.

"Stop!" Paislee knocked the glass from Lydia's hand, reaching for Blaise's, who had been too stunned to drink, thank God.

Christina had though—a sip to savor. "What, Paislee?"

"I think it's been . . ." Paislee watched Lara in horror, then Mari. "Poisoned." *No more death, please.*

"Did you poison this?" Lara glared at Mari, fingers at her throat.

"Morphine. Dying willnae hurt a bit. A hundred capsules crushed in the wine." Mari's eyelashes fluttered and she swayed, holding the edge of the wood table with her fingertips. "I realized afterward that it wasnae just Kirsten who was mean and cruel—it was all of us!"

Christina pushed back from the table. "You're sick, Mari! You told John you needed that prescription for pain."

A knock sounded behind them at the front door. The DI pushed it open and took in the scene.

"I *am* in pain." Mari held her hand to her stomach. "I have nothing left tae live for. Charlie will take care of Mia." Mari fainted to the ground.

Lara collapsed at the table, face-first. Christina ran to the bathroom, already retching.

Zeffer, cool and calm, joined Paislee as she stood up. "Mari killed Kirsten—not Lara." She'd texted Lara, incorrectly. Paislee pressed her forearm to her roiling stomach.

Lydia remained seated as she stared at the tableau of a lunch gone wrong. Paislee put her hand to her best friend's shoulder. "You didn't drink it?"

"No. You stopped me in time." Lydia looked up at Paislee and squeezed her fingers, which were like ice.

The DI gestured for the EMTs he must have called to come in.

"Morphine in the wine. Lara and Mari drained their glasses. Christina had a drink." Paislee touched his arm. "Mari wanted tae die and take us all with her in the name of friendship."

"Not nice ladies." His sea-glass green eyes darkened.

"No." Tears welled as she watched the EMTs take care of Lara and Mari. It reminded her of Kirsten and Paislee's head swam.

The men ran in from where they'd been smoking cigars outside. The other guests had gathered in clusters; the pale maid hovered near the children, her hand in Maxim's. The boy's eyes were huge with fear. Paislee, Blaise, and Lydia stepped away from the table to give the EMTs room to maneuver.

"What happened?" Gerard asked. Lara was being treated where she sprawled unconscious on the table, and Mari on the floor.

"Bad Aunt Mari," Maxim said.

"We'll need two stretchers," the DI instructed Constable Dean and Constable Rory, who'd followed him in.

Blaise ran to Shep, who hugged her close.

"Where's Christina?" John asked with concern.

"Bathroom," Paislee answered. "She only had one taste, but I don't know the strength of capsules Mari put in. Morphine you'd prescribed?"

John's face darkened and he brushed by her in search of his wife. "Christina!"

"Three stretchers, possibly," Zeffer amended, arms crossed.

Constable Payne ran out to the front where the ambulance was parked to call for more help.

"How are you?" Zeffer asked, watching the people closest to Kirsten and how they were reacting.

"Fine."

The DI turned and scanned her from head to toe. "This time, I believe you. It was a close call. If you'd had that wine . . ."

"Mari said she brought it over on Friday night, after she'd shared with Kirsten about Charlie leaving her for another man. Kirsten behaved cruelly." Paislee rubbed her arms. "When she and Kirsten didn't drink the wine together Friday night, she must have decided tae add the peanut topping tae the crumble on Saturday. They rode together tae the club."

"Fergus finally started talking when I warned him someone else might die. I asked Fergus who he and Hendrie saw that day, and who might have access tae the Bentley. He told me Mari and Christina, but Christina had an alibi: she was on the phone with her husband—we checked the phone records—or in plain view of everyone the whole time. Mari does go back and forth from the kitchen on Sonya's video. She holds the door for Kirsten and Fergus. Lara is there, too."

"Were all the shortbread doctored?"

"No. Twenty of the dishes had a slightly different scalloped edge, so slight that only a perfectionist would notice. Those twenty had the peanuts. Mari must have wanted tae make sure that Kirsten would get one of those."

"There was going tae be shortbread and a dram for everyone, as a thank-you from the Buchanans. Kirsten would have eaten one. Mari must have put the EpiPen on Blaise's chair as she brought Kirsten's purse from the conference room. She had access tae the Bentley tae take it from the car." Paislee hugged her waist. "Mari was there all along, pointing fingers everywhere."

"Stirring trouble in plain sight. Why dinnae you and Lydia give your statements tae Constable Rory, and then you two can go."

Paislee nodded at Zeffer. "Thank you."

She walked around the EMTs, thinking of when she'd tried so hard to save Kirsten's life. And failed. Life was a fragile thing.

Mari was being wheeled out in a hurry. Lara, strapped in, called for Gerard in a slurry voice. Gerard stayed with the men and turned his back.

"Ready, Lyd? The detective said we can give our statements and go." Paislee glanced back at the giant photo of Kirsten.

Stay here, Kirsten. Your murder is solved.

Blaise hugged her tight. "Thank you. This is so awful. I just cannae believe it. We're yanking Suzannah from Highland Academy and will have her at Fordythe for the rest of the year. Mary Beth's girls sound like nice girls."

"They are," Paislee said.

Shep nodded, his expression more serious than Paislee had ever seen it. "Moving tae Nairn was the best thing we could have done for our family. Blaise, you were spot-on with that, love."

Blaise blossomed under her husband's approval. "Let's get our daughter and get oot of here. Paislee, would you ask the nice detective if we can go, too?"

"Detective Inspector Zeffer . . ." Paislee waved at him, and introduced Shep O'Connor, since he'd already met Blaise.

"Do you golf, DI?" Shep asked.

"I've been known tae go a few rounds."

Who knew that golf was so popular? Paislee gave her statement to the constable, then searched for the maid, who remained by Maxim, Robby, and Mia. "Thanks for looking after the kids while that happened. You have a cool head. Sorry if I came on too strong about Fergus."

"It's okay." She patted her eyes with the edge of her apron. "You were right. I knew it wasnae Fergus driving, but I didnae know who, and I was tryin' to protect my job, that's all. Hendrie murdered, Mrs. Buchanan killed. I've been scared out of me mind."

"It's over now."

"Do I have to tell the truth?" She shuddered.

"Aye. See that tall, thin officer, Constable Rory? He's a sweetheart and can take your statement. Good luck tae you, and your mum. If you ever need a reference, come find me at Cashmere Crush."

"What's that?"

"A sweater and yarn shop in Nairn that specializes in bespoke items using local yarn." Paislee spoke with confidence in herself, and her place in the world. She'd earned it.

Chapter 29

Sunday afternoon, the Shaw family was enjoying the brilliant blue sky at the beach. She and Grandpa relaxed on the plaid blanket and soaked up the sun. Last night, Paislee had slept free of Kirsten haunting her dreams, the woman's murderer found, so she could be at peace. *Not sure if she made it to Heaven, Gran, but if so, keep an eye out.*

Paislee watched Wallace chase an orange ball in the surf with Brody—her son hadn't wanted a friend to spend the day. Considering the way they'd acted, she didn't blame him. They'd both have to work on seeing the good in others.

"Shortbread cookie?" Grandpa asked her. He offered her the open tin.

"No, thanks. I'm still full from the cheese toasties." She'd given her grandfather the option to stay home by himself but he'd chosen to come with them.

She, Brody, and Grandpa were family. She was about to ask Grandpa about her da and what he'd been like, something she hadn't had the strength to do until now, but then a tall, russet-haired shadow became the figure of a man, a detective inspector to be precise.

"May I join you?" Zeffer peered down at them.

"How on earth did you find us?" She'd hoped to not talk to anybody but family for the whole day.

"I'm a detective, Paislee," Zeffer drawled. "It's me job."

Grandpa chuckled.

"Why don't you sit down, then, rather than hover? Why are ye wearing a suit tae the beach?" She sat cross-legged and scooched closer to Grandpa.

Zeffer knelt down on the blanket, careful to keep the top of his designer shoes out of the sand.

"Lemonade? Tea?"

"I'll have tea, thanks."

Paislee poured him an icy cup of Brodies from a thermos. "It's sweet, is that all right?"

"It'll do." He sipped and nodded. "Nice."

"Shortbread?"

He shook his head and reclined back, legs stretched out, on one elbow, holding the cup to his stomach as if he were dressed in beach attire and comfortable. "You could be a model," she said without thinking.

He flinched. "I dinnae approve of your methods, Paislee, but you have a natural gift for seeing beneath the surface."

"That would be intuition," she quipped, noting that he hadn't at all cared for her model comment. She'd keep that in mind for when she needed to needle him next.

"Whatever you call it, your instinct saved Lara, and Mari, all the ladies at the table, when you realized there was something wrong with the wine."

She breathed in deep and said a prayer of thanks. "They're both all right?"

"Lara will be released this afternoon. Gerard was there tae take her home, but he said that her services as a tutor, and Kirsten's assistant, would no longer be needed."

"Ouch. Lara cared for him. Not that she had the right, really."

"You cannae say who someone will love or why." Zeffer shrugged. "The emotion is unpredictable."

"And Mari? What will happen tae her?" The woman had more issues than Paislee could count.

"Christina and John were both at the hospital tae visit her, though she's unable tae see anybody. She's under arrest. We found peanuts in her house. An EpiPen that might be the one missing from the Bentley. A black hoodie. The clincher was finding the matching dishes. She had boxes of white that were just a wee bit different around the edges than Kirsten's."

"She's slender enough to resemble Fergus in the CCTV." Paislee twisted her loose hair into a braid. "John prescribed the morphine tae her."

"He was her doctor for bulimia. I understand that sufferers often have issues with addiction. Whatever is causing the need tae binge and purge affects the same part of the brain as the euphoria one gets from being high."

Paislee looked at Grandpa, then the detective. "So why did John give her that prescription?"

"She'd broken her leg last year—legitimately—and he thought she was still suffering."

"Oh. Does her husband know—*ex*-husband?"

"Charlie was also at the hospital, with their daughter, Mia. He feels responsible for not realizing how far she'd sunk. John told him that sufferers of bulimia get tae be very tricky tae hide their disease."

Paislee reached for her glass of lemonade. "In her mental state, Mari probably thought she had tae kill Hendrie before he told the police what he'd seen: her in the Bentley. But then she would have had tae go after Fergus . . . What an awful spiral. It's good she's getting the help she needs."

"Now, we won't know for sure until she regains consciousness and can answer questions," Zeffer sipped his tea, "but I think you're correct. Her fear of getting identified spurred her into action. She had tae understand that Fergus would eventually be released from jail, so she donned a hoodie like Fergus wore, stole the Buchanan Fiat—the keys were hung up in the kitchen—and ran the Bentley off the road after drugging the driver."

"That's diabolical," Grandpa said.

"Hendrie was *drugged*?"

"Maxim finally told his dad why he'd been so upset on Friday morning: seems 'Aunt' Mari had been waiting at Highland Academy tae talk with Hendrie. She'd brought the chauffer breakfast, a hot cocoa and bacon sarnie—all nice, aye, but she had a scary smile. Maxim hid and heard Aunt Mari whisper-shout at Hendrie, whom the lad considered a mate as well as his driver. Maxim didnae know what it meant, but he was scared and just wanted his mum."

"Oh, that poor child." Paislee's stomach spun and she tasted lemonade at the back of her throat. "Let me guess—morphine in the food?"

"The cocoa."

Paislee sighed and scanned the blue-gray waters of the Firth.

Zeffer balanced the cup on the blanket to peer at Grandpa. "And you, Angus? Any word from your son, Craigh?"

Grandpa froze in the action of lifting a shortbread biscuit to his mouth and then lowered it. "What do ye mean?"

"When you first were in Nairn—what, two months ago now?—you said you were looking for your son. On the *Mona*. But the oil rig doesnae exist."

Prickles raced up her spine. He'd been listening.

Grandpa was not a happy man. "I've heard nothing from the station in Dairlee, where I filed my complaint." In other words, back off.

"I've asked around." Zeffer observed Grandpa like a hawk about to dive for a rabbit.

"Oh? Thanks. Dinnae bother." Grandpa brushed the crumbs from his fingers.

"Why not come tae me at the station here in Nairn? If I had more information, I might be able tae uncover what happened. I have a braw talent for finding the truth." He tapped his nose.

Well, that was mighty egotistical. Paislee was about to say so when Grandpa got awkwardly to his feet, knees popping. "I'll keep that in mind. Paislee, I feel like a game of catch with Brody."

Grandpa ambled off without addressing the detective's offer of assistance. What was that about?

Paislee longed to accept the offer, but felt as if she couldn't do anything behind Grandpa's back.

"What aboot you, Paislee? Anything you want tae share with me—say, regarding a storage unit in Dairlee?"

She gulped and shook her head. "Naw. Sorry."

He exhaled and finished his tea. "Stubborn. Runs in the family, then." Zeffer rose in a single motion that was a thing of beauty to watch. He had grace, and elegance. Not a single bone popped into place.

"Thank you for arriving when you did yesterday." She squinted up at him, the sun behind his russet head like a golden halo, like the saints at Saint Mary's church. She doubted she would ever know the exact details of how he'd shown up in the nick of time.

"Aye. As I said, it's me job to lock up the bad guys." Zeffer stuck a hand in his pocket. "How did Amelia work oot?"

"Grandpa said she was a natural with the customers, since she knits herself. Did you know that she used tae be close with Inspector Shinner?"

"I'd heard. I thought at one point she might have been the leak from the department, but it wasnae her."

It had been the other receptionist.

"She wouldn't. Amelia has integrity." And she was thinking of becoming an officer one day.

"And during the Knit and Sip nights?" His tone held levity. "What kind of gossip passes around while you're all blethering?"

"You'd have tae join us with a knitting project tae find out," Paislee teased. "I'd teach you, if you'd like. It's very relaxing." She pointed to her bag with yarn and needles. "I always have something at hand."

Zeffer smiled at her, then looked away. "Ye're an interesting woman, Paislee Shaw. Stay oot of trouble, if ye can?"

He strode off and she grinned at his straight back.

He found her interesting?

Grandpa joined her on the blanket as soon as he was gone. "What did he ask ye? What did you say? Aboot Craigh?"

"I kept your secrets, Grandpa." She stretched out her legs. "We're family."

He nodded, worry clear on his wrinkled face. "Well?"

"He knows about the storage unit in Dairlee." Grandpa winced. "He knows there was no oil rig." She watched him carefully and suggested, "Maybe you should talk tae him."

He'd said their family was stubborn. Could he have been referring to Craigh Shaw?

Her breath caught in her chest and alarm raced through her. She jumped up but Zeffer was long gone.

"What?" Grandpa asked.

Wallace raced toward them as if chased by the hounds of hell to bring the orange ball to Paislee. The pup dropped it at her feet.

"It's time you come clean, Grandpa. Tell me everything you know about Craigh."

"No. I need his trust for when he returns. He has tae return— Craigh is me only child left."

Paislee took Grandpa by the hands and stared into his brown eyes. Warm brown that were so like her son's. Like her da's had been.

"I think the DI knows more about Craigh Shaw than he's letting on."

Grandpa trembled. "I cannae break his faith."

Her mobile rang—it was Lydia, family by choice. It must be important for her to call on a Sunday. "We aren't done, Grandpa." She cleared her throat to answer her best friend. "Hiya."

"Paislee—I have special news," Lydia spoke in a rush. "Corbin asked me tae elope! Can we do lunch tomorrow, Paislee? I have tae find the nicest way tae let him doon."

What? "Lydia, this is happening so fast. Maybe you just need time."

"I need *you*, Paislee. I'm losing my mind. Lunch at the Lion's Mane tomorrow. You have tae."

Paislee sighed. "Can we do breakfast instead? I'm so over lunch."

Connect with Us

Visit us online at
KensingtonBooks.com
to read more from your favorite authors, see books
by series, view reading group guides, and more.

for sneak peeks, chances to win books and prize packs,
and to share your thoughts with other readers.

facebook.com/kensingtonpublishing
twitter.com/kensingtonbooks

Tell us what you think!

To share your thoughts, submit a review,
or sign up for our eNewsletters, please visit:
KensingtonBooks.com/TellUs.